Toxic

by

Debra Jupe

Toxic

Cover Art by *Diana Carlile*

The Wild Rose Press, Inc.
PO Box 708
Adams Basin, NY 14410-0708
Visit us at www.thewildrosepress.com

Publishing History
First Crimson Rose Edition, 2015
Print ISBN 978-1-5092-0316-1
Digital ISBN 978-1-5092-0317-8

Published in the United States of America

"A model employee, that's what you are.
I'll tell Mike to give you a raise." Gracie abruptly broke their connection. "Thank you for the dance. Now excuse me." She whipped around on the slick floor. One leg slid in front of her, while the other slipped behind. She struggled to regain her poise and not perform the splits in front of the entire nursery industry.

Rough hands glided over her bare arms to steady her. "You okay?"

"I'm fine." She didn't bother to look in his direction as he set her back on her feet.

"Might want to go easy on the margaritas."

She ignored his recommendation. Though grateful for stability, she wanted to get away from Ethan McCarthy pronto. She stood in mid-indignation not sure of her next move. Everyone seemed occupied, and she had no place to go. The bar caught her eye. The hell with his suggestion. Tonight the section of the restaurant was her only true friend.

A large hand encircled her forearm. "Easy, Ms. D." Ethan pulled her to him. "It's an observation. I need to know the feelings weren't mutual."

"Mutual feelings? With Reed? Why would you want to know that?"

His lips curved. "'Cause, I prefer not to make a move if you're otherwise involved."

"Make a move?"

"I'm pretty sure you understand the concept, but in case you don't." He brushed his mouth against hers, then smiled. "Consider yourself hit on."

Dedication

For shoe shopping,
chai tea drinking,
and my book buying partner.
This book is dedicated to my favorite daughter,
Hannah Michelle.
Thank you for all the support and fun.
Love you bunches.

Chapter 1

Gracie Desoto glanced at her watch. Nine-thirty. With loads of work piled on her desk, she should place her plant material order and hurry back to the office. Instead, she wandered through a near deserted nursery, baking in the morning sun. Normally she wouldn't waste her precious time, but she needed to find her friend Krystal to get her input for an upcoming project. Peering in greenhouse after greenhouse, she searched for someone who could point her in Krystal's direction. She wanted to get all work related discussions out of the way now, and later they could move on and talk about her own drama. Like her life's latest implosion.

She cruised the nursery's perimeters. The scorching June sun reflected off the fly ash, making the Texas morning seem twice as muggy as the thermometer indicated. But she no longer cared about the heat. Her mind had refocused on the previous evening. Doubtless the whole town was aware of this newest development. They probably guessed how her former spousal unit's delightful news threw her for a major loop. So much so, she'd eaten an entire pan of brownies—with nuts—for dinner last night. After she went to bed, she tossed and turned, and even cried some—okay, a lot, which made her angry. The bastard didn't deserve a tear, much less the onslaught she'd shed.

Forget about shop talk, Gracie wanted to vent. She wandered into the secluded greenhouse Krystal liked to hang out in when she wanted privacy. They needed to get this discussion underway.

Sweat trickled down the back of her neck the moment she entered. Odors of stale humidity, aged soil, and overripe foliage lingered. Pebbles crunched under her sneakers as she trekked through lush ferns and enormous potted palms only to find the greenhouse empty. She hurried to the exit, eager to leave the makeshift sauna. She took a step outdoors, her thoughts still sucked up into her personal crises while she searched for her friend.

A roar of an engine yanked her attention back to the present. She leaped backward, inside the threshold. A four-wheeler with a flatbed attached missed her by a centimeter as it sped by. The trailer gracelessly bounced with each dip and bump in the graveled road, leaving a cloud of dry dirt to dangle in the air. She coughed and fanned at the dust, moving back into the doorway.

"You need to watch where you're going. That guy almost hit you."

She flinched and twisted, stumbling into the doorframe, knocking her off balance. A pair of rough hands grasped her shoulders and stopped her from toppling to the ground. Her palms skated over warm, muscular skin and rested against soft material covering a solid torso.

She cranked her head up, and froze. A sharp tingle traveled throughout each body part causing her stomach to drop to the ground. Every issue evaporated in an instant. Serious gray eyes coolly regarded her. "This isn't a good place to walk around and daydream. Could get you hurt."

His voice was low and easy. Sexy.

"Daydream?"

"I've followed you for a while. You've roamed in no particular direction and never noticed me behind you. You were zoned out. So, yeah, I'm guessing your mind was somewhere else."

"You were following me?"

A slight grin played at the edge of his lips as his fingertips traced down her upper arms and dropped to his sides. "Doing my job, ma'am."

"Ma'am?" she repeated indignantly.

He ignored her piqued resentment although his gaze stayed on her. "Are you lost?"

"Oh, no, I'm just waiting." Heat saturated her face. Shocked to find her hands still bonded to his chest, she released the T-shirt, one finger at a time and took a step backward.

He dipped his fingertips into his shirt pocket and extracted a pair of Maui Jims to cover his gray eyes. "The area is restricted. Only certain employees are allowed in this section." He lightly took her arm to escort her away from the greenhouse. "You'll have to wait somewhere else."

"Yes, I used to…" Her voice trailed. *Did he just tell me to leave?* She stopped and jerked away from his grasp. Her eyes narrowed. "Who are you?"

"I'm the person informing you that you need to stay out of this area."

His words hung in the air between them. Gracie stared at the man, keeping her face impassive, though inwardly she fumed. First, he insinuated she was directionally challenged, and now he was giving her orders. The guy certainly didn't have a clue as to who he was dealing with.

He'd have to carry her out if he wanted to get rid of her. Raising her chin, she spun to face deeper into the nursery, and took an awkward step which caused her to lose her balance. She caught her breath as her arms flew out to her side, catching herself before she toppled onto the gravel.

Upright and stable, she was glad the situation didn't end with a clichéd plunge, especially in front of this guy. Although there was no way he missed her slipup. She glanced at him. He remained in place, arms folded across his chest, his shaded gaze never wavering.

"Hey Gracie," called someone from behind. "Is your truck parked in the front?"

She turned. Good. Somebody who knew her. He could tell this—person—where to get off. Gracie gave the young man strolling toward them a friendly wave. "Hello, Reed."

Reed Doliver shot a significant glance at the guy next to her before he flashed a charming grin. "Have you placed an order? No one's called me to pull any plants for you."

"I haven't been to the office. I wanted to speak with Krystal first."

"Wait a minute. Gracie." The outsider snapped his fingers and pointed at her. "Are you the same Gracie who used to work here? The landscaper?"

Gracie returned her attention to the stranger. "Yes, I'm Gracie Desoto. I did work here, but left five years ago to start my own landscaping business."

"Explains a lot."

Gracie cocked her head. "What is that supposed to

4

mean?"

"You're legendary."

Her brows rose. "Legendary?"

His lips lifted in a grin as he looked her over, but he didn't respond. Gracie folded her arms across her middle and took him in. Chestnut hair combined with the scruff spread over his jaw gave him a mysterious, bad-boy façade. His entire aura whispered extreme confidence, yet his attitude infuriated her.

"Okay, you've heard of me, but I have no idea who you are. Care to change that?"

His grin turned into a full-blown smile, displaying a set of straight, white teeth. "We'll become acquainted soon enough, I'm sure." He rotated to Reed. "Doliver, a moment?" He nodded at Gracie. "You can wait in the office for your order."

Gracie scowled at the man, exasperated. Who did he think he was? She'd spent twelve years of her life at this wholesale nursery. The owners—and many longtime employees—were her close friends. Yet, he acted like he held some sort of authority over the entire place. How dare he behave in such a condescending way? She was a customer, after all. A very good customer. Krystal would get an earful later.

She watched as he ambled farther away and stopped to wait for Reed to join him. For a moment she forgot about being miffed. He was tall. Good looking in a rugged, virile way. He possessed an edginess. His T-shirt stretched tight across what appeared to be a well-built physique, arms muscled and taut. His stance reminded her of a gunslinger in an old western movie showdown.

Gracie pictured a holster wrapped around his waist,

a hand positioned as if ready to draw. He looked like he'd know how to use a gun. An upsurge of restlessness flowed through her. There were boys, and there were men. This was definitely a man.

Gracie pulled herself together and jerked her eyes away. What was she doing? She didn't openly gape at guys. Especially one who irritated her so much. And he called her ma'am. Plus, this particular man might be a smidgen—or a lot younger than she. With a final glance, she took a step, ready to check out.

The words "sweet ass" drifted through the gentle morning breeze followed by a roar of laughter. She stopped to look at the men again. The serious discussion appeared to be over, and the two engaged in a lively conversation.

Were they talking about her sweet ass? Surly not. Though the dress style was causal, and the work atmosphere was laid back, the higher ups were encouraged to behave professionally. Therefore, they shouldn't be commenting on her hind quarters, sweet or otherwise.

She refocused on the new guy.

Or would they?

The man's head swiveled in her direction. Although his eyes were covered, Gracie sensed his gaze resting upon her. A combination of indignation and exhilaration rose in her chest as he and Reed returned to where she stood.

"Ms. Desoto, the rumors about your resilient determination appear to be fact," the man drawled. "I realize you are a former employee and a valued customer, but in the future, you'll need to stay out of this area. As you're aware, this is where we store chemicals. All are hazardous." The corners of his mouth lifted. "Wouldn't want to put you in any kind of danger."

"I know the drill, and I am mindful of what is kept here. I've maintained my chemical license and am well versed on all elements usages. I'm not at risk whatsoever."

"I'm sure you're skills are excellent, but things have changed. We don't make exceptions for past employees. Reed will escort you to the office so you can place your order." He gave a slight nod and spun away. "Have a nice day, Ms. Desoto."

She and Reed watched him until he vanished into a distant greenhouse. "He's certainly arrogant. He acts like he runs the place."

"Yeah." Reed cleared his throat uneasily. "He kinda does."

"What do you mean?"

"Mike hired him a couple of weeks ago. He's the nursery's foreman. Whatever Ethan McCarthy says, goes. He's got everybody jumping. No playing, no goofin' off. He's all about the work. We follow his orders to the letter if we want to keep our jobs." Reed laughed nervously. "Sorry, Gracie. You'll have to stay outta here—well the new rules say you're not supposed to be inside the nursery unless authorized personal are with you. And I don't qualify."

Gracie glared at the younger man, not believing what she was hearing. Yes, the nursery did need a revamping, especially where employees were concerned, but these updated policies were past the point of being ridiculous.

He gulped loudly. "I'm gonna have to take you

away from here. Like I was told." He gently touched her arm. "Let's go find Krystal."

She stepped farther from Reed. Arms crossed around her middle, she glared at him, as if to dare him to remove her. "I don't care what this Ethan McCartney says—"

"McCarthy."

"Whatever. You may take orders from him, but I don't."

Reed's shoulders slumped. "Please don't do this, Gracie. I understand where you're coming from, but if I don't do what he tells me to, he'll write me up."

She dropped her hands to her side. She didn't want to give in to this, intriguing yet tyrannical man, especially after the years of service she'd contributed to this operation, not to mention the business she awarded them. On the other hand, Reed was one of the good guys, and she'd rather not cause him any trouble.

With a huff, she nodded and fell into step, allowing an obviously relieved Reed to lead her away. It was probably best to not be obstinate and follow proper channels for now, but she and the owner, Mike Manzel, would have a major discussion about his newest employee.

Reed interrupted her thoughts "You can't blame Ethan. He's doing what Mike wants him to do."

"I'm aware that Mike can be a hard ass, but there is a right way to do things and there is a wrong, and—"

"Help," a strained, bass voice floated through the warm breeze.

She and Reed skidded to a halt. Both stretched their necks and looked around. A faint pounding reverberated, seemingly far away.

"Is that coming from the nursery?" Reed asked.

"Somebody," the person coughed. "I'm trapped. Get me out, quick."

"I'd say so." Gracie continued to comb her surroundings anxiously. "Someone's in trouble."

Accidents had occurred at the nursery ever so often, though most due to employees not following regulations, the worst being a broken leg. Either this person was in severe peril or they were into some major drama.

"Crap, not again."

Gracie's brows lifted. "Again? What are you talking about, Reed, what's been happening?"

"I need to find out what's going on." Reed gazed at her, his face distrustful. "Can I count on you to go to the office by yourself?"

"I'm not the issue."

Another distant cry called out and hung in the breeze. The voice sounded weaker this time, farther away.

"As a matter of fact, I think you need all the help you can get." She took off in a full run, leaving Reed to stand in her wake. "You coming?" she hollered over her shoulder.

Reed sprinted to catch her, and together they jogged deep into the compound on the graveled roadway. Greenhouses were lined in long rows on either side, separated by weedy drainage ditches in between. Inside, the light winds swayed lines of hanging baskets, creaking from their hooks into a rhythmic lull. Foliage filled pots were scattered on the ground, their leaves gently fanned in the breeze as the sun's heat radiated off the semi-clear tops. Just being near the greenhouses shot the temperature past sweltering.

Gracie and Reed slowed as they entered the mid-section. An odd eeriness enveloped the atmosphere. Only the wind's quiet whistle accompanied by a soft hiss disturbed the stillness.

Gracie skimmed the boundaries, her ears fixated on the strange fizzing sound. Her gaze settled on a greenhouse situated beyond them. It was closed and locked from the outside. Unusual. The only reason to shut a house in this heat was for fumigation purposes or because it was empty, and it was obvious this one wasn't. If the infestation was so bad it couldn't be drenched manually, then the insecticides were set after hours, once employees had left due to risks of toxic gas release.

Reed lumbered farther from her. Hands on his hips, he turned, looking from side to side. "Don't see anyone. I guess whoever was in danger managed to get out."

She didn't miss the relief in his voice.

Gracie stepped closer to the house. The outer lock was in a horizontal position, the insides fogged. A pungent odor of pesticides seeped through the slender cracks.

"I'm not so sure anyone escaped." She squinted toward the heavily misted greenhouse. "I'm thinking we may be too late."

Chapter 2

Gracie rushed to the entrance, flipped the latch, and slid the door open an inch. Hoary fumes billowed through the crack. A sharp, bitterness saturated the air.

She jumped away and covered her breathing cavities with a palm.

Reed's head whipped as his gaze followed Gracie. "You don't think someone's inside, do you?"

Her arm fell to her side. "The person said they were trapped. We haven't heard from anybody in a while. It's a definite possibility."

Reed came up behind her. "Do you see anyone?"

She strained to distinguish something unusual through the haze. "Too foggy." She paused. "Why is this greenhouse being fumigated now? It's always been taboo to spray poisons of this magnitude while the nursery is in operation. You don't even have a sign posted."

"This house has a major bug problem, and it's up to be sprayed. And yeah, you're right. Even if we're closed, a warning should be outside." Hands on hips, he shook his head. "I don't know what's going on."

A mournful groan ricocheted from the fog. Reed leaned over her shoulder. "My God, someone *is* in there."

Gracie flattened a hand across her forehead and squinted against the sun.

"Yes, but where in there? I can't see a thing." Vapor's swirled within the house. Her gaze traveled the building's entrails, concentrating hard on the floor. "There." She pointed. "Near the back." A body lay sprawled across the soggy ground cloth amid a crop of zinnias.

"Oh shit, it's Ethan. Ethan," Reed shouted. "Hang on." He rushed to the door, shoved it all the way open, and then back peddled. He hacked a stiff cough, waving the fumes away. "Not sure how to get him out."

"Somehow we have to. We need masks before we even try to go inside."

"I'm on it." Reed took off in a run.

Gracie gazed at the motionless torso stretched across the floor. She yanked her cell from her back pocket. No bars. She wasn't surprised. The service out here was iffy at best. Not that it would make a big difference if she did manage to call for help. The nursery was located in the boonies. By the time assistance arrived, they may be too late, if it wasn't already. She studied the stilled Ethan with a combination of dread and unease. Reed's silhouetted form reappeared in the distance. He rushed to her at top speed, a facemask in each hand.

"I could only find these disposables," he panted as he approached. He stopped next to her and passed her a mask. "But we won't be inside long, these should work."

"The material is heavy enough." She should've gone for the protection since she knew where the professional heavy duties were kept. She extended the rubber holder and pulled the cover over her head, fitting it across her mouth and nose. "They'll do."

She shot a glance at Reed, who squeezed the second facemask between his hands. He surveyed the murky greenhouse, his face pale. Gracie motioned toward the mask. "We need to hurry. Put that on."

He chuckled anxiously, his complexion whitening more. "Insecticides make me sick. I'm already nauseous from the smell. I'll go in if you need me to, but I'm afraid you'll end up rescuing the both of us."

Gracie nodded, understanding that even the slightest contact with the toxic fumes made some people violently ill. Gasses of this magnitude would put those affected under. "Fine, but don't stand too far from the entrance. He's a lot bigger than me. I can drag him for a ways, but I don't think I'll be able to get him outside."

"I can go get some more help."

She glanced at the lifeless Ethan draped across the asphalt shaded ground-cloth. "No time," she said as she stepped through the door.

"Call when you're ready for me."

The interiors of the sealed house stifled from lack of oxygen combined with toxic spray. The spewing fumes overwhelmed her as the lethal mist dusted her uncovered skin. Even with the protection, she was forced to hold her breath, taking a small gasp each time she required air. She blinked repeatedly and wished she had goggles, too. Carefully, she paced across the soaked tarpaulin, Ethan becoming clearer with each step. After what seemed like forever, she finally reached him. He lay on his stomach. He'd removed his shirt and wrapped it around his head, holding the fabric secure with his fingers.

She bent and placed a hand onto his bare shoulder.

His torso felt warm and wet. He spun around. A pair of gray eyes peered through a makeshift hole in the material. She straightened, bouncing backward, shocked he was alive, much less conscious.

Once relief set in, she leaned over him. "Are you okay?"

He extended his palm. She nodded, thankful she wouldn't have to carry him since she'd misjudged the amount of gushing toxins. No way would she be able to rescue him alone.

She took his hand between hers, giving him a firm tug, and slowly drew him to shaky feet. He rocked back and forth, and his body swayed before he collapsed into her. Gracie struggled to stay steady.

Finding his stability, he rested an arm around her shoulder. He situated his shirt over his nose and mouth, then gave her a solid head bob to indicate he was ready. They took a step. Again, he went off-balance and fell into her. Her knees buckled from the added weight. Once more, he fought for strength while Gracie wrestled to keep them on their feet.

"Are you going to be able to walk out?"

"Let's go," he choked.

Gracie gauged the extended length between them and the exit. Reed stood far away from the gap, observing them with a worried expression. Gradually they made their way toward the opening, stopping several times for Ethan to recover. Gracie eyed him worriedly. His breathing was labored, his skin saturated, though she wasn't sure if the wetness was from the spray or perspiration, probably a blend of both. After what seemed like a twenty-mile hike, they reached the outlet. Reed slammed the door behind them once they crossed the threshold.

Ethan toppled to the ground, landing on the hot gravel, though he didn't seem to notice the roughness or the heat. He took a series of short gasps, coughing in intervals.

Workers had caught on to something was amiss. They gathered around, eyeing the situation either curious or concerned.

Gracie removed her mask, shaking the dampness from her hair and shirt. She slanted over him. His skin was pasty white as he struggled for air. She considered the fastest routes to the emergency room, debating whether someone should drive him or should they call in the EMTs. Probably best to have the experts transport, in case the unthinkable happened along the way. She looked at him again. Hopefully, he wouldn't get any worse before help arrived.

Reed jogged to her side, then stepped around her to kneel next to Ethan. "Are you all right?"

"No, he's not." Gracie straightened. "He needs medical attention immediately. Call an ambulance."

Reed turned his head, looking at the group of employees. "We're not supposed to bring phones into the nursery, but everybody carries one. Someone dial 911."

Gracie shook her head "I tried earlier." She flipped her cell from her pocket and held it up. "No service."

Reed wiped the sweat from his brow. "Somebody go to the office and call from the landline."

Ethan shot out a hand and shook his head. "I'm fine," he insisted in a rasped tone. He scrubbed the shirt over his damp face, gulping for another breath. "Never realized how much I enjoy clean air."

He rose to his elbows, triggering his muscular arms to ripple. Gracie's mouth dried. Though inappropriate, she battled not to stare. Her gaze flowed to his flat stomach, perfect, muscled chest…and those firm, powerfully built arms.

Shunning the memories of their recent closeness, she fought to regain her faculties before she lost all semblance of professionalism and common sense. "You don't look so fine," she said in a tight voice.

He glanced in her direction. His color was beginning to return, and his eyes held a slight twinkle as a grin played at his lips. His expression told her he read her mind perfectly. He tilted his head and studied the insides of the cloudy house. "Damn. Left my sunglasses. Hope they won't ruin."

"Really? That's your worry?" Gracie asked skeptically. "I'm not sure what took place, but I'm guessing you don't normally just walk into fumigating houses. How did this happen?"

He coughed again then wrestled to a sitting position. He raked a hand through his moist hair and turned his attention to her. "You're still here. Though I suppose your inability to follow orders is a positive, considering the situation."

Gracie folded her arms across her chest and gave him a scornful look. "You mean considering I saved your life."

"True. But I believe it's time you did what you were told, and go wait in the office. You see what can happen out here, even if you're careful."

"You're still on that?" She released a sarcastic chuckle. "May I remind you, it didn't happen to me? You were the one who was trapped. Shouldn't you be bothered by the fact someone locked you in a greenhouse full of poison?"

He appeared shocked. Like the thought hadn't occurred to him.

"Instead of harping on me for not obeying your stupid rules," she continued, "how about a thank you for saving your life?"

He dipped his head. "I suppose I owe you."

"If that's your idea of a thanks, I suppose I'll take it."

A putting sound had everyone temporarily forget Ethan's dilemma and stand at attention.

"It's about to hit the fan now," Reed murmured at a nearing golf cart. He rose and backed away from Ethan.

"No joke." Ethan edged to his feet, weaving as he stood. He let go a loud stream of air as the nursery's owner maneuvered the miniature vehicle in front of the stationary cluster of employees.

Mike Manzel killed the engine and exited. Krystal, Gracie's friend and the nursery's head grower was next to him, also climbed from her seat. She caught Gracie's eye and gave her a small smile before her mouth altered into a flat line. Mike took in the assembly, his expression blank though Gracie knew better. Her years here made her acutely aware Mike didn't tolerate workers loitering on his dime. He wasn't happy.

He glared pointedly at Ethan. "What's going on?"

"We've had a…" Ethan glanced at Gracie. "Situation."

"I don't do vague, Ethan." He stopped to scowl at the inactive crew. The group took a back step. "Explain to me why my entire staff is standing around instead of doing what I pay them to do."

Reed turned to the employees. "Shows over." He clapped his hands. "Back to work." The crowd instantly dispersed, Reed hurrying after them.

Ethan swiped his shirt over his forehead one more time before he poked his arms and head through the holes to cover his torso. "I can't give a lot of details, Mike, because I don't know any. I was doing a nursery walk-through when I noticed this house sealed. I went in to investigate. Once I reached the back, I heard a hiss, similar to cans spraying. Before I realized, the door was shut and locked from the outside, the area filled with poison." He hesitated. "If not for Ms. Desoto's unwillingness to follow procedure, the outcome may be much more dismal. At least from my perspective."

Mike scowled at Ethan in disbelief. "You're telling me you were locked inside during a fumigation?"

"That's what I'm saying. I tried to break through the plastic, but the double layer of polycarbonate is so sturdy, along with the house filled poisonous fumes, I couldn't even tear an inch."

Mike rotated to Krystal, who'd walked to the spewing greenhouse. "Krystal?"

She spun around, shaking her head with a shrug. "No idea, Mike."

He sighed loudly, his face turned purple with rage. Fists clenched into tight balls, he visibly shook. If he'd been a cartoon character, smoke would blow out of his ears. "Where the hell is Quinn," he said through gritted teeth. "I want to know who did this, and I want to know now."

Quinn was the third woman who'd replaced Gracie, and although it'd been a while, the transition had been less than smooth. This situation wasn't going to help her cause.

"I'll speak with her, Mike," Krystal assured.

"Find out what's going on. She's responsible for chemical outtake. She should be on sight and or at least be aware what is being sprayed and where." Mike cleared his throat. His glance bounced between Gracie and her friend. "Krystal. Why don't you show Gracie the new selection of ground covers that just arrived?" He motioned for Ethan and said to the women over his shoulder, "You can take the cart."

Gracie and Krystal looked at each other with raised brows. Mike never relinquished his mode of transportation. Evidently he wanted them out of hearing range while he and Ethan continued their conversation.

They mounted the transport without question, Krystal at the wheel. She finessed the vehicle past the men in a whispered huddle.

Gracie glanced at the two as they passed. Ethan ripped his attention away, his gaze instantly linked with hers. His lips slightly lifted, his gray eyes sparkled. Her heartbeat increased to lightning speed, smacking into her chest. She swallowed hard and whirled away, trying to control her sudden heavy breathing.

Krystal pointed the golf cart toward the premises outer range. Neither spoke on the ride over. This place had its moments, but the tension had never been this elevated.

"Rather an edgy day," Gracie commented dryly.

"It's been a stressful few weeks, but yeah, you're right. This incident will up the strain a notch."

"A notch? Someone was nearly killed."

"The welcome hasn't been so hearty for our new

supervisor." Her friend tried to be flippant, but the tremble in her voice showed how upset she was over the occurrence.

"This is disturbing, but the outcome could've been much worse."

Krystal guided the cart over a long graveled road, bridged between two cooling ponds. "Did I understand correctly? You saved him?"

Gracie nodded, then gave an abbreviated version of the event. "What's Mike's thinking by bringing him in, anyway?" she asked at the end of her story. "Just his presence seems to have added to the anxiety."

Gracie wondered why she bothered. Tall and exciting, yes, but bossy and condescending too. Not her type. Something told her his knowledge about the workings of a nursery were nil. His demeanor didn't jive with the normal horticultural persona, so what was he doing here?

And again, why did she care?

"Mike wants his employees to have more structure."

Krystal parked near the border of the growing area. Hundreds of gallon pots of tall grasses wisped in the hot breeze. Normally, the plants would've grabbed Gracie's interest, but not now. She couldn't free her thoughts from Ethan McCarthy.

"Mike's been trying to do that for years. Has this Ethan managed to implement organization?"

"Well…" her friend paused. "Not exactly, but not for the lack of trying. He hasn't been here that long. I'm sure he'll get the job done eventually. Change doesn't happen overnight."

"The shortage of stability has always been an issue.

Heck, it's prevalent in this business. I deal with the same problem."

"Our troubles go beyond that." Krystal gave Gracie a grave look. "There's been some other stuff happening."

Gracie frowned, recalling Reed's response right before they'd discovered Ethan. "Like what?"

"Weird things." Krystal appeared uncomfortable. "That no one can explain. Be glad you're gone. I've had to make myself come to work lately."

Chapter 3

"Weird as in what happened to Ethan?"

Krystal spread a hand across her chest, her expression uncomfortable. Like she'd revealed too much. "Not as serious, but we've had a lot of little issues—almost as if we're being warned that something, or someone is out to harm us." She stopped to look around. "There's a couple of other things, too. Bigger."

"Such as?"

"We can't discuss the details here. The nursery has ears. You know Mike. He's hell bent on keeping negativities private. Most employees aren't aware of our problems. Although after this latest incident, I suppose he has no choice. He needs to call the authorities."

Krystal was right. Mike was protective about his business and careful not to allow pessimisms to get out into the community, even if he sometimes looked the other way where the law was concerned.

"I don't disagree, but it's too late for the police to do a thorough investigation considering we were everywhere and contaminated any evidence."

"True, but the incident should be reported." Krystal stepped from the cart. "We'll talk more on the subject at lunch. Come look at these beautiful, accent grasses."

They viewed the products, keeping their

conversation focused on plants, and Gracie's latest landscaping venture. She took plenty of notes, then they climbed back inside the golf cart. Krystal drove them through the compound, pointing out other new intakes that may interest Gracie until they arrived in front of an older doublewide, which served as the office.

"I need to speak with Quinn, per Mike," Krystal told Gracie as they mounted the stairs leading to the entrance. "I'll do that while you place your order."

"Quinn's inside? When I worked here, I was outside nearly the whole day. What's changed?"

"Nothing. She just stays in a lot." Krystal gave an exaggerated eye roll. "She and Vivian have something of a friendship."

"I thought the new foreman had whipped everybody into shape. No more goofing off. Her inside sounds like goofing to me."

"You're right, it is. Ethan works more with the supervisors and crew chiefs. I don't think he enjoys interacting with Quinn either. She's more of an internal issue, anyway."

"Still, I'm surprised Mike puts up with her not doing her job." Gracie relished in the cold blast from the air conditioner as they entered the building. "And Vivian's been his office manager for years. She knows better."

"You'd think." Krystal rolled her eyes again. "Those two have become tighter than pages in a book."

They separated to take care of their business, agreeing to meet in Krystal's private office once they'd finished.

The indoor staff remained subdued. Doubtless the news of Ethan's near demise had reached them. Gracie walked down the short hallway, passing Mike's private sanctuary. His door was shut, but a hint of muffled voices seeped through the thin wood. He and Ethan must be continuing their pow-wow inside. She found the usual animated sales team was also low key. Ethan's episode had really affected everyone.

After she placed her order, she went to find Krystal, who was in her one windowed office, the smallest in the building. Seated behind a large, laminate desk, she waved at a worn chair across from her before she returned to typing into a computer from the Stone ages. Piles of file folders, plant magazines with pages eared to be read later, and a soil sample kit, among other work related odds and ends surrounded her.

Krystal entered in another notation before her attention returned to Gracie. "Is the new deli in the town square okay for lunch?"

"Works for me." Gracie fidgeted now feeling cold from the blowing cool air after being in the heat for so long. "I need healthy. I ate a pan of brownies for dinner last night. With nuts."

Krystal studied Gracie with a worried expression. "A whole pan?"

"With nuts."

"Must be a hell of a mess. As a matter of fact you look like you've already been through the wringer today, and I'm not talking about the earlier chemical disaster. What's up?"

"Nothing much." She paused. "Stewart stopped by yesterday."

Krystal's eyes widened.

"To tell me he's getting remarried."

"Didn't he move in with his girlfriend before the

ink dried on your divorce papers? I'm surprised he's bothered with legalities."

Gracie winced. She tried not to let the fact bother her that her ex-husband had another woman on the side during the final two years of their marriage except she was a mere mortal, and the thought still kicked her in the stomach.

"Yeah, but here's the wrinkle. He isn't marrying the one he left me for. She's new."

"Not so shocking. Statistics show when men leave their wives for someone else, they rarely marry the other woman. He probably found this squeeze while still with the one he left you for. Once a cheater, always a cheater, right?"

Gracie raised her eyebrows. "Just make that up?"

They burst into giggles.

"So how are you? You like to put on a brave front, but the situation upsets you, doesn't it?"

Gracie could be honest with Krystal without judgment. They bonded years ago, but what made them close is their marriages disintegrated at the same time, and they leaned on each other through the rough days and even rougher nights. Both ended up head of households, working single mothers. "I'm confused and I am mad. It's almost as if he betrayed me again. Is that crazy or what?"

"Understandable. He's found someone and he's happy. You're alone. You didn't do anything wrong except love him. You were a good wife. He treated you like crap and forced you to seek a divorce, and he made the failure of the marriage your fault. No, it's not fair."

Gracie folded her hands and placed them in her lap. "He put me through hell. I jumped through hoops, leaped tall buildings at a single bound, and groveled at his feet, yet I couldn't make him happy." Her voice cracked. "I almost killed myself trying to please him, and I failed miserably."

"Things have been rough for you, but you've done quite well for yourself. You have every reason to be proud of what you've accomplished. You're so much stronger now." Krystal stopped briefly. "When's the big day?"

"Next month."

Krystal pursed her lips and whistled. "Kind of quick."

"Oh, did I forget to mention? She's twenty-nine and pregnant? About three weeks. She prefers a lavish ceremony though that'll take too much time to put together. She's willing to sacrifice amenities as opposed to her pregnancy showing on their wedding day. Priorities, huh?"

Krystal's mouth dropped. "She's young, but old enough to be aware of how not to get in that predicament."

Gracie flashed a cynical smile. "Unless she wanted to trap an affluent, well to do doctor." She laughed. "Good luck with that. I begged him for another baby, and he refused. He didn't want any more kids. Good thing, I suppose, he barely made time for the one we had."

"No worries there. Mason turned out to be a wonderful young man in spite of an inattentive father. Who's the woman? Do we know her?"

Gracie shook her head. "She's new to the area. Stewart hired her to manage his office. He did slip and reveal she was engaged to someone else when they met."

"The two prizes deserve each other. Whether the relationship works or not doesn't matter. He's officially moved on." Krystal gazed at Gracie. "Perhaps you should think about doing the same."

Gracie shifted uneasily. Krystal's words stung. Her friend usually sugar-coated her advice. Her putting things in such a matter of fact perspective left the sugar off.

Krystal propped her elbows onto her desk, her chin rested on her fists. "Probably the best way for you to get past this is for you to find someone new. When was the last time you had a date?"

An image of Ethan McCarthy zipped through Gracie's mind followed by a rush of heat. She shook away the picture and lifted her shoulders. "To be honest I can't remember. Pretty sad, because I haven't dated much since my marriage disintegrated."

"Well honey. Get out there. Find you someone. A younger guy would show Stewart you can go youthful, too."

"If I follow Stewart's age range, my new guy would have to be about twenty-eight. That's awfully young in man years, especially for a forty year old."

"Yeah, but they're trainable. Youth equals more stamina. You need one who goes the distance and get you laid. A lot."

Hot sex with the hot and sexy, younger Ethan. *Stop.* "I don't know…"

"Well, I do. Believe me, once I met Charlie after I waited for so long." She smiled, with a satisfied sigh. "Let's just say I felt like a different women."

Gracie grinned, happy her friend found love again.

"But what are the odds I'll get a keeper like Charlie?"

Krystal held up her hand, spread her fingers, and gazed thoughtfully at her new wedding band. "The right guy will find you if you let him. That's how things happened for me. You never know. He may not be far away. Charlie and I were friends before we realized we were meant to be."

A loud knock hammered at the office entrance. Krystal opened her mouth. Before she had a chance to utter a word, Quinn peeked inside, a self-important smile painted on her face.

"Yes, Quinn?" Krystal asked in a cool tone, her expression annoyed.

"Ah-what's happening." She nodded toward the nursery. "Shouldn't be talked about to just anybody." Quinn glared at Gracie then pointedly scowled at Krystal. "Not everybody needs to know everything that goes on here."

Gracie shook her head. Not for the first time wondered why Krystal kept this woman. She was so aggravating.

Krystal's eyes darkened. "Thank you, Quinn. Please shut the door on your way out."

"I'm only saying—"

"Thank you, Quinn."

The door banged closed.

Krystal returned to Gracie. "Sorry."

"I consider the source, although I can't understand why Mike keeps her. Her behavior is so unprofessional."

"She is rough around the edges. Plus, she's threatened whenever you're here."

"She shouldn't be. I'm happy doing what I do and

have no desire to come back, even if I could. She ought to be secure by now."

"I've spoken to her about her behavior numerous times. Since we have a hard time keeping employees, we can't always be choosy over manners. Quinn's my third assistant since you left. I've scouted for a replacement, but applicants are slim pickin's." She gave Gracie a half grin. "I agree, her people skills suck, although when she puts her mind to it, she can be an asset. She does know her stuff."

Gracie bit her bottom lip. She didn't agree with her friend's assessment, but she respected her enough not to argue.

A salesman stuck his head inside to inform Gracie her order was ready. They settled on a lunch time before she retrieved her paperwork, and then she returned outside. She attempted to wave at several former co-workers, but everyone had their chins tucked to their chests, appearing too busy to look up. She supposed the recent incident had everyone on edge. She let the employees be and circled the trailer to inspect her material.

"Ms. Desoto. I see you can follow instructions. I'm impressed."

Gracie jumped and turned. A powerful forced arced through her shadowed by sheer panic. Ethan stood next to her, arms folded over his chest, his crafty grin in place. Where were these odd feelings coming from? This man irritated her, yet she was fighting an unexplainable attraction. His smile widened as if once again he could read her thoughts.

"Isn't there someone else you can terrorize?" She tried to keep her response airy and carefree, although her attempt flopped miserably.

"You're the only one who can't follow rules." He gestured toward the trailer. "Material up to your high standards?" His easy, low voice impelled her amorous radar to soar, placing her desires on high alert.

"Looks good."

The man was so much better than good. Moving away, Gracie needed to regain composure and keep this uncontrollable hormonal outbreak in check. She retrieved a pot from her trailer for something to do. "You've recovered quickly, but you should take things easy."

He strolled to where she stood and bent so his face was even with hers. "Careful Ms. D." His tone was low. "I might start to think you care."

Gracie licked her lips, unsure how to respond. He stirred sensations she'd neglected for years, or maybe she was oblivious to their existence.

"You found your sunglasses," she observed weakly. "Any damage?"

"Better shape than me."

She picked at a dead leaf from the flowerpot she clutched. Ethan straightened, simultaneously reaching for same withered foliage. Their fingers brushed. The contact scorched her hand. Her arm jerked, triggering the pot to vault and tumble to the ground.

They glanced at the damaged plant before their gazes locked.

****

Ethan intentionally held her stare. Her obvious discomfort was humorous, and he wondered if shyness invoked such a strong reaction or if something else made her so jittery. A tiny blip wished he was the

30

reason of her uneasiness.

Then he backtracked.

He needed to keep his thoughts in check, no matter how minute. He didn't travel in this petite woman's social circle, anyway. Even in shorts and a tank top, she wore a solid air of refinement. Sun streaked hair smoothed into a ponytail. Cute little tendrils escaped and flowed over her dimpled cheeks. He'd always been a sucker for big, green eyes. And even though she didn't look it, he guessed her to be slightly older than him. She may reject the idea of a younger guy.

Therefore, he should forget about olive colored irises and watch his behavior. He had other things to concentrate on, like his job. Flirting with customers, even former employees, wasn't a part of the plan and forbidden to boot.

Her tongue slowly traced her top lip. "So you're not as intact as your shades."

He wiped a hand across his forehead, trying to focus on procedure and ignore the sexy tongue swipe or the rising entity between his legs. "I'm a little queasy from inhaling so much poison. Mike insists I see a doctor. I'm on my way now." If he hadn't caught sight of her, he'd be halfway to his appointment, but he couldn't resist. Maybe he'd huffed too much insecticide, and the fumes had affected his better judgment. She bent and scooped up the destroyed plant and the pot, exposing her tight round, butt. He became lightheaded again, but this dizziness wasn't from the pesticide.

His dick surged into his jeans zipper. "Nice."

She attempted to straighten, knocking the back of her head on the edge of the trailer. He fought to keep from smiling over her constant clumsiness. She ignored the thump and gazed at him with raised brows. "Did you say something?"

"Nope." Resisting the urge to touch where she'd hit, he forced his expression to remain cool though this woman had his libido wandering into a much warmer territory. "Just admiring your plants."

"Do you know anything about my plants? Or about any of the products in the nursery? Where did you get your education?"

"Excuse me?" He wondered where this came from and what direction the conversation was about to turn. Instincts gave him a slight push, telling him to shut her questions down.

"You're the new foreman, and you're whipping everybody into shape work wise, but how experienced are you in the industry." She gave him a stern glare.

Ethan almost chuckled at her tough-girl wannabe glower. This was too much fun to miss. Except to pull off the hard ass disposition she aimed for, she needed life to knock her down a few more times. "You're interviewing me? I thought I already had the job."

"I'm just curious. A supervisor in this field should have a horticulture background, and since you insist on ordering me around, I'd kind of like to know if you're qualified."

"You're correct. One would need cultivation skills, and I don't have any. I was hired for my management abilities, not for plant knowledge although it's something I'm working on." Ethan stepped forward and relieved her of the dumped pot. While he'd like to hang around for amusement sake, it was time to hit the road. "Does that answer everything, or have you prepared an entire questionnaire?"

"Don't get offended." Her confident expression turned uneasy. "Management abilities or not, only certain types succeed in this line of work, and the environment seems too out there for someone like you."

A corner of his mouth lifted. "Again, you are correct."

This woman was far too intuitive. He enjoyed infuriating her, and he owed her a mass of gratitude, but the time had come to wind up their budding relationship.

An expensive, newer model car roared into the parking lot and saved him from further conversation. Both turned their attention to the automobile as it screeched to a halt behind them. A well-dressed blonde stepped out of the driver's side. She ripped off her sunglasses and glared at him, then she replaced her shades and hurried up the steps into the doublewide.

Inwardly, he groaned as he glanced at Gracie. Her expression appeared a mixture of curious, surprise, and perhaps—disappointment? Nevertheless, he didn't have time to analyze this intriguing woman's reaction. He had a doctor's appointment, and his attention was needed elsewhere before he could go.

"I am forever grateful for your heroics today, but I have a date with the doctor." He raised a hand and saluted her as he turned, holding up the damaged plant. "I'll tell Reed to get you another one on my way out. You have an awesome life, Ms. Desoto."

Chapter 4

"Sorry I'm late." Gracie slid into a faux buckskin booth across from Krystal.

She shuffled to get comfortable, tugging at her shorts, trying to alleviate the scratchiness against her bare thighs. "I had to make an unscheduled stop at a customer's home to re-explain my crew's instructions over the care of their new trees." She shifted again still searching for a softer spot until she finally gave up. "My crews tell each customer how to take care of their new materials, and I give them explicit written outlines, yet some people still don't get it. I mean, it's not hard."

"The cons of being a business owner." Krystal smiled as she slid a laminated menu over the Formica table to Gracie's side.

"Tell me." Gracie glanced at the selections, then pushed the menu aside, already knowing what she wanted. "Was the rest of your morning calmer?"

"Nope. The craziness escalated." Krystal paused. "We're waiting for someone from the sheriff's department to stop by and question us on the Ethan situation and everyone's panicked. Mike gave them your number, by the way. They'll be contacting you since you were involved."

"I'll keep my cell by me so I won't miss their call."

The waitress interrupted to take their drink orders.

"Then there's the Quinn thing I had to deal with,"

Krystal said, after she left.

Gracie looked up, surprised. "What's up with Quinn?"

"I want all my ducks in a row and be able to answer the authority's inquiries about any chemicals that may be missing."

"Makes sense. Quinn's not cooperating?"

"I'm at a loss on how to handle the woman." Her expression morphed into a look of frustration. "To get to the bottom of this morning's fiasco, I needed to examine her spray charts. Come to find out, she's overdue in posting her logs—and she's not just a little behind—she's a lot. If OCEA were to come in, we'd be facing a hefty fine. Either way, I don't think there is any way I'm going to be able to figure out if any chemicals are missing."

"I don't understand how she can't keep up with her records. All you do is key the chemical, date, and objectives into the computer, and do it on a daily basis. Simple."

"She says she's swamped." Krystal rolled her eyes. "Her and Vivian's nail polish and perfume discussions takes up a lot of her time, I guess. I spent the rest of the morning muddling through her mess of unorganized paperwork, while trying to calm Mike. He's still livid over Quinn's un-organization skills and the Ethan incident, among other things. Plus I'm having to keep up with my own duties." She exhaled with a smile. "Are you sure you don't want to come back? I'll give you a raise. Hell, I'll even throw in my entire salary."

Gracie laughed and shook her head, though the thought of seeing Ethan every day was appealing and a little frightening.

The waitress returned with their drinks and took their orders. Krystal sifted the paper away from her straw and speared it inside her glass before she took a sip. "Quinn's biggest problem is she doesn't like to spray chemicals."

"That's one of her main responsibilities. Does she enjoy anything outside the office?"

"Yeah, she loves to police everyone else. She goes into the nursery and bosses everybody, which created a huge conflict now that Mike hired Ethan. Her directing crews was never in her job description, but she still thinks he took over her duties." Krystal's mouth flat lined. "Then there's the other thing."

Gracie's gaze lifted. "What other thing?"

"You noticed, right?" Krystal raised her eyebrows. "Ethan is extremely attractive."

"I only met him today." Gracie cleared her throat and spoke in a non-committal tone. "Yeah, I suppose very attractive describes him."

"So you understand. I'm a newlywed, and I do double takes when he walks by."

"He does seem to possess the physical package, but the little time I spent with him, he comes off as arrogant. And he's not familiar with the plant material. He even admitted it."

Krystal's brow knitted. "Did something happen with Ethan you'd like to share?"

"Aside from him trying to kick me out of the nursery, no."

Gracie wasn't ready to admit her encounter with Ethan McCarthy rattled her to the point to where she either simmered because, oh wow, or she seethed from his overconfident attitude. Plus, he may've dismissed her for good when they'd parted ways this morning.

Krystal chuckled. "He's only doing what he was told, but I'll make sure he's aware you're an exception. He should anyway, since you saved his life."

"Doubtful. I practically had to drag a thank you out of him, and he still ordered me to leave." She snatched her glass for a long drink of water. Even though the guy infuriated her, talking about him left her mouth parched. "I ran into him as he was leaving for the doctor. Have you heard how he is?"

Gracie cast her gaze downward to avoid the knowing glint in her friend's eyes.

"He doesn't go through me, although I expect some news when I get back to work. He reports directly to Mike, so he'll contact him for an update."

"No wonder he's so full of himself."

Krystal looked thoughtful. "I suppose he does possess an alpha quality. Either way, his appearance has gotten a lot of attention from the women. This is a big part of our problem. Besides being angry by his presence, Quinn's developed a crush on him. An unrequited crush."

"Talk about inner conflict. So her feelings are hurt twice."

"They shouldn't be, but yeah, she's offended. And because she's upset, she's angry. Her rage makes her do stupid stuff or she neglects her responsibilities. I'm unsure how to manage her. My degree is in horticulture; I'm not schooled on supervising a grown woman crushing on the resident hunk."

"Don't know what to say, my friend. A pro of owning a business." Gracie grinned. "Mike needs to hire unattractive employees."

Krystal chuckled. "Thankfully, he won't be there that long."

"Who won't be there long?"

"Ethan. He works in a consultant capacity, which is why he's not too familiar with plant material. His job is to get the nursery running smoother by implementing better operating procedures, and train the supervisors to use them. Then he'll move on to another company."

"Oh." Disappointment flooded over Gracie. He'd only be there for a short time. She'd best start to let go of any ideas of him before she started acting like Quinn. "Even if he's not permanent, I'm shocked Mike allows Quinn to behave so unprofessionally. That's so unlike him."

"Mike's had other issues to deal with." Krystal hesitated. "Although we'll be meeting to discuss her once Ethan returns from his doctor's appointment."

"Doesn't sound good."

"No, her jobs going to be on the line after this little stint, I'm sure. But I can't do anything about that. Quinn's going to have to save herself." She glanced at Gracie. "Speaking of distractions, I need to ask you about something on another topic. This pertains to our conversation this morning."

Gracie frowned.

"Please keep this quiet. If Mike found out I'm telling you, he'd fire my ass on the spot, too."

"Now I am intrigued. You'd never risk your job for anything."

"Count this as a first." Krystal paused again and leaned across the table and spoke in a quiet tone. "Plants are being stolen from the nursery."

"Plants are what?"

Krystal did a lowering motion, her voice soft. "Not so loud." She cleared her throat. "They're disappearing. Not many and not all the time but it seems as if they're evaporating. Someone must be taking them. That's the only thing I can figure."

"How?"

Krystal shrugged. "The place looks like a prison. The game fence surrounding the site should keep people out. Plus we're located in such a remote area. Evidently neither is an issue."

"I thought we put in an alarm system years before I left."

"The office has one, but the greenhouses don't, although they need to be installed. They use to leave the gates unlocked, but that's changed now."

"Then how are the thieves getting in and out?"

"Not sure. Either they've somehow made a duplicate key, or there's a hidden exit."

Gracie bit her bottom lip. "Do you think the thefts have something to do with what happened today?"

"No idea. But it would almost make sense."

"What kinds of plants are they stealing?"

"Everything." She pointed a finger and motioned in a circle. "Different varieties, sizes, and never out of the same house."

"So how can I help you?"

"I wondered if you've seen or heard anything unusual. Is someone selling plants cheap, perhaps in some sort of black market scheme?"

"Like underground plant thieves?" Gracie swallowed a laugh. "Rogue landscapers?"

Krystal scowled.

"Sorry."

"This sounds crazy, but I can't think of why anyone would want them other than for profit. Although I'm not sure the amount a person could get for stolen plant material. Mike's driving me nuts. His mood swings go from euphoric to explosive."

"How long has this been going on?"

"He's been suspicious for about a year, although he thinks thieves may've been active longer. Apparently the losses started out small, where no one would notice. Now it's obvious. They're gone." She snapped her fingers. "Just like that."

"Bold thieves. Perhaps an enemy of Mike's or a bitter competitor could be the culprit?"

"Possibly. He hasn't come out and said it, but I think he suspects the thefts might be internal."

They stopped the conversation as the waitress returned with their meal.

Gracie adjusted her plate, then unfolded her napkin and placed her it in her lap. "Did he report the thefts to the police?"

"No. You know how much everyone in town likes to gossip, and he's so protective of the nursery's image. The plant farm was his late wife's baby. He won't tolerate any bad talk. He did mention something about bringing in a private detective, but that thought was fleeting, one he won't go through with."

"Hiring an investigator isn't a bad idea." Gracie shook pepper onto her food then pierced a bite with her fork. She gazed at Krystal, uncertain this wasn't a huge joke.

"He and his son are policing the place at night."

"His incompetent, spoiled rotten son or the sensible, decent one?"

Krystal made a face. "Mickey."

"That's asking for trouble."

"I agree. They got into a sticky situation the other evening, or at least Mike did."

"Is this what you were referring to earlier?"

Krystal nodded. "Mike decided to hang around after their inspection and do some work."

"Not unusual."

"It's normal and everyone knows. He went inside his office, about to sit down—Gracie, there was a copperhead curled in his chair, ready to pounce. He almost sat on it."

Gracie slapped a hand over her opened mouth. "A snake in his chair?"

"Not a big one, smaller, easier to miss, but still could do some major damage. Somehow the word got out and employees are aware. Mike's done his best to play it down and claimed it got in through an air duct."

"People bought that? Seriously, how did a snake manage to get inside and into Mike's chair?"

Krystal lifted a shoulder. "We've found a lot of creepy crawlers sneaking into the office over the years, but we've never had a snake slither inside."

"The implication is someone put it there?"

"That's what I'm thinking." She gave an exaggerated eye roll. "Leave it to Quinn to think it was cool."

"You're joking."

"One of her crazy ex's was a snake handler. She's learned the craft, and she still enjoys interacting with the slimy varmints."

Quinn thought snakes were okay; add another reason to dislike her to the list.

"Gracie, please don't say anything to anybody. Mike will kill me. Keep quiet about the missing material, too. The employees were told the plants are diseased and are thrown away."

"I won't. But with everything, you'd think Mike would welcome outside help."

"He's carrying a lot of secrets lately. Can't put my finger on anything, but more stuff is going on than he's telling." Krystal dipped an onion ring into catsup. "What's your plan for Friday evening?"

Gracie blinked, startled from the sudden subject change. "I'm going to a lawn care seminar on Friday, although no plans for later. Why?"

"I thought you might enjoy a night out." Krystal grinned. "We can go on a Mr. Right or for a Mr. Right now search."

"You're talking about a sympathy evening?" Gracie's eyes widened. "Oh no, you're not thinking of fixing me up? I hate that."

Krystal shook her head. "Mike booked a room. He's throwing a party for workers, spouses or significant others, and a few select customers at the new restaurant Saskia, located on the riverfront. Suppose to be an upscale place. Free food and drinks. They may set up an area for dancing. Should be a lot of fun. Consider this your invite."

Gracie gnawed her bottom lip. Her first instinct was to turn Krystal down flat. Then she rethought the offer. A party. The inclusion of employees meant Ethan might attend, maybe she could—why did she care if that overrated, walking pin-up would be there. Okay, so he tickled her secret places with a meager glance, and his body was god-worthy, but his condescending

42

arrogance ruined the illusion of perfection. Besides, someone that hot probably had a girlfriend, or even a wife.

And he was a short-timer. Would never work.

"Gracie?" Krystal interrupted her thoughts. "You drifted off?"

"Oh, yeah, I'm sorry. I was deciding if I could make it. The seminar ends at about five-thirty, and I'll socialize after to do some networking. I probably won't leave until around six-thirty. It might be too late to go to a party."

"Six-thirty is too late to go to a party? Honey, you really do need a night out."

Gracie tried to come up with a pliable excuse to decline. She didn't want to go to a get together, especially if there was a possibility the overhyped but hot, temporary foreman with attitude was attending with another woman. "Most of your co-workers are married or will at least be with a date. I'd be a third wheel."

"There's nothing wrong with you hanging out with Charlie and me. We've never considered you any kind of wheel, third or otherwise. Friday night with the weekend ahead." Her voice grew excited. "Your son is gone, working in Alaska all summer, so you don't have to behave. Margaritas will be flowing. When's the last time you got good and drunk?"

Gracie giggled. "I'm beginning to wonder about you. First you think I need sex, and now I should get bombed. too?"

"Either one wouldn't hurt. Both would be better."

"I'll consider going, minus the sex and booze. If I decide to come, I will need to get home early."

Krystal looked annoyed.

"No, for real. My neighborhood had some break-ins. I prefer not to leave the house unattended too long, especially at night."

"Your subdivision has gated security."

"And several houses have been robbed. The thieves are after jewelry and small, pricy items. I don't have any jewels worth stealing, but still."

"Stewart gave you a ton of expensive bling throughout your marriage."

"Yeah, he was especially heavy on the pricy gift-giving during the cheating years. I didn't want to keep anything from him after we split, so I sold everything to a gold and silver dealer." She smiled. "Used the cash to buy two zero-turn mowers for the business."

"Good for you."

After they'd finished eating, they paid their bill then rose to leave. Outside, they walked to their vehicles.

"Keep your eyes and ears open and keep me informed of anything out of the ordinary concerning plants," Krystal reminded as she headed toward her car. She opened her vehicle door. "I'll see you Friday."

"Krystal, I didn't say I was going."

"Oh, you are."

Gracie's mouth flattened as she reached for the truck handle. "If you say so."

"You'll be there." She smiled. "And so will he."

"Who?"

Krystal laughed. "Whoever."

Chapter 5

"We'll have your results soon, Mr. McCarthy."
The nurse flashed Ethan a flirty smile as she shut the
door behind her, leaving him in the room alone.

"Not interested, Nurse Nirvana," he mumbled,
sliding off the icy x-ray table. While she was attractive
enough, he had too many things on his mind to consider
the obvious "he and she" waltz she tried to lure him
into during his examination. He snatched his clothes
from the chair, eager to dress, and be on his way.

This trip had been a total bust. Other than a
scratchy throat, and a slight catch in his chest when he
inhaled too deep, he was fine. More troubled someone
tried to kill him, he'd rather direct his efforts and
pursue that person than spin his wheels listening to a
diagnoses he'd known.

Within minutes he'd ripped off the hospital gown,
dressed, and was out the doctor's office, and back into
the scorching sunshine, ready to return to work. His cell
rang the moment he stepped outside the building. He
glanced at the caller ID and groaned before he punched
the on button. "McCarthy."

Mike's booming voice reverberated from the other
end. "Ethan, what's the good word?"

"Esophagus is burned. Doc expects it'll be okay in
a few days. He gave me antibiotics and some throat
spray for relief. My lungs sound clear, but he did a

chest x-ray to make sure no serious damage occurred. He'll let me know the results later today."

"Good. Good." A silence lapsed for several seconds. "Exactly how did you explain the injuries?"

"I told him the story we agreed upon."

"Did Doc accept it?"

"He didn't question me." Though Ethan was unsure the doctor bought his account he was "accidently" trapped in a greenhouse full of pesticides. He certainly would've raised his brows an inch or two if someone tried to sell him that load of crap. He'd arrived at his truck, pressing the keypad to unlock. "You get everyone on board on your end?"

"Krystal's at lunch. I'll speak with her when she returns."

"You're sure you can convince her?"

The line went quiet for quite a few seconds. "Krystal is a straight arrow, but she always does what is best for the nursery, even if she doesn't agree. Quinn won't be an issue, because as usual, she's oblivious to what's going on. You'll talk to Doliver? Make sure he gives the rest of the crew the appropriate update?"

"As soon as I get back." Ethan inserted his key and turned his truck over. Then he flipped the air conditioner switch to high to cool down the oven-like conditions inside his vehicle. "What about Gracie Desoto? She witnessed everything and then some. Can we trust her?"

Mike sighed loud from the other end. "She's on the nursery's' side, but she'll be a little more difficult to sway. Krystal invited her to the get together, Friday. I'll talk to her then. Maybe you could drop by her office, soften her up before then? Before the sheriff calls her?"

"I don't know…"

The last thing Ethan wanted was another encounter with the strong minded, Ms. Desoto. Something about the woman made him forget he was a professional. Her stubbornness was maddening, yet she had an unexplainable quality that drew him. A disturbing quality. He'd planned on steering clear of her at Mike's party, and he'd definitely avoid any more nursery encounters. Now, if he could just get her out of his head.

"She and I didn't exactly get off on the right foot. I'm not sure she'll be receptive to even a gentle push from me."

Mike chuckled. "Maybe you should extend an olive branch. Turn on the charm. After all, she did save your life."

He forced a swallow past the new lump that formed in his throat, grimacing from the bitter taste of his saliva.

"Yeah, that'll work," he said dryly.

"Give it a shot. Can't hurt."

He struggled to find patience. The man was his boss for the moment. If Ethan wanted to continue this project, then he had to play his game to some degree, even though the idea was ridiculous.

"I'll stop by now."

"Just set it up, and make sure she stays quiet until Friday. I'll do the rest. As a matter of fact, I'm going to phone Bud now. See if I can't get him to hold off his deputy from interviewing her until later in the week."

"Shit," Ethan muttered, after he'd rung off.

He summoned his GPS for Desoto Landscape Design and Lawn Maintenance and pointed his pickup to follow the instructions until he arrived at a coffee colored building located on the outskirts of town. He sat in front of the office for a long while, not knowing what to say, or how he would say it if the words came to mind.

Finally, he opened the door and stepped into the hot sun. He'd like to do what he normally did. Turn off his emotions and wing it. The winging part he may get, but shutting down his feelings would be near impossible with this woman.

****

Gracie breezed into her office and sang a strained, "Hey, Betty."

Her secretary sat at her desk, her iron gray head bent over an electronic tablet, a steaming cup placed within arm's reach.

Betty peered at her through thick lenses, her sharp features enhanced by a mouth that always seemed to frown. "Gracie."

Gracie paused to gather the unopened mail laid neatly at the desk's edge "I am so far behind today." She sifted through the stack giving Betty a quick glance. "Anything I need to attend to right away?"

Betty shuffled the tablet aside. She slid a hand into her stackie tray for a small notepad, tearing off several pages. "A few phone calls, but that's all."

Gracie extended a palm.

Betty adjusted her trifocals and laid the posts in front of her. Fingers interlocked, connected hands rested onto the desks surface. She stared at Gracie.

Gracie's eyebrows rose. "Messages?"

"Stewart's gonna remarry, huh?"

"Good news travels fast. You spoke with my

mom?"

Gracie stifled an eye roll. Her mother probably wore out the speed dial with this information. Betty and her mom had been friends since their schooldays. Betty's name would've been first on the call list.

"Of course, I talked to your mama. A dang idiot, isn't he?" She didn't give Gracie a chance to answer. "Don't you worry over that sorry excuse of a man. He's shown his behind on more than one occasion. He's only acting like himself again."

"I'm not worried, Betty." She closed her eyes, mindful of what was about to come, though powerless to stop it. "I don't have time to discuss this now, but I'm dealing with the fallout."

"Just like you dealt with the divorce?"

"Excuse me?" She straightened, arms folded over her chest. She glared at Betty. Though grateful for her loyalty, Gracie wasn't prepared to suffer through one of her self-proclaimed "expert" opinions. Not today.

Betty shook a finger at her. "You heard me. Just like you dealt with the divorce. Or haven't. How long since he left you? Two years? I guess you'll throw yourself into this business again. Keep on ignoring the other aspects of your life."

"I don't overlook anything in my life."

"All you do is work, girl. You need to socialize. Shake things up, go out for some fun."

"I enjoy time with my friends."

"You only associate with woman friends. Married, lunch buddy, female friends. I'm talking about mixing with the single population. The unattached, male population. You should get out some. Date. "

"I date."

"Not for a while. From your description, they're all duds."

Gracie shrugged and made a face. She couldn't argue. To say her social life was at a standstill would be an understatement. But she'd already had this conversation with Krystal, in a much more dignified way. She didn't care to repeat it with her secretary, old family friend or not.

"Time goes fast, Gracie. You need to start living again. You played the part of the wronged ex-wife long enough. Deal with the heartache and move on. Get out. Raise some hell, girl. Do something that'll shock your mother."

The office door opened. Intense light from the mid-afternoon sun blazed through the gap, a rush of hotness heated the entryway, triggering the air conditioner to click on.

The brightness reduced the visitor to nothing more than a shadow. The large, silhouetted frame stepped inside from sunshine. He stopped to tuck his sunglasses into his shirt pocket.

Gracie's mouth dropped, and for once Betty was silent.

"Ms. Desoto."

Gracie managed to choke out a squeaky, "Ethan."

Betty grinned at her with raised brows. "Ethan?"

Words failed her. She'd done nothing but think about him since they'd parted earlier. Even so, she'd decided their one encounter would remain a single, which shouldn't be a problem if he wasn't going to hang around long. She could avoid the nursery until then, and she'd planned to feign sickness to get out of going to Mike's party.

But here he was, all rugged and muscled. His high testosterone level overpowered her small office.

Ethan looked at Betty. "I'm Ethan McCarthy. Ms. Desoto and I met this morning."

Betty's smile widened. "Oh you did?"

"He's Mike new foreman." Gracie's voice still high pitched and unnatural sounding. "For a while, anyway."

Betty glanced at Ethan, then leaned across her desk and whispered to Gracie, "Now that's what I'm talking about."

Ethan's gaze zeroed in on Gracie. "Is there a place we can talk?" He glanced at Betty. "In private?"

Alone? Gracie's once inactive libido suddenly stood at attention followed by a firm salute. She motioned toward her office, stretching for the knob and missed it completely.

"In here." Making a second stab, she grabbed the handle and twisted, standing back to let him pass through then followed him inside. She peeked around at Betty as she closed the door. "Hold my calls."

Betty shot her another crafty grin. "For as long as you need me to, honey."

She turned to Ethan, hoping the heat on her face wasn't apparent. He paced about, as if inspecting her office. The space was small, with only enough room for her desk, a file cabinet, and a tiny credenza placed behind her chair. And her fridge.

Ethan's tremendous presence made the minute size seem even tinnier.

"You're okay now?" She realized his health wasn't the reason for his visit but she was too flustered to ask why he was here. "What'd the doctor say?"

"No permanent damage. I'm just thirsty."

She stepped behind her desk and gestured to her little refrigerator. "I have drinks."

"I doubt if you've got what I want."

"I don't keep alcohol here," she stated primly.

A corner of his mouth lifted. "You look like someone who does only healthy, and I'd prefer something bad, like a soda." He stroked his throat. "Relieves the scratchiness."

She bent and opened the fridge and removed a can, handing it to him.

"Looks can be deceiving. I have a slight chocolate addiction. Soda enhances the buzz."

He chuckled and eyed two candy bars lying on her desk.

A palm snapped to cover her treats. Her gaze narrowed. "Don't think about it or getting poisoned won't be the worst thing that's happened to you today."

"Lady likes her sweets."

"I do." Then she stopped, recalling their previous encounter. Her face reddened even more. Her earlier demands of his credentials had been way out of line and embarrassed her now. "Um, I am sorry about my questioning you over your plant knowledge this morning. I wasn't aware of your employment situation."

"I should've explained."

Gracie gave a slight nod, glad he easily moved past her impoliteness. "How long are you going to be at the nursery?"

"Three months tops. Then I'm on to other assignments." He smiled. "Any other questions?"

God, she was doing it again. Why couldn't she just

bite her tongue and let this guy go. She wanted to know the reason for the visit, but after her over the top inquiries, the words wouldn't form. Even though he'd been agreeable so far, she got the impression he didn't appreciate her constant queries, even if the habit was second nature. A nervous smile flickered across her lips. "That's all."

An awkward silence followed as seconds turned into minutes. He took several long sips of his drink. "I suppose you're wondering why I'm here."

Finally. "Well...yes."

"I came to apologize." He hesitated. "For my behavior. I'm afraid I wasn't particularly gracious earlier. You risk your life to save mine when you clearly didn't have to. I do appreciate the efforts."

Gracie struggled, taken aback by his frankness. "I only did what anyone would."

"Not so sure, but if that's a "you're welcome" I'll take it." He scanned the piles of paperwork on her desk. "Looks like you have a lot to do, so I won't take up any more of your time. I need to get to the nursery, anyway."

"You're going back?"

"I work there, why wouldn't I?"

"Someone made an attempt on your life."

He gazed at her, his expression matter of fact as if someone trying to kill him was commonplace.

"How come you're not more upset about this?"

"Former military. Did a couple of stints overseas. Afghanistan." The corners of his mouth twitched again. "Not my first rodeo."

"This is a little different. Someone targeted *you*."

He didn't respond. Steel, gray eyes penetrated her,

cutting though her, hitting her straight to the core.

"Um, have you talked to the police, yet?"

He looked surprised. "The police?"

"Yes, somebody tried to kill you. Krystal said Mike had an appointment to speak with the authorities. They'll want to speak with me, too. Please tell me Mike called them to investigate."

He took a long swig of his drink, finishing off the soda. Crushing the can between his strong, deft fingers, he tossed it into the trashcan next to her desk.

Gracie planted her hands onto her hips. "You're kidding me. Mike didn't call anyone, did he? He loves to sweep negatives under the rug, but this is crazy." She pointed a forefinger in his direction and stabbed the air. "And you're letting him get away with it."

He turned away, lifting a shoulder. "I'm not letting him do anything. The nursery is out of city limits, therefore, not in the police's jurisdiction. He contacted the sheriff, and they discussed the issue. He'll also speak with me, and yes, he'll get in touch with you later."

"Right," she said caustically. "He and Sheriff Bud are super close—golf buddies. I bet the issue is no longer one."

"We're doing what's best for the nursery." Ethan strolled to the exit, his fingers tapped the doorknob. "Mike needs you to do the same. Can you keep this quiet, please? At least until the investigation is completed?"

"So that's why you're really here. You want me to keep my mouth shut."

He twisted the knob and stepped through the door. "Thanks for the soda. Ms. D. Have a lovely afternoon."

Chapter 6

"First I see you on Monday and now again today. Two visits in one week. What do I owe the pleasure?" Hands thrust into his jean pockets, Ethan lumbered into an unused greenhouse. He preferred to skip this summons, but due to the circumstances, he had little choice other than to comply, unless he wanted trouble. Which he did not.

The blonde woman waited. She regarded him through narrowed eyes. He gave her a onceover and marveled at her composure. The interior of the hothouse were stifling, yet her business suit remained crisp as if she'd just put it on. And though she walked across a long, graveled path to reach the secluded area, her dress shoes appeared clean and without scuffs. Even her hair stayed in place despite the hot, blowing winds.

"I wanted to check on you before I took off."

Ethan set his shoulders. "I don't need a babysitter, Becca."

She raised her perfectly shaped brows. "That's not my intention, Ethan."

He wasn't interested in her objective. While he respected her, even liked her to some degree, their personal and professional relationship staggered on a delicate, fine line and at the moment she'd crossed over.

"Someone tried to kill you the other day. That may

lead to lots of questions."

"How did you get back here without anyone noticing you? There'll be even more questions if you're spotted."

Situated almost behind the nursery, the house's view was obstructed from the compound by overgrowth and low hanging tree branches, sitting far enough away from the activity that unless someone sighted anybody going in, no one would have a clue anyone had ventured inside.

"No worries." Her lips lifted into a cool smile. "I have my ways."

"I bet." He combed his fingers through his hair. "As you can tell, I'm fine."

"This incident certainly has put you in a horrible mood, which I can understand." She stopped and shot him another severe look. "But I don't understand how you managed to get trapped in the first place. What happened to your ever so sharp skills?"

"Let one slip by me, I guess," he said, not thrilled to be reminded of his recent sting.

"Lucky your little landscaper was such a quick thinker."

"She's not my little anything." He gazed at the tips of his work boots.

"Not from what I hear."

Ethan's head jerked up. What had she heard? Probably nothing. Her tone sounded smug, and she was undoubtedly on the warpath with the intent of smacking him below the belt. Somebody must have pissed her off. Possibly him, since her usual critique of his behavior was always harsh lately. Either way, he doubted she knew much about his recent encounter with

Gracie Desoto.

Or how he couldn't get her out of his head.

He'd enjoy getting to know her or would if she didn't infuriate him so much. And the woman was way too perceptive. His gut told him she was probably diligent when she wanted answers. Instincts also alerted him that she was attracted to him too, although she'd never admit it.

Images of her large, green eyes, and her sexy, little body swept through his mind. Pictures of her naked and underneath him had his cock nudging his jean's zipper as beads of perspiration dotted across his forehead. He inhaled, forcing himself back to the present. Now wasn't the time to allow his fantasies take over. His current situation needed his full attention.

"I strongly discourage any contemplation you may have in getting close to this woman."

"I'm not contemplating anything. I'm just happy she was here to save my ass."

"Yes, well…we all are." She fidgeted with a heavy beaded necklace that draped around her neck. "I'm thinking we may need to remove you."

His entire body stiffened. "Remove me? The job's not done."

"Your work here *is* finished, whether the assignment is completed or not."

She walked across the torn ground cloth, careful not to snag her heals in one of the frayed rips, to stand in the doorway. She used her hand and fanned her face to stir the air. "I can't afford to have any more mess ups."

Shit. He should've guessed something like this was in the works. Getting locked in an insecticide-filled greenhouse was huge, but his pride, among other things were on the line, and he'd fight to stay on this job. He wanted this SOB's head on a golden serving dish and the body buried in an unmarked grave.

"The decision has been made."

"Without including me?" He swung a leg and kicked a cracked, plastic flowerpot lying in the middle of the dirty sheeting. It bounced across the floor and smacked against the flexible side, landing on the ground with a plop, slitting in two. "Listen, I know you're still pissed about a lot of things—"

"No, Ethan, I'm way beyond ticked." She spun around, her hands settled on her hips. "You weren't paying attention." She pursed her lips and cast him a death glare. "I call the shots, and I'm taking you off this assignment."

Ethan opened his mouth to argue, then he stopped to consider his line of reasoning and how to persuade her to recant her ruling. "You are my superior, true— but I strongly disagree with your choice. I've been on this project since the beginning. Things are coming together. Bringing in a replacement will put you back at square one. We've made too much headway to start over. A lot of time and money will be wasted, and my knowledge won't be useful because I'm the only person who understands the process. Everything is too complicated to explain, it'd take forever for someone new to get it."

She sighed and dropped her arms to her side with a slap. By the look on her face, he could tell he'd made his case. He wouldn't be going anywhere just yet.

"You must be more careful," she warned.

"I will now that I know what I'm up against." He

turned to leave. "I gotta get back to work."

"This is your final chance."

He came to an abrupt halt.

"No more mess ups."

"Of course."

He walked away without looking back, satisfied he'd saved his assignment, for now at least,

It was a little after noon, and the heat scorched past one hundred. The breeze had all but disappeared. Sweat instantly covered him as he entered outside into the blistering temperature. He headed toward his truck. He'd left his shades inside, and the sun's intensity made seeing almost impossible. On his way, he caught sight of Reed and his crew and made a detour.

"How's it going?" he asked Reed as he approached the workers laying a new sprinkler system in a newly built greenhouse.

"Almost done." Reed grinned. "Your *boss* paid you another visit?"

"I wish she'd stay inside and chitchat with Mike."

"Guess she can't help herself." Reed chuckled. "She wants to be with you, heartbreaker."

"Whatever." Ethan squinted against the sunshine, studying a greenhouse behind them.

A ladder was placed on the far side, in the house's shadow almost as if somebody wanted to conceal its existence. A silhouetted figure was on top of the house, ducking low as they carefully straddled the roof's beam. Ethan glared harder, before he aimed Reed a confused glance. "What's Ortiz doing up there? We didn't have any roof cover work scheduled today, did we?"

"As far as I know we didn't." Reed frowned

looking in the direction of the employee's outline. "Quinn may've sent him with one of her hair brained schemes."

"Yeah, that's a possibility. Somebody needs to reel her in." Ethan took a step, still watching the guy on the rooftop. He'd maneuvered off the gable's edge and stepped onto the extension ladder, a foot planted onto the top rung. He started to climb down.

The ladder swayed, then tilted to one side. The man clutched the edges, stuck in the middle with no means of escape. He attempted to step down to the next rung.

"Ortiz, stop." Ethan took off in a full run toward the catastrophe in progress with Reed at his heels. "We're on our way."

The stepladder lurched, the right side completely lifted off the ground, and toppled over in what seemed like slow motion. Ortiz dropped, his body smacked into the dirt, bounced once, then lay still in the graveled dust.

Ethan and Reed rushed to him. He wasn't moving. Ethan knelt down beside him and gave him a gentle shake hoping the unthinkable hadn't happened. "Ortiz. Ortiz, wake up." Bit by bit, the man lifted his head, his expression dazed. "You okay?"

Ortiz nodded and groaned as he pushed himself to his butt.

"Can you stand by yourself?"

Again he bobbed his head with a grunt. Ethan put a hand around the heftier man's upper arm and helped him to his feet. "We should call for an ambulance. You need to be checked out."

"I'm okay." Ortiz insisted. "Maybe a little bruised is all."

Ethan observed him. He didn't appear to be in any obvious pain, and his limbs seemed to be working properly. "Fine, but you still need to have a doctor look at you."

Reed motioned for an employee from his crew over. "Take Ortiz to the office. He needs to fill out an accident report, and then send him to Vivian. She can make an appointment for the doc to examine him. Ethan and I'll be up later and explain everything to Mike."

Ortiz opened his mouth to protest.

"If you want to work, you'll get a doctor's okay." Again Ethan wondered why this guy was on the top of the house. He resisted the urge to interrogate him now, but he'd be sure to question him later.

Reed walked over to investigate the extension ladder's placement. He swiped a foot at the dirt. "One leg was set in a hole. Looks fresh." He glanced at Ethan. "Wonder if the leg was sunk in after Ortiz placed the ladder."

"Without anyone noticing?" Ethan strolled to where Reed stood.

Reed shook his head. "We were busy. Had no idea Ortiz was up there."

Ethan stroked his chin, studying the situation. Why anyone would want to harm Ortiz?

The nursery had become quiet, as the crews had broken for lunch. The engine of a tractor rattled nearby. Ethan's brows lowered, his attention drawn to the sound. If everyone was gone, who was on the tractor?

An urgent chill dashed through him.

His eyes narrowed against the burning sun. The huge piece of machinery was on the path nearby and seemed to be closing in on them. The operator was a mere shadow but appeared to be covered from head to toe, their identity enigmatic.

Within seconds, the tractor was upon them. The driver suddenly bailed, vanishing into a nearby greenhouse. The machine continued to roll toward them at a high rate of speed. Ethan pushed an unobservant Reed hard. He fell to the ground. Ethan dived in the opposite direction, the instant the monstrous contraption barreled between them. The forks attached to the front, ripped into the greenhouses sturdy Polycarbonate as it bowled inside, crushing pots and flats and an assortment of plant material before hitting an iron pipe, bending in the conduit, before coming to the stop.

Reed was laid out in a muddy ditch. He pushed to an elbow, ignoring the wet dirt. "What the fuck?" Scrambling to his feet, he sprinted inside to inspect the rumbling machine.

"Pretty obvious, I think." Ethan followed Reed. Gassy fumes saturated the small area, the stench almost overpowering.

He stared at the tractor as the motor chugged slowly then whizzed to a stop.

"Someone tried to take us out."

Chapter 7

"Good morning, Betty." Gracie struggled through her office entrance, her arms full. Betty stood near the doorway, fists planted on her hips, and her scowl deeper than normal.

Gracie squeezed past her secretary to get inside. "This is terrible. I'm never late, and here I am running so far behind. On a Friday, no less."

This week had been a hectic one. New landscaping jobs, dodging questions, or sympathies over her ex-husband's pre-nuptials, and the *very* brief interview with Sheriff Bud took turns occupying her thoughts. To top things off, she had Mike's party to contend with-Krystal was still insisting she attend.

Then there was Ethan McCarthy. He remained a constant in her mind the entire five days. The guy unraveled each and every nerve in a way she'd never experienced. Despite a previous firm decision to avoid him, she wavered, seesawing from excitement from seeing him again to wanting to hide until he rode out of town.

Most of last night was spent awake, debating whether to attend tonight's get together or stay home with a good book. The chance of another encounter sent her over the edge. She'd drifted off to sleep around five, snoozing through her alarm, hence the reason for her tardiness.

Betty dropped her arms with a shrug. "I guess it's okay if you want to run your company into the ground. The business is yours to lose."

Gracie spun around almost spilling her armload. "What's wrong?"

Betty's fists returned on her hips only this time she added a foot tap. "Where to start? Pea gravel order didn't show up at the Sable's residence. The customers won't let your crew onto the property until the shipment arrives. Your lead guy phoned the rock company. They can't find the truck. Looks like the cargo is lost."

Gracie sprinted toward her office.

"Also—"

She stopped and twirled back to Betty.

"Flu's going around. Three people called in sick, with a couple complaining of upset stomachs and threatened to go home if they weren't better soon. Your able crews are at the condo job, which means there's no one at the Hawkins Court subdivision."

"Is that all?"

"Let's see." Betty pulled at her chin. "Ronnie's made it to the Anderson's. He can't get the riding mower to turn over. They're trying to find a mechanic who can come right away, but they haven't had any luck."

Gracie flew into her office, dumped her work in a pile on her desk, and picked up the phone. The business issues took her nearly all morning to resolve, therefore she was late getting to her seminar. Her tardy arrival forced her to copy notes from other attendees, which made her departure later from the conference.

She weaved through the crammed, parking garage. With each step, her confidence waned over attending this party. She was exhausted, and she preferred to go home. Pajamas, reading, and bed superseded loud noise, overindulgence, and small talk. After all, she was a grown woman. If she wanted an early night, who'd tell her no?

Key inserted, she started her pickup and maneuvered the garages heavy traffic, her body tense as she manipulated the aisle's tight squeeze until she exited into the late afternoon sunshine.

After a quick stop by the office, she'd be heading for home.

Betty was tying up loose ends when she arrived.

"How'd the meeting go?"

"It was good." Gracie strolled inside, bending at the mini-fridge for a soda, then opened the bottom drawer of her desk for several bites of chocolate. Because of the hectic, problematic morning, she forwent lunch, and she was starved. She plopped down behind her desk with a sigh. "Right now I want to enjoy my drink. Then I plan to pack up and go home for a quiet night."

Betty had trailed in behind her. She sat down in a chair across from Gracie. "I'm ready to head that way myself." She hesitated. "You're not attending Mike's get together?"

She unwrapped a piece of candy, barely glancing at her secretary as she stuck it into her mouth. "I thought about it, but no."

"Why? I hear the place he's holding it is real nice. Good food, located on the river. Pretty area."

"I live on the other side of the river. My backyard is on the water. I even have a pier leading into the canal. It's lovely there too, and much quieter. Not a huge draw for me." Gracie reclined and tilted her head against the chair's back. "After the week I had, I'm worn-out. I want to sleep the entire weekend."

Betty studied her for several seconds. "Are you sure tired is all you are?"

"What else would it be?"

"Ethan?"

Gracie's head popped up. Her face heated with a loud gasp. "Ethan?"

"You didn't forget tall, dark, and dangerous. You haven't been the same since his visit."

No she hadn't. But seeing him again wouldn't change that. Even with his overconfidence, Ethan somehow managed to seep under her skin, and if she saw him once more, he'd never go away until she got him out of her thoughts if that were possible. A motive to avoid him at all costs.

"Will he be at this shindig tonight?"

"No idea. I don't know much about him other than he's worked at the nursery for several weeks and caused quite a stir with his rule changes."

"This guy is the real reason you're bowing out."

Gracie's gaze dropped to her desk as she tucked her bottom lip between her teeth. "I've decided not to go because I choose not to."

Betty eyed her, evenly. "You're not going because you're attracted to him, and it scares you."

Gracie picked up her soda and took a lengthy drink, then undid another chocolate. "I'm not afraid. This isn't the right time for me."

"If you're not ready, you're not ready. You should most definitely skip this evening." Betty pushed out of her chair and onto her feet. "Just remember one thing while you're enjoying a peaceful, uneventful night alone." She smiled and reached into the slacks pocket and brought out an envelope. "Stewart didn't find his new fiancée by sitting at home in sweatpants, watching television, and eating chocolate." She paused. "Speaking of your ex, he stopped by a while ago."

"Stewart was here?" Gracie asked her voice high and squeaky.

Betty tossed the envelope onto the desk, landing in front of her. "He feels you two are on good enough terms that he can invite you to his wedding. Here's his invitation." She turned and walked toward the exit. "Enjoy your solitary weekend."

****

She was so firing Betty on Monday. Gracie stomped down the pier leading to the restaurant. A young hostess opened the door as she approached the Saskia's Fine Food and Dining. The girl ushered her inside and directed her to a private room where Mike's festivities was already in full swing.

She froze in the doorway. The interior was lit in a dim, smoky almost romantic glow. Cuisine aromas seeped through the atmosphere inciting her empty stomach to rumble. Krystal gave her the impression this was to be a small gathering, but a swarm of guests filled the place with wall-to-wall people. The music was loud, the dance floor packed.

"Gracie." A voice yelled above the crowd. "Gracie. Hey girl, over here." Krystal stood at a table near the dancing area, swinging an arm over her head.

Gracie stepped inside, maneuvering through multitude of individuals. She hugged Krystal when they met, shook Charlie's hand, and sat down. Quinn was on the other side of the table. She shaded her eyes in dark blue giving her a raccoon appearance, and she lined her mouth in bright red, which was stuck in a frightening smile.

Gracie said hello, but her only answer was a moaned grunt. Two full shot glasses of clear liquid sat in front of her. Five empties sat in a row next to the filled ones. Gracie raised her eyebrows at Krystal, who shrugged in return.

"I'm so glad you came. I was afraid you'd chicken out and go home to your pajamas and novels."

Gracie interlinked her fingers and clasped her fists, resting them in front of her on the table. "Stewart dropped off a wedding invitation by the office."

Tiny lines puckered between Krystal's brows.

"He left me a note telling me how excited he is because of my supportiveness over his remarrying, and he believes we've bridged our gap. He thinks we are now at a place where we can be happy for each other." She rolled her eyes. "Friends."

Krystal picked up her glass and drained the contents. "Kinda makes me glad my ex just left to get a pack of cigarettes and never came back. Trust me, if I ever see him again, it won't be to rekindle a friendship."

"I'm not excited about the new direction our relationship is taking either." Gracie glanced at Quinn's empty shot glasses. "Quinn, I think you have the right idea. Which way is the bar?"

Quinn picked up the glass of liquid and downed it in one gulp. She glanced at Gracie with glassy eyes, her mouth opened wider, but she didn't say a word.

Charlie scooted his chair away from the table and

stood. "I'll go. What are you drinking, Gracie?"

"A margarita, frozen no salt."

"Krystal, another?" Her husband didn't wait for her to answer but picked up her empty and disappeared into the crowd.

"Bring me one, too," Quinn shouted.

Gracie took in the huge gathering and nodded at her former boss, who appeared jolly, holding a drink, and laughing. "Mike looks relaxed."

"For once," Krystal agreed. "After this week, he needs to wind down."

"Anything else happen?"

Krystal leaned closer and lowered her voice. "A ton of plants came up missing this morning, and as of yesterday we had two more mishaps."

"Like Ethan's?"

Krystal nodded. "One of the big tractors crashed into a greenhouse, right after an unidentified driver jumped off. Ethan and Reed jumped away to avoid being crushed."

Gracie gasped. "They weren't hurt, were they?"

"Thankfully no, though there's some minor damage to the house and a little dent in the tractor. Right before, Ortiz was on top of a greenhouse roof. Somehow one side of the ladder he'd used was placed in a newly dug hole and tipped over on his trip down."

"Is he all right?"

"Bruised and understandably shaken, but yes, he's fine."

"Did he see anyone mess with the ladder?"

Krystal shook her head. "It's like we have a ghost."

"Has Mike conceded and brought in the real police?"

Krystal lifted her glass and took a long sip. "Nope. He and Sheriff Bud are still conferring, but that's about it."

"In other words, they're scheduling a tee time."

"Hey," Quinn shouted and pointed to the dance floor. "Who's the woman with Ethan?"

The women whipped around. Gracie's heart raced, beating twice its normal speed. Her jaw dropped. Ethan was only a few feet away, dancing with a tall, cool blonde. Together they gyrated, as he spun her, keeping in time with music.

Krystal stared. "I've never seen her before."

"She was at the nursery the other day," Gracie said. "He and I were talking, then after she drove up, he kinda made a quick getaway."

"Must be his girlfriend."

Charlie returned with their beverages and set glasses in front of them. Gracie picked hers up, taking a lingering swallow, and then she gulped a mouthful, still staring at the impeccably dressed woman dancing with Ethan. Her clothes, hair, and jewelry shouted sophistication. Gracie zeroed in on the sparkle, blinking from the woman's left hand. Her heart stopped. An engagement ring. The lady had to be Ethan's fiancée.

An instant jealous rage ballooned in Gracie's chest as the couple moved compatibly across the floor. He was engaged. Her throat constricted. She forced the liquid in her mouth down. Never the bitter type, her instant fury caught her off guard.

It took every morsel of willpower for her not to rush to them and pour her drink over their heads. Several deep breaths later, she calmed. She'd need two beverages to make that plan work. She glanced at them again. One question answered. He definitely liked older women.

She looked one more time. Her eyes narrowed.

Much older.

She downed the rest of her margarita and pushed back her chair. "I'm going to get me another and do a little circulating."

She sashayed past Ethan and his lady friend, keeping her focus on the bar. After she placed her order, she mingled with some of her competitors and former co-workers. Reed strolled in her direction.

She peeked at Ethan, who was still on the floor with his woman, doing her best not to stare as she sipped her drink. Someone stroked her arm. She jerked.

A smiling Reed stood next to her.

"Gracie. I haven't seen you on the dance floor yet. How 'bout I be your first partner?"

Her initial response was no thanks, but again her gaze gravitated toward Ethan and his date swaying in time. She tipped her mug up and guzzled down the rest of her margarita.

She set the empty glass on the bar and held out her arms. "Love to."

He took her loosely into his arms and guided her onto the floor. The song was a lively one, and Reed was an excellent dancer. Gracie struggled to keep up. It'd been years since she'd danced, and the alcohol didn't help. Maybe younger wasn't the way to go, especially if she wanted to avoid humiliating herself.

She did her best to not watch Ethan and his friend, although her head seemed to automatically drift in their direction. The couple laughed and talked, while their bodies shifted together in rhythm.

Winded by the time the song ended, Gracie pulled away and walked toward the bar with Reed close behind. No more dancing. Jealousy wasn't worth a heart attack.

A feather stroke skimmed across her shoulder. Gracie jumped.

"May I have the next one?" asked a deep, smooth voice from behind.

"Hey Ethan," Reed said. "Thanks for the dance, Gracie. Enjoy the rest of the party."

Gracie stood motionless. Her gaze embraced his steely, intense stare. She wanted to say something except all words vanished before they reached the edge of her tongue. She tried to drag her stare away. He looked good in his work duds, but dressed nice shot him to the tiptop of the gorgeous benchmark.

Not waiting for an answer, he caught her wrists and slid his palms over her forearms. He drew her close, crushing her into his body. She glided her hands over his chest, locking her fingers behind his neck. The two began to rock to the slow music.

His dancing skills weren't as good as Reed's. Didn't matter. She released a deep, unsteady gasp, then sighed, relishing in the sheer feel of being against him.

"That boy has a fascination for you," he whispered next to her ear.

She wrenched her body away. "What?"

His lips slightly curved. "Doliver. He likes you."

"I'm sure he's as charming as the over processed blonde you've spent most of the evening with. Where is your lovely date anyway?"

"Don't have a date. But it's interesting you noticed."

She'd given away too much. "I didn't, ahm…you were right in front of me. How could I not see you?"

"Then you were making a casual observation."

"Exactly." Relief swept through her. He didn't seem to be engaged or otherwise. At least that's what he was telling her, but on the other side of that coin, she'd tipped her hand. "I don't understand the fuss—what's it to you if he likes me?"

Ethan's smile broadened. "You're a good customer. I'd hate for him to overstep any professional boundaries and lose your business."

"A model employee, that's what you are. I'll tell Mike to give you a raise." She abruptly broke their connection. "Thank you for the dance. Now excuse me." She whipped around on the slick floor. One leg slid in front of her, while the other slipped behind. She struggled to regain her poise and not perform the splits in front of the entire nursery industry.

Rough hands glided over her bare arms to steady her. "You okay?"

"I'm fine." She didn't bother to look in his direction as he set her back on her feet.

"Might want to go easy on the margaritas."

She ignored his recommendation. Though grateful for stability, she wanted to get away from Ethan McCarthy pronto. She stood in mid-indignation not sure of her next move. Everyone seemed occupied, and she had no place to go. The bar caught her eye. The hell with his suggestion. Tonight the section of the restaurant was her only true friend.

A large hand encircled her forearm. "Easy, Ms. D." Ethan pulled her to him. "It's an observation. I need to know the feelings weren't mutual."

"Mutual feelings? With Reed? Why would you want to know that?"

His lips curved. "'Cause, I prefer not to make a move if you're otherwise involved."

"Make a move?"

"I'm pretty sure you understand the concept, but in case you don't." He brushed his mouth against hers, then smiled. "Consider yourself hit on."

Chapter 8

Gracie hurried to get her purse. Vivian had joined Quinn and the two were huddled together. They looked up from their discussion and eyed her curiously as she approached.

She ignored the nosy bodies, went to Krystal, and leaned down to whisper into her friend's ear. Krystal tilted her head, catching a glimpse of Ethan who lingered by the restaurant's exit. Her eyes widened, her mouth dropped before her lips transformed into a huge smile. Bouncing in her chair, she flashed two thumbs up with a vigorous nod. Heat saturated Gracie's face. She swiped up her handbag and rushed to where the gorgeous man waited.

Hand against her spine, he guided her toward his pickup outside the restaurant. "I'm over here."

"What about my truck?"

"I'll bring you back later."

"Seems complicated. We can leave separately and meet somewhere."

"If you want."

Gracie twisted to face him, ready to tell him she'd rather travel alone when she really wouldn't. It seemed like something a nice girl would do. His look caught hers. Lips curved, his eyes glittered silver in the moonlights glow. His gaze glided over her, taking his time, lingering in certain places. She almost wilted. It seemed like thousands of years had passed since someone looked at her with such naked desire. Sensations of her own rushed through her, and she was instantly in a hurry to make up for lost time.

As if knowing her thoughts, he tugged her to him. He lowered his head as she tipped her face and stretched to meet him halfway. Their lips touched for a brief moment, and then the kiss deepened. A whirlwind rocked her to the core. Intense, sizzling—dangerous. He crushed her against his truck, pressing his mouth harder onto hers. Heated tongues tangled as the growing hunger between them mounted.

Fingers raked through her hair; he stroked her body until he reached her bottom. He gripped tight, lifting her, urging her legs apart with his solid erection. A hand skimmed her breasts and lightly edged across the peak. His palm curved around her mound and pressed.

Gracie jerked, breaking away.

"Something wrong?"

"No."

He studied her through narrowed eyes. "Tell me."

"You touched me."

He released her and backed up, his fists placed on his hips. "We know where this is going. At some point in the very near future, I plan on touching you more." He flashed a wicked grin. "And tasting you—everywhere." His expression turned uncertain. "Unless you've changed your mind."

Changed her mind. Gracie tucked her bottom lip under her teeth. He'd given her a way out. She could walk away and forget about this. Forget him. When he suggested they leave the party for a more private meeting, his intentions were clear. Gracie still couldn't believe her reaction. Instead of turning him down flat, she'd simply agreed. Now she was with him, and she had the opportunity to back out.

She shook her head.

He opened his truck door and reached inside to push up the middle console. "Where to?"

"My place?"

He stepped aside and allowed her to get in. Her dress wasn't short but not long either and on the tighter side. Scooting across the seat was a struggle. He climbed in behind her and leaned over her to find the seatbelt, and buckled her in.

"Leave it up." His fingertips traced the hem and skimmed her exposed thigh. He brushed his lips over hers. "I might want to explore at stop lights."

Her insides trembled from the mere thought. "There aren't any lights on the way to my house."

"We'll have to improvise, won't we?" He turned the ignition and put the truck in gear.

Thirty minutes later, they pulled into her driveway. Her panties lay in the floorboard, the top of her dress gathered around her waist. Not that she cared. They could've driven all night if he continued working his incredible magic. They parked for several minutes.

Ethan finally raised his head and smiled. "Are you ready to go in?"

Eyes closed, reclined, she released a faint groan.

"I'm about to lose control," he whispered against her ear. "Do you want our first time to be in your driveway inside my pickup?"

She was beyond worrying where they did it, just as long they did. And quick.

"Let's go," he said quietly.

She wiggled into the top of her dress and tugged to lower the bottom. Ethan opened the door and slid out and offered her a hand. Her legs trembled as she led him to the entrance. She stopped halfway and frowned at the truck.

"What's wrong?"

"I left my underwear in your pick up."

"So you did. And there they will stay." He grinned. "Souvenir."

She struggled inserting the key into the front door. She was in such a state, she couldn't make the connection. "You get a memento from this night and I don't?"

"I'll leave you my boxers if you like." He snatched the keychain from her and threw her a mischievous glance. "You're taking too long."

"You're awfully sure of yourself. I should make you go home."

"You should." He put in the key, twisted the lock, pushing the door open, and stepped back. His grin widened. "But you won't."

Gracie grabbed his arm and yanked him inside, slamming the door with a foot.

Hands on her shoulders, he backed her into the entryway wall, his body melted into hers. A white-hot ache throbbed between her legs. She craved a fiercer bond, to be a part of him, and a need for him to be inside her.

"I've wanted to be with you the second I laid eyes on you," he said in a hoarse voice.

"Me too," she purred.

He slanted his lips over hers. The kiss was slow and burning. His tongue explored the inside of her mouth. A cascade of pure heat seeped through every vessel, in and out of her body.

He dipped his knees, slid his arms round her and lifted her so her feet came off the ground. Her fingers clasped behind his neck, instinctively her legs opened and wound around him, ankles crossed and rested on his hips. He pushed his firm penis into her softness between her bare thighs.

A low moan escaped from his throat. "Bedroom?" he murmured against her lips.

"Upstairs."

He glanced in the direction of the staircase. "Never going to make it."

With his hands under her butt, he turned toward the dining room, sitting off to the side of the entryway. Her legs squeezed round his middle as she unconsciously elevated, shamelessly pushing herself further against his hardness.

He lowered her onto the table, letting his weight press into her. He pulled away, or as much as necessary to remove her dress and bra before his impatient lips clasped over a nipple. Sucking hard, his tongue circled the tip over and over. She clenched her jaw. He moved to the other side. He lifted his hips to slide a hand between her legs. Her back arched as his caresses demanded control. She clutched both sides of his head, biting her lip to keep from screaming.

Ecstasy was near, and she was drowning in an upsurge of raw need. She wanted him, and she wanted him inside her now.

Abruptly he rolled off her just long enough to wrestle out of his clothes.

He braced himself above her, using a knee to urge

her legs to open further. Gracie clasped his arms, her hips elevated, anticipating the incoming thrust. He lowered, with one rapid push, he was in her. A sharp pain rose throughout her inner core, her center tight. She froze with a hiss.

"You okay?"

"Better than I was but not as good as I could be."

"Let's get you there."

He slowly eased deeper into her as his mouth found hers again. Her hips instinctively revolved, keeping in time with his steady movements. Together they rocked back and forth with strong even strokes. Her mind drifted into a euphoric elation. Fiery sensations pulsated between her legs twisting a vortex of pleasure through her. Then her world exploded, bursting into a blazed rapture. Her body stiffened. She released a loud breath, stilled briefly, and she relaxed with a soft moan.

Ethan allowed her to rest but only for several seconds. He brushed his lips over hers as he pushed against her again. She flexed her muscles around him. He let out a groan. Intensity sparked and surged between them, their entangled bodies moved rapidly in a gripping rhythm. Another fierce blast ignited inside her.

Gracie stifled a scream into his shoulder, her arms and legs squeezed, hauling him closer as she shuttered. Ethan made a satisfied sound and collapsed on top of her. She let out a long exhale as she slid her hand over the tabletop. No meal would ever be the same. And she'd never get rid of this table.

****

Ethan fought to wake up. Bright sunlight beamed through a tripled set of veiled bay windows. With a hand raised to shield the glare, he propped to an elbow, trying to remember. Purple walls, lacey shades, a twisted quilt covered with hearts lay at the foot of the queen size bed. A whiff of feminine aroma combined with the scent of recent sex lingered, teasing his nostrils.

Two glasses, quarter-filled with amber liquid stood on the nightstand next to the bed. Gracie Desoto sat next to him. He was in her bedroom. He'd spent the night with her, but this wasn't a typical sleepover. There wasn't much sleep involved at all.

She placed a palm on his arm.

"Again?" He fell back into the pillow. "My god, woman, you're going to kill me."

"No. I want food. I think the last time I ate was yesterday morning, and I need sustenance." She stopped and looked at him curiously. "You're not hungry?"

"I'm not awake enough to know." He rubbed his face with a large hand. "Are you offering to make breakfast?"

She tossed her pillow, hitting him in the nose. "It's after two, past lunchtime, and no, I don't cook on Saturday's. Or ever."

"Watch the attitude or you'll have to satisfy me again before I take you anywhere. You want to go out, right?" He stuffed the extra pillow behind him and lay back, stacking his hands underneath his head.

"Unless you prefer to take over chef duties, but you'll have to make a trip to the store. It doesn't matter to me. I'm starved." She gave him a meaningful glance. "For food."

She wanted him to take her to eat. What was he

thinking? On a whim, he made a move, not believing she'd agree. It turned out to be a hell of a night. He wouldn't mind spending more time with her, except he'd played this game before. She'd get the wrong idea if he stayed much longer. He didn't want to be a jerk, but he needed to make a break soon. The plan; feed her and move on.

He rolled out of bed, his feet hitting the cool floor. "Get dressed."

"Okay if I shower first?"

"I need one, too." He stretched across the mattress for her hand and tugged. "We can share."

Long after the warm spray turned ice cold, they exited the oversized shower stall. They leisurely dried, dressed, and headed toward his truck.

Ethan found this lady to be amazing. Their physical connection was mind-blowing, but it was also scary. Unfortunately, there was no room in his life for her, which was too bad. Sans the frightening aspect, he enjoyed her company inside the bedroom, and he was pretty sure he'd find her exciting outside, as well. He'd relish the little time they had left, then sadly be on his way.

Ethan backed out of the drive. "I'll take you to your vehicle after we eat."

She tucked her bottom lip and nodded, staring at her panties lying in the floorboard.

"Something wrong, Gracie?"

She shook her head and leaned back against the seat. "Just tired." She straightened and stared at him. "You called me Gracie."

"That is your name."

"Up until now, it's been Ms. Desoto or Ms. D."

"I assumed since we've been naked together, we'd be on less formal terms. Unless you prefer Ms. Desoto."

"Gracie is fine."

"Will your stomach hold up if we take a side trip and stop by my place? I'd like to change."

"I can manage." She stifled a yawn and relaxed into the seat, closing her eyes.

He pointed the truck in the direction of his house. Twenty minutes later, he drove down an obscure road leading to his small cabin. He glanced at Gracie, who was sound asleep. Setting the gear in neutral, he turned off the engine.

Gracie immediately sat up and blinked. "Where are we?"

"My place."

Gracie nodded toward the cabin that set off outwardly in the middle of nowhere. "You live here?"

He exited from his pickup. "I call it home for now."

He enjoyed the secluded little cabin, surrounded by pines and live oaks. A small pond situated near the back was great for fishing. The backside of the house was mostly all glass; he always had a panoramic view of the wildlife that frequented his home, especially in the evenings. On one side, sat a small deck. Perfect for having a cold one while listening to the tree frogs sing late at night.

Yeah, he really liked it here, and he was kind of sad the place was only his temporarily.

"It's cute." She opened her side and got out.

"Cute," he repeated dryly. "Thanks."

"Is something wrong with that? Tiny houses are adorable."

"Men don't live in adorable."

"Touchy. I'm sure you have an oversized TV with three hundred plus channels. All sports. I'm also guessing there's enough beer in the refrigerator to guy up the place and stamp out the majority adorability factor."

"A stash of alcohol and a big television is considered…?"

"A single man's staple."

"You're profiling. I suppose a readymade bag of salad, an opened bottle of wine, and near empty sack of chocolate bites signify the mantra of unmarried women?"

"You snooped in my fridge?" Her eyes widened. "Wait. I just bought that candy. It should be full."

He snatched her hand and pulled her onto a miniature porch. "My stomach was empty." A corner of his mouth lifted. "Pretty much like your pantry."

He released her to unlock the door and led her inside. Although dark, the room held a cozy atmosphere, the warmth enhanced by the scent of natural wood. He went to a large double window to crack the blinds, ready to bring this budding "relationship" to a halt.

"This is nice." She stood in the middle of the room and did a slow twirl. "Belong to you?"

"Nope. It's a loaner."

"Right. You're not a permanent employee at Mike's, are you?"

"I'm there on a consulting basis."

"What company do you actually work for?"

Ethan smiled. Too many questions. "Thought you were starving." He gestured at the sofa. "Sit if you want. I won't be long."

He hurried to dress. Ten minutes later, he returned to her. She sat straight on the couch, her hands folded in her lap, biting her bottom lip. Time to start their final goodbyes, though he was unsure what to say. Thank you for a lovely evening, didn't quite mesh after spending most of the night naked together. But thanks for the mind-blowing sex seemed too insensitive.

"We'll have to make our meal a quick one," he said uneasily. "I have some work to do this afternoon."

"At the nursery?"

He shook his head. "My weekends are spent filing reports and recommendations to my superiors. It'll take me several hours to type them up and email them off. I'll also run them by for Mike to review, and we'll discuss them afterward."

She looked disappointed. A twinge of guilt twisted in his gut. He ran a hand through his short hair. "But if you're okay with later, maybe I could stop by?"

Gracie hesitated. Ethan's entire self-became motionless. Her pause shook him all the way to his heart.

"I'd like that," she finally said.

He walked to the door and opened it, standing back for her to exit.

So much for putting an end to this. He was gearing up for a full fledge relationship with her. The idea terrified him, in a good way, which worried the hell out of him.

Chapter 9

The past twenty-four hours had been wonderful, but by the time she got home, Gracie was exhausted. She was thrilled Ethan expressed interest in seeing her again. She'd hesitated when he asked, although she didn't have to consider her answer. Instead, she had to taper the impulse to jump and scream "yes" to avoid seeming too eager.

But if she were going to be in shape for a repeat performance later, she'd need some sleep—a lot of sleep. Younger was definitely exciting, though Ethan had worn her out.

She slowly climbed the stairs and fell into bed, asleep the second her head touched the pillow.

****

What seemed like only moments, Gracie flinched, abruptly awakening. She perched on her elbows, her brain fuzzy from slumber. Her room was dark except for shadowed streetlights glowing through the opened blinds. An odd sound resonated from downstairs.

Her thoughts leaped to her mother's voicemail earlier, alerting her of another robbery taken place in her neighborhood. She feared the noise was the result of a possible break in. Quietly, she rolled out of bed and crept down the stairs, leaving the lights off. More clattered bangs came from outside. Swallowing a scream, Gracie froze. Tiny spikes pricked across her neck and pierced her spine. She needed to call for help, but her cell was in her purse, which she'd left in her truck. Though she'd parked her vehicle in the locked garage, she'd prefer not to leave the house.

Tiptoeing through the living room, she headed into the kitchen for her oversized flashlight. She snatched the torch, bounced it in her palm, and nodded. She sneaked to the front, holding the thick roll above her head. She inhaled, then yanked the door open and swung the beam. The heavy cylinder made contact with something solid.

"Son of a bitch." Arms flailed, grasping at the air. Her "intruder's" large body rocked backward and tumbled into a bed of rosebushes.

Gracie flipped the light switch. "Ethan?" A palm covered her opened mouth.

"What the hell is wrong with you?" He struggled to escape the thorny branches.

"I'm so, so sorry." She hurried outside and held out a hand. "Let me help you."

He waved her away as he wrestled from the barbed clutches. "Shit. These fuckers hurt." He escaped and marched to her, jerking the metal cylinder from her grasp, and held it in front of her face. "Why are you trying to knock me out? If you don't want me here, tell me. Don't take my head off."

"I'm…" Explanations whirled through her mind, none plausible, and the truth certainly wouldn't work.

He grabbed her upper arm and dragged her inside. He gave the door a hard shove and spun back to her. He held the flashlight to her again. "Explain."

"You didn't use the doorbell. The way you were pounding, I thought you were a burglar."

"The damn thing wasn't working. It's hanging off the hinge, and I was trying to make repairs in the dark." He rubbed his forehead. A small knot was already swollen over his eye. The rest of him was a mess, too. Black marks and mud covered his clothes, his hands soiled. Blood trickled down his bare arms where he'd been cut by the plant's spikes. "Besides, how many burglars knock before they break in?"

"Did you get that dirty from your fall?"

"I had a flat tire. I slipped in some mud getting the jack from underneath my wheel well. I figured since I was so late, I'd come straight here instead of stopping for clean clothes. Obviously a bad idea."

"I'll get ice for the swelling, and I can put ointment on those scratches."

"I'm fine. I need to use your shower again." He narrowed his eyes and smoothed a filthy hand over his shirt. "Unless you have your hair dryer plugged in by the stall, waiting to finish me off."

"Of course. I mean, yes, you can use the shower, and my outlets are grounded. No risk, whatsoever."

"Tired of people trying to kill me." He pressed the flashlight into her chest as he walked past her, mumbling, "Sorry I scared you."

"And I'm sorry I almost knocked you out. I'll put your clothes in the washer while you clean up."

Ethan stopped and whirled around. A hand clutched her shoulder and pulled her to him. He planted a kiss on her mouth, then gently pushed her away. "You owe me." He smiled, ran a thumb, and smeared her nose with dirt. "Now you need some scrubbing yourself. And after today, I don't bathe alone."

"Did you get dirty on purpose so we can shower

again?"

He took her hand as they climbed the stairs together. "A definite incentive."

Gracie had a wonderful large shower-stall for which they utilized the benefits to the hilt earlier today. An experience she would enjoy repeating many times and never tire. The selling point of this house for her was the huge garden tub made for two, equipped with a soothing Jacuzzi jets that sat in the corner of her bathroom beckoning.

Ethan released her when they entered and walked to the sink. He unbuttoned his shirt and dropped it to the floor. He tapped the facet to wash away the mud and blood. Gracie hopped on the countertop, legs crossed, biting her bottom lip admiring his bare chest.

She traced a finger down his muscled arm. He took her hand and kissed the palm, and then he released her to kick off his shoes. Belt unbuckled, his jeans dropped and lay in a pile on the tiles. He stepped out of them.

He flashed a wicked grin, popping the elastic in his boxers. "You want more?"

Her teeth sank further into her lip. She hoped drool wasn't trickling down her chin. He pushed his shorts from his waist and over his legs.

"Slow down."

He chuckled. "So that's how you like it." He turned his back to her, shoving the boxers to his ankles, and then he punted them away.

Gracie's tongue ran over the outer edges of her mouth, admiring his tight backside. "You could turn around."

"I could." He looked over his shoulder wearing a naughty smile. "Tell me why I should."

"I like the view."

He raised an eyebrow and snatched a towel off the rack to wrap around him and lowered onto a vanity chair. "You're going to have to wait."

"This isn't fair. You get a girl all riled up and then you hold out?"

Arms across his chest, he frowned. "You've got some making up to do." He raked a gaze over her. "A private show for me is in order. Your turn." Ethan's smile widened. "Take it off."

"What?" Though they'd been intimate many times, Gracie wasn't comfortable undressing *that way* in front of him. "I'm supposed to—?"

"You want me to forgive you. This is the beginning."

"The beginning? You're going to milk this, aren't you?"

"Oh sweets, I've got a long list. Expect years of atonement before you get back into my good graces." He leaned forward and tugged at her top. "Off."

"You're not serious, right?"

"As serious as snow in the desert."

Gracie pulled away from him and sighed. She couldn't avoid this. "Fine." Gingerly, she grasped her t-shirt's hem and lifted it over her head.

A hand shot out. "No, wait."

Gracie dropped the shirt, confused. "You don't want me to undress?"

"Of course I want you to undress." He extended a thumb, motioned upward, and pointed to the long strip of marble. "On the counter."

She gnawed her bottom lip and stared at him. Was he kidding?

"You want forgiveness, right?"

She giggled and glanced at the countertop. "We'll be even?"

"Hardly." He nodded at the bathtub. "Not until we have sex in there. In any position. My choice. New place, new position, new record breaker. Plus, stripping gives me extra points."

"Record breaker? Points? You keep score?"

"Not literally." He pointed at his head. "Up here."

"Shallow, don't you think?"

"I don't disagree, but I can't help it. It's the way my mind works."

"You keep a running track of everything?" Gracie asked her tone disbelieving.

"Yes, but some records are more interesting than others."

"Like sex?"

He laughed. "What do you think? Of course sex is by far the most intriguing. By the way, I'm getting a bonus as we speak. I can see your nipples through your shirt. They got hard just from me looking at them. That's a talent."

"Mine or yours?"

"Mine, of course. How else would I get the points?"

Gracie rolled her eyes. "Okay, strip, sex in the tub. Your position choice. Got it. Is that all?"

He rubbed the small knot on his head. "You sound smug. You almost knocked me out, you know. I'd think you'd be more accommodating."

"You have a teeny, tiny bump."

"Teeny, tiny?" His voice elevated. "You nearly took my head off."

"Fine. I'll help you break your silly records." She climbed upon the marble slab. "But my action was a reaction to you scaring me. So you're required to assist me in advancing up the woman's ranks."

"How many more orgasms can you have?"

"That's not what I'm talking about."

"I'm almost afraid to ask."

"The tub has to be filled with bubble bath."

"No. No way." He shook his head, folding his arms over his chest. "Men don't get into fizzy water. Especially smelly, fizzy water. Not going to happen."

She tugged at the bottom of her shirt. "If you can't help me, I can't help you. I should've given you a real head injury. Incidentally, that's a different woman record all together."

"What's the purpose of stinky water? I think I get the gist of the knocking a guy senseless."

"Getting strong manly type bathing in a tub full scenty bubbles record. Difficult to achieve. It falls between watching chick flicks together and shoe shopping."

"What kind of scent are we talking about? Nothing citrusy. I prefer not to smell like fruit. Too womanly."

She gave him a lazy smile. "After the performances you've given, you could wear ruffles and high heels and I still wouldn't consider you womanly."

"Somehow that entire scenario disturbs me, but I'll table the idea for now." His gaze traveled the length of her body. "Pour in the super-suds. But no gossiping at Tupperware parties or whatever you females do when you drink too many strawberry banana daiquiris. I don't want rumors floating around the nursery I do this kind of thing. I have an image to uphold."

Her eyebrows rose. "The fact you know strawberry banana daiquiris exist will raise my status. But we need to educate you on today's female events. This is a different millennium. Forget burping plastic tops. We have lingerie and sex toy get-togethers nowadays."

"Ohhh, now that's interesting." His expression brightened. "Got any lingerie?"

Gracie smiled.

"Toys?"

"Do you want to talk all night?"

"Nope. Take it off." He clapped his hands. "But count on more discussions about those slinky nighties and your sex toy collections."

She climbed onto the counter and pulled her shirt over her head.

"Slowly."

She made a face and dropped it to the floor. Shorts unbuttoned, she slid them down her legs and then stepped out and tossed them away with her foot. She stood in front of him wearing only her bra and panties. She rotated away and faced the mirror.

"I'm waiting."

She glanced over a shoulder.

"Everything."

She unhooked her bra. The straps slide over her arms. She spun, flinging it at him. An easy catch. He held it up. "I need the match."

Gracie bit her lip as she stepped out of her panties, then bent to snatch them up. A low, throaty groan came from behind as he swept her from the counter and carried her to the tub.

"Don't we need to fill the bath?"

He sat her down.

93

"This'll take a few minutes." She twisted the knobs and held her fingers under the stream, testing the water.

A large hand stroked her bare bottom. "We'll have to improvise until it's full."

The digital clock read after two when they finally finished. Bodies laced with a fruity fragrance, their skin wrinkled from the long soak. After she toweled off, she went into her closet for her robe.

Ethan tugged at the tie. "What is this for?"

She gathered up his things. "I'm going to take your dirty cloths downstairs to be washed. I have neighbors, lots of windows, and I don't want them to see me naked."

"It's late. Do you think anyone is awake?"

"I'd rather be safe than sorry."

"You sure none of them caught our performance last night? The blinds were open, and the streetlamps blared through like spotlights."

"I hope not. I'd hate to be the newest neighborhood gossip."

Clothes in the washer, she downed several pieces of chocolate before she returned upstairs. Ethan was already asleep. She took off her robe and crawled in bed, cuddling close to him, hoping they would become a habit.

****

The bed vibrated. Like someone was restless. Gracie instantly woke. A silhouette of Ethan sat beside her, his torso stiff and erect. Streetlights glowed through the opened blinds, the glimmer centered on his face. His expression was…odd.

Unsure if he was awake, she grasped his shoulder and gently jiggled.

"Ethan? Are you all right?"

He didn't respond. She shook him again. His entire body remained rigid beneath her palm. Anxiety choked her. Something was definitely off kilter. Maybe she should call for help.

She leaned across him, to the nightstand searching for her phone. He abruptly whipped around and pushed her onto her back, hurling his body on top of her. Pinned to the mattress, she fought for air underneath his weight.

His fingers tightened around her wrists as she resisted, his legs buried into hers trapping her, holding her in a position to where she could barely move. Her face was smothered into his chest.

"Ethan." She struggled beneath him. "Ethan get off, you're hurting me."

The pressure stopped. He rolled away, raising his head to search the room, his face blank. Perspiration sparkled over his forehead. He swiped a shaky hand across to wipe the sweat away.

"Where am I?" Even his voice sounded different. As if he were in another world.

Gracie slowly rose to her elbows. She stretched to flip on a light, then she studied him. He appeared confused.

"You're at my house."

"Who are—?" His puzzled gazed rested her, staring at her as if he didn't recognize her. Seconds extended into minutes before recollection noticeably set in.

At first, he appeared alarmed. His shoulders slacked. "What happened?"

"I'm not sure. You were sitting up. You had a

strange look on your face, and then you attacked me."

"Attacked you?"

"Yeah, you held me down. I thought you may be having a nightmare, so I tried to wake you and you jumped me. Not in a good way, either."

"I'm sorry." He took her hand and squeezed, tugging her to him. "I'm so, so sorry. I did have a bad dream. I guess I acted out. Are you okay? I know I scared you, hell, I scared myself."

She worked to control the rupture of tension that struck now the ordeal was over. "I'll be fine."

His hands smoothed over the curve of her waist. His arms surrounded her as he drew her closer. His body trembled next to her. His lips found hers. Her frame braced against his. He kissed her harder, urging her into submission. She relaxed a little as her palms on his chest tenderly shoved him from her.

"I can't," she said shakily. She couldn't believe she pushed him away. "Not now."

"I understand." He pressed his lips together. "I'm being selfish."

"Selfish?"

"I need your forgiveness."

"Nothing to forgive. You can't dictate what you dream."

"It doesn't make what I did right. I feel terrible."

"It was bad, wasn't it? The dream."

"I can't remember." He looked at her, his eyes pleading. "I need you, Gracie. I need to connect with you, to recover."

She sat motionless, staring at him, unsure how to respond. He hadn't hurt her, nor did she believe he would intentionally. But could she give herself to him right now, after such a near violent episode. Then again, his dreams weren't his fault, and he did seem remorseful.

She nodded nervously.

He closed in on her, wrapping his arms around her. "Thank you," he sighed into her hair. His mouth found hers again. His tongue pressed to slide though her teeth, touching, dancing with hers, and attempting a complete surrender. She tensed, her arms slipped across his shoulders, giving into his advance.

After a long while of kissing, he pulled away. "We okay now?"

Her head bobbed, her features relaxed. "Do you want to talk about your nightmare some more?"

He gave her a lazy grin. His head lowered to find her lips again. "Later."

****

Sunlight shimmered through the window. She shook her head, trying to assimilate. What had awakened her?

"Your phone's ringing, Gracie." Ethan mumbled. He rolled away, hiding his face with a pillow.

She stretched to her nightstand to retrieve her cell, but it wasn't there. Right. Her phone was in her purse which was still inside her truck. "Not mine, Ethan, it must be yours."

"Shit." Ethan rolled off the mattress, surged to his feet, and rushed into the bathroom. He answered in a clipped tone. "McCarthy."

She got out of bed, put on her robe, and hurried downstairs to give him privacy. She headed into the laundry room to switch his clothes to the dryer. She would've preferred to stay and eavesdropped, but she didn't want to be one of "those" women.

While she waited, she stopped by the refrigerator for a soda, then went to her double secret stash of candy for some chocolate and emptied the supply she kept for when she was low in all her other storage places. Definitely time to make a trip to the store.

Fifteen minutes later the candy and soda were gone. Ethan marched down the stairs, a towel around his waist. Ignoring last night's off episode, her stomach lurched. It didn't get much better, and she was sleeping with him.

"I have to go," he said as his foot slapped the bottom step.

Shock jolted through her. "Now?"

He nodded, not meeting her gaze. "Where are my clothes?"

"In the dryer."

"I need them."

"They aren't ready."

"Doesn't matter." His voice was cool and polite. Like they were almost strangers.

A sharp sting vaulted inside her stomach as she went to retrieve his things.

Moments later she returned. He took his almost-dry clothing without a word and hurried upstairs. Within minutes he was dressed and headed to the door. He touched the knob. What might've been an afterthought, he skidded to a halt and turned to her.

"Sorry for the rush, but...I just need to go." He pushed his fingers through his hair. "And we need to keep our little interlude between us. Are you okay with that?"

Gracie's insides took a nosedive. He was ashamed

of being with her. Slowly, she nodded, as if she could do anything else but agree.

"Thanks." The relief in his expression was obvious. "Enjoy the rest of your weekend, Ms. Desoto."

Chapter 10

Ethan raced away from Gracie's house without a glance behind. His conscience wouldn't allow him to look back. Badgered with guilt, he cerebrally kicked himself. Why didn't he go with his first plan and cancel—no, he'd been aware of their mutual attraction the moment they met. He should have steered clear of Gracie Desoto from day one.

His brain definitely hadn't been involved in the thought process where she was concerned. He'd disregarded every respectable instinct to answer his primal urges, and he loathed himself for what he'd done to her.

Massaging her small memento on his forehead, he knew the moment would come when they had to part ways. He thought he was prepared and was surprised how much he'd dreaded leaving her, and he hated doing so in such a cold manner. But it had to be done.

The woman was now his past, and that's where she must stay.

The next few days would be tough. His focus from here on would be on the bigger picture and find the person who tried to kill him. Plus his damn nightmare had returned. Hopefully it was a onetime thing, but if not, he'd have that trauma to contend with again. Then there was this newest catastrophe.

He rammed the accelerator and retrieved his cell at

the same time. One press of a button and the phone automatically dialed the number.

"Okay, I can talk now," he growled when his connection picked up. "What the fuck happened?"

"Exactly what I told you. I got the word, and I called you right away." The other end paused. "The boss tried to get in touch with you too, but you weren't available. Where the hell did you disappear to?"

"Busy."

"I bet."

"My private life isn't open for discussion. We've got more important things to talk about anyway."

"You're right. Just be forewarned. She's is super ticked over your," his cohort hesitated to do a throat clear. "Unavailability."

"No one's business. I made no promises to anyone; therefore, I maintain exclusive rights on my free time."

The last thing he needed was someone making more demands of him, especially her. He worked twenty-four seven, and he made sure he took advantage of the few off moments of his own he had. She and all of them could go to hell if they had any problems with his attitude. He'd tell them to their face, too. Right now he was tired, mad, and he didn't care who he pissed off.

"I'm not going to argue, except to suggest you might want to consider lowering your profile."

"My visibility is already minimal," Ethan said. "Or minutest as it can be, given my situation."

"You're still too obvious. You can tell me to fuck off, but here's a word of advice. Make yourself undetectable. It'll keep you safe, and ensure your new lady friend stays out of harm's way."

"No new lady anything. We had a weekend and

that's all. We're done. Finished. You know I don't get too involved. Her safety isn't an issue."

"Just making sure nothing's changed."

Ethan bounced the foot on the brake pedal as an amber stoplight switched to red. His truck screeched to a halt. Frustrated, his eyes seesawed from one side to the other, glaring at the empty crossroad in front of him. Fingers drummed the top of the steering wheel. "Has the news been made public?"

"Not yet. Only a matter of time, though. Prepare for the worst once the word gets out. Every local media outlet will blast the story along with their spin, no doubt."

"No doubt." Ethan repeated. "God, this is a major fuck-up."

The signal went to green. Ethan punched the gas; the vehicle roared forward.

Tires squealed against the pavement.

"No shit. All our efforts shot to hell. Everything's at risk now. We need to regroup. Back to square one." A long silence stretched between them. "We've been summoned to a meeting later this evening."

"Got it." He rolled into his secluded drive, skillfully guiding his truck around the snaky bends until he pulled into the driveway. He killed the engine.

"What time is the meeting?"

"Seven-thirty. You plan to show, right?"

"Count on it."

****

Betty swung her chair away from her computer screen and eyed Gracie as she strolled into her office Monday morning.

"Hey Betty." Gracie did her best to project a feign

calm. After the weekend, Ethan's dream, and the abrupt way she'd been left, she didn't want to give away the anxiety twisting through her.

Betty would nag her to death if she had a clue.

"Any messages I need to attend to?"

"I printed the Griffin contracts for you to sign so I can scan them and email back." Betty reached into a basket and retrieved a folder filled with a stack of papers and handed them to Gracie. "A humdinger of a weekend, huh?"

"I'll say. With a huge day ahead." Gracie opened the file and thumbed through the pages. "A busy week for that matter."

"I wasn't referring to business."

Gracie's face reddened. Her chin dipped to stare at the paperwork. The typed words blurred together. "What exactly are you referring to?"

Betty's gaze bored into her. "Don't play dumb with me, missy."

Gracie raised her head. "Betty, I have no idea what you're getting at." She hurried toward her office, hoping to end this conversation before it began. "I should get to work."

"Sex, girl. I'm talking about sex."

Gracie stopped. The folder slipped through her fingers and plopped to the floor. Sheets floated and scattered across the tiles.

"It's written all over you." A broad smile extended over Betty's face. "You got lucky this weekend, didn't you? More than once, from the looks of you." She reached for her steaming cup and blew before she tasted a tiny sip. "'Bout time too, that's all I got to say."

"You mean, you can tell?" Gracie remained still as

a statue, gazing at Betty, disbelievingly. "No you can't. You're guessing."

"I'm a widow, Gracie. For a long time I grieved the loss of my husband and my marriage, same as you. I know the look. You're glowing like a beacon in a dense fog. So who's the lucky guy? The luscious Ethan, I hope?"

Gracie hurried into her office to the small fridge for a soda. She would need a double dose of sugar to get through this. She kept talking, knowing Betty would follow. "I'd rather not discuss my private life, Betty." She was also aware her secretary wouldn't let this go. She only hoped she'd keep her "discovery" to herself and not blab everything to anyone, especially her mother.

"Suit yourself." Betty almost huffed, standing in the doorway. "I understand."

"I'm sure."

"I do. Not many people are aware of this, but I've had a gentleman in my life for some time. I keep what happens between the sheets confidential."

Gracie's lips twisted. This big secret didn't transform into shocking news.

Everyone in town was aware of Betty and her man's lengthy affair. She stayed quiet and let Betty believe her relationship remained hush-hush.

"I always had a healthy sexual appetite and like you I didn't have a physical outlet for a long while."

"Oh my." Gracie preferred not to talk about her mother's best friend's carnal relationship, and yet— "And because of this, this common ground, you can tell I had sex?"

"You're radiant, sweetie. I wish that ex of yours

could see how much you glow. He'd be dumping that youngster and begging you to come back." She chuckled. "In which your reply would be to tell him to go to hell."

"Not a good idea." Gracie laughed too. "I'd rather our next encounter happen when I'm in love with a man." She cerebrally retracted the statement. It would be awesome to run into Stewart while together with Ethan. She'd even fantasized the scenario as they ate at the restaurant Saturday. Taller, much better shape, and younger than her ex. Though she'd yet to meet his fiancée, but she bet she'd win in the good looks department.

"I wouldn't be surprised if you aren't in love. Or at least telling yourself you are."

"I'm not in anything, Betty." She sat her drink down and walked past her secretary to her strewn pages. She kneeled to pick them up. "This was a onetime thing." A quiet, between them, single occurrence, per Ethan. She shoved the papers into the folder and stood, raising one leg then the other to dust off her knees. "I don't plan on seeing him again."

"If you say so."

"I do." She strolled back into her office. She stopped and turned to Betty. "Why would you think I can't have just a sexual relationship? I'm single, and woman like me engage in physical activities without emotional ties."

"It's not into your make up. You being alone isn't by choice." Betty adjusted her glasses. "Some women are programmed for carefree behavior. You're not. You're an all or nothing kind of woman."

"Maybe I was." Gracie rushed inside her office. "I

think after this weekend I can do causal, at least this once."

Or not. Her knees gave way to sink into her chair. Betty was right. She wasn't an emotionless person. When she accepted Ethan's proposition, she thought she could handle physical and leave the sentiments behind. Truthfully, she couldn't. She liked Ethan, although she didn't know him. An understatement for sure. She'd like to understand his nightmare better and fathom his odd departure. The fact he'd asked her to keep quiet about their weekend nearly devastated her, though she hadn't planned on telling anyone but Krystal.

Still, instincts told her he was a good guy. But even good guys are able to have sex without feelings. For a few hours, she'd hoped they'd defy the odds and their chance hookup would evolve into something more. But that was before the callous way he'd left her. Any hopes of a growing relationship after had died a bitter death.

****

Gracie did her best to ignore her weekend activities and concentrated on locating supplies for a new client she'd just secured. The process took her most of the morning and a better part of the afternoon.

Finally, curiosity got the best of her. She fired up her computer and typed Ethan's name in the search engine. Many Ethan McCarthy's popped up, but none was the man she'd been intimate with over the weekend.

In a day where almost everyone had a virtual presence, he didn't exist in the cyber world. She continued her research for a while, still coming up with nothing, deciding to stop when Betty poked her head in to inform that she was on her way to get them lunch.

Gracie didn't reveal that her appetite had disappeared, and she hadn't eaten a bite since Saturday. She refused to hear again about the importance of regular meals for the rest of the day. And she preferred not to give away how upset she truly was over Ethan's heartless departure. That conversation would be never ending. So, she played along and pretended she was famished.

Thirty minutes later, the food was in front of her. She ignored the cuisine and hoped to give off the appearance she was too involved in her work to eat. With Betty's constant checking, she was finally forced to pick up her fork.

Her cell buzzed and gave her a sound excuse to avoid the dreaded first bite.

Already given up on Ethan calling, she glanced at the caller ID and pressed the on button. "Hey, I've been meaning to call you."

"I've been waiting. I figured you were busy."

Krystal's voice sounded peculiar, but Gracie chalked it up to stress from work. Whenever Mike was unhappy, he made sure his top employees were aware of his dissatisfaction and thus, they weren't happy either.

"I wanted to talk to you about Ethan and get your take on how to handle the situation. We had a great weekend, Krystal. I'm talking hurdle the moon sex. He spent Friday, and most of Saturday with me, and then Sunday morning, he received a phone call and abruptly left. I haven't heard from him since. I realize our weekend was spontaneous, but...I don't know?"

"I don't either, Gracie." Krystal's voice cracked. "I'd need more details."

"How about we meet for a glass of wine later in the week?"

Gracie waited for Krystal's response, but a long silence dragged from the other end of the line. Something was up. Krystal should be pumping her for details and suggesting they go for wine now.

"Krystal? Are you still there?"

"I'm here," Krystal sobbed.

Gracie braced herself. "Krystal, what's wrong. Why are you crying? Did something happen between you and Charlie? If you had a fight, it's okay. You'll make up soon, I'm sure. We can talk about that, too."

"Charlie and I are fine. The nursery is the problem."

"What happened at the nursery?"

"We had another incident."

"Another incident." Gracie took a moment to process. Someone was big into sabotaging the place lately. A new disaster had occurred.

"It's worse than before."

"How could things be as bad?" Gracie's heart jumped into her throat and stopped. Ethan. Something had happened to him. He was hurt. "Another attempt was made on Ethan's life. Is he okay?"

"Not Ethan," Krystal paused for long, sobbing breath. "Mike. He's dead, Gracie. Somebody killed him."

Chapter 11

Krystal's words hit Gracie like a load of cement.

"Mike is dead?"

"Yes."

"How did he die?"

"In the worst way," Krystal sniffed. "They found him underneath a tractor. His skull was bashed, and a bullet was in his head."

Gracie choked on her saliva. "Oh, that's awful."

"Terrible. They found him yesterday, though they hinted he might have been killed before then." Krystal appeared to have regained her composure and spoke without emotion.

"How long ago do they suspect?"

"He may have died on Saturday."

Gracie tried to find some air. Mike was gone. This would be a huge loss to the community and for her personally. He'd maintained a hard ass, take no prisoners persona, but he'd treated her just as an employee and a customer. The man had been more than generous when she started her business, plus he'd been instrumental in sending leads, which helped her succeed. Many former employers wouldn't lift a finger for an ex-worker, yet the man went out of his way to assist her and continued to support as her company grew.

"A ton of detectives met us at the nursery this

morning. It appeared to be a set up so they'd catch the crews by surprise for questioning."

Gracie wiped away a tear. "Do they think someone from the nursery murdered him?"

"I'm sure they're covering all the bases."

"It's too late to speculate, but if he'd called in the police when the trouble started, he may still be alive."

"I'm not disagreeing, although we can't focus on that now. Our concern should be finding out who killed him." Krystal gulped. "A lot of people thought Mike a jerk and sometimes I agreed, but he always stood by me. He was family, Gracie. How could somebody do this to him?"

"Mike was important to me, too." Gracie rose from her chair, swung her door shut, and paced the small space. "Did the police give you any information?"

"Not really. The lead detective corralled the entire staff into the main office. The only specifics they told us was how he died, and those details were sparse. They wouldn't even disclose where the murder took place, but the emergency vehicles had parked near the statuary. Yellow tape is strung around that area, so it's easy to put two and two together."

"You're not at the nursery, are you?"

"No, they sent us home after they questioned us."

"I hope the cops turn every pebble until they discover who did this." Gracie walked to a small window, cracked the blinds, and peered outside. "No one's been arrested, right?"

"Not yet. I'm scared someone we work with did this."

Gracie's thoughts drifted to Ethan, his near out of control dream, and his odd behavior when he left her yesterday. Did the phone call have something to do with Mike's death?

"The police interrogated all of Mike's employees?"

"Yes. They spoke with us individually. They queried me on my whereabouts Saturday from six to ten, and asked if anyone might vouch for me during those times. They were also interested in our professional relationship. Our closeness, if we argued. That sort of thing."

"Did everyone show up this morning?"

"Yes—no wait. Ethan…" Krystal stopped. "Gracie, I didn't see Ethan."

Gracie's fingers tightened, crushing the phone. "Are you sure? Things were probably crazy. You might've missed him."

"I don't think so."

She sounded certain. Gracie stumbled to her desk and sank into her chair.

"Strange he wasn't there. Maybe because he isn't a hired worker. I'm sure they'll talk to him later."

"Possible." A smidgen of relief swept over Gracie, but the uncertainty lingered.

"Still, he wouldn't have known about Mike's death. He should've been at work this morning. Unless he called in and Vivian forgot to tell us because of all the commotion."

Suspicion instantly plagued her again.

"Gracie, I'll have to call you back later. This is going to kill me, but I need to go back to the nursery and take care of the plants in the sections I'm allowed in. The investigators gave me special permission to go inside."

"Will you be okay? Do you want me to come with

you?"

"I'll be fine. Charlie should be home soon. He'll keep me company. And there will be detectives to guide me."

"Call later if you need to talk."

Gracie remained at her desk. This must be how shock felt. She gazed at her untouched salad still in front of her. The food looked worse than before. She was sure now she couldn't stomach a bite.

Thoughts of Ethan and the mysteriousness surrounding him swirled in her head. She couldn't shake the sensation his phone call and abrupt exit yesterday had something to do with Mike's death. He wasn't forthcoming about himself. And then there was his terrifying reaction to his nightmare.

She tried to remember if he'd mentioned anything during their time together that would give her any insight to who this man was. She pushed away from her desk, rising to her feet, and hurried to the door. She may be making a huge mistake, but it was hers to make.

"I'll be gone for a while, Betty. Call my cell for any emergencies, otherwise please take messages, and tell everyone I'll get back with them tomorrow."

"Wait." Betty laid down her fork. "You're three shades whiter than a ghost. What happened?"

Gracie spun back around. "I just found out Mike Manzel has been killed."

"Oh no." Betty's hands flew to her cheeks. "How did he die?"

"Someone murdered him."

Betty shook her head, her expression grim. "In such a small town, too. This used to be a safe place and now…did they catch the killer? I bet drug dealers had a hand in this. I heard a rumor a group set up a meth lab not too far from his place. Being out in the middle of nowhere, they probably tried to rob him, and he caught them."

"No one is talking."

Betty gazed suspiciously at Gracie. "You don't need to get mixed up in this. Let the authorities handle it."

"I'm not. Mike and the nursery were a big part of my life for twelve years and then some. I'm upset and want to get out of here for a while."

"Makes sense, 'cept I'm not buying what you're selling, missy. Mike was special to you, I get that, but you don't act like someone mourning. You're pale, though not traumatized. You seem determined. And a little scared. If you know anything about Mike's death, then you should take it to the police."

"How would I have any information?"

Betty's eyes narrowed. "You tell me."

"I can't because I don't know anything. And if did, I'd do the right thing."

"The right thing can be subjective. Especially when it concerns someone you're in love with."

"What are you trying to say? I have no knowledge about this killing." She moved to the door. "And stop saying I'm in love. I had sex. That's it."

"Keep telling yourself that."

Gracie ignored Betty and stepped out of her office. She rushed to her truck.

Bright sunshine glimmered across the cloudless sky. The heat index inside her vehicle soared to the brink of suffocation. Air conditioner on full blast, her thoughts drifted to her days working at the plant farm.

She had many fond memories. Besides the friendships she'd made and a glimmer of a professional dream had begun there, the place had been her refuge when she and Stewart's situation escalated, and she couldn't bear to go home. She wondered what would become of the business now Mike was gone. She hoped the family wouldn't shut it down.

It occurred to her the police may want to speak with her. Former employees might be on the list if no other suspects emerged, and her association with a presumed missing Ethan could erect some red flags.

She'd be okay. Though she hadn't worked for Mike in a long time, the two maintained a friendly business relationship and never shared a cross word. Didn't matter how far back the authorities went, she had no doubt she'd be in the clear.

As for Ethan McCarthy, she was not so sure.

Almost as if the truck guided itself, Gracie drove down the road leading to Ethan's property. His house wasn't visible from the street, which produced a dilemma. How could she tell if he was home? Did she have enough nerve to walk up and knock on his door? What would she say if he answered?

Slowly, she passed his graveled drive, did a turn around, and went by again.

She searched the lonely street. Houses sat in the distance, sporadically dotting the landscape, many similar to Ethan's, not evident from the pavement. Only ribbons of gravel revealed their existents.

She backed into a treed cove located near Ethan's land and hid her truck. Keys in hand, she hurried across the street. Though late in the afternoon, the sun beat hot down on her head, the scent of dry grass and cow manure drifted in the light wind. A barbed wire fence surrounded his acreage. She crawled between the spiky ropes, and then took off in a run over an exposed gap, ducking into a thicket. Weed stalks brushed against her bare legs, making her itch, and wish she'd worn jeans instead of shorts.

She followed a weaving trail through the undergrowth until she approached the backside of his house, which was mostly glass. The blinds were open wide. If he stood anywhere near a window, he'd spot her.

Gracie pressed into the brush, moving closer to the front. No vehicles were parked in the drive. She could assume no one was home. She stepped from her hiding place and returned to the rear of the house. The windows were low enough for her to view the inside. She crept to the glass, standing on tiptoe, and peeked in.

An unmade king size mattress on a frame sat in the middle of the room. A long dresser had been placed across from the bed. A set of built-in mirrors faced out, toward her. Probably a closet. Bedroom, obviously. She crouched to duck-walked along the back wall until she reached the next set of windows. She stood and pressed her face to the pane. This room was dark. She wondered where Ethan had disappeared to. His absence this morning didn't look well, and then him not being home wouldn't help his cause.

A flash filled the room. An Ethan-sized shadow crammed the lighted doorway. Gracie dropped to the ground. When did he get here? She didn't hear him drive up. On her hands and knees, she crawled toward the grove of trees, stopping below the bedroom window.

His voice boomed from the inside. She gazed up. He stood right above her.

She hugged the house's side. A glance down and he'd catch her. Her heartbeat clobbered her ribcage as she held her breath.

"What do you mean I can't leave town."

His tone carried through the glass, clear enough for her to eavesdrop. She flattened further into the house's side, ignoring the heated slats burning against her skin.

"Hell no, I didn't go to the nursery this morning. I have no desire to be questioned by homicide. And since I was the supposed last person to be with him alive, you can bet they'll look at me long and hard. I might be the only suspect they consider." It went quiet. "You need to get me the hell out of here. I must leave town now."

Gracie inhaled. So he knew about Mike's death. But was he involved or just aware?

A purr of an engine combined with the sound of tires crackling over the gravel came from the front of the house.

"Shit. Someone's here." Ethan's voice faded like he'd backed off. "I gotta go. Do something to make me disappear and keep my ass out of jail."

Gracie inched to the cabin's edge and stole a glance around the side. She leaped back. Strobes flung a rhythm of color into the surrounding woods. Two men in uniform exited the car, their voices hummed in the wind. A loud knock echoed off the trees.

Time to make a getaway. She scouted for an escape route. She had only a couple. Either go the way she came in, or leave by way of the drive. Whichever course she took, she stood a good chance of getting caught by Ethan or the police. Neither idea appealed to her.

She sat back on her knees and sighed. Staying wasn't an option either. She rose on all fours and peeked around the corner. The officers had moved out of her viewing range. They must be inside the house. She gazed upward to listen. No sound. Hair stood on the back of her neck, her entire body stilled.

They were behind her. The cops. She had to come up with an excuse as to why she was lurking around Ethan's house, but her mind went blank.

An arm snaked around her waist and tightened, jerking her to her feet, pulling her against a rock-hard torso. Her mouth and nose were covered with a large palm. Warm breath stroked against her skin.

"Ah, Ms. Desoto," a deep voice whispered. "You have a knack of being where you're not supposed to at the most perfect time."

Chapter 12

"Don't make a sound, understand?" Ethan commanded.

A blast of panic shot through her, but she ignored the terror and nodded slowly.

"Good."

He released her and gently drew her back down to her knees. He maneuvered beside her on all fours to peek around the corner. His shoulder pressed into hers as he leaned in. The simple touch set off a swirl of tiny rockets. Though the circumstances were bleak, Gracie felt ecstatic from his nearness.

Until she came to her senses. Then she quickly jerked away.

He sat back and whispered, "They're coming around from the other side of the house. Time for us to leave." He stood, grabbed her hand, dragged her to her feet, and took off in a run. "Let's go."

He yanked her into the same cluster of brush she'd fought through earlier, veering from the trail and into a mass of brambles and thorny branches. Overgrown thatches ripped her skin, leaving red scratches over her bare arms and legs. They squatted in the middle of the brushwood to wait.

Several scrapes bled. She wiped the worst with the hem of her shirt, and then stared at Ethan.

Why was she here?

All she'd wanted to do was talk to him. Find out what was going on, and put her suspicions to rest. No matter how much she liked him, she wasn't interested in going on the run with him. The cop's appearance and the conversation she'd overheard not only increased her doubts, but almost convinced her he'd been involved in Mike's death somehow.

She needed to get away.

Perhaps she should call for help since the police roamed the grounds. Except if they got caught, she could be inadvertently implicated just from being on his property. She looked at Ethan again. Like he read her mind, he put a forefinger to his lips and slightly shook his head.

Unfamiliar voices rang out, disturbing the quiet.

"Told the sheriff he'd be expecting us. I knew he'd run," one of the deputies remarked.

"Said the same thing. With this many acres, he could be hiding anywhere," the other commented.

"Well, I ain't trekking through thick brush and crap to search for some no account foreigner."

"Me either. This time a year, these fields are full of snakes and fire ants. County don't pay me enough to get my ass bit or stung."

"Trip's got my stomach growlin'. How 'bout we head on over to the Dairy Cone. Ice cream whiteouts are on sale, two for one."

The clap of car doors slamming followed, then a motor revved from behind. A white blaze passed by, rushing down the coiled drive. It quickly disappeared once it turned onto the main road.

Neither Gracie nor Ethan moved until they were certain the car was far gone.

"They're sure in a hurry to get the Cone," Gracie mumbled.

Ethan glared at her. "You want to tell me what the hell you're doing here?"

"A better question would be why the police are here?"

"I think you can guess. But that still doesn't give me a clue as to why you showed up."

She didn't have to take this. She should walk away. Get out of this while she still had time. She gazed at him. A twist of compassion riveted through her. Somewhere deep down she couldn't believe he murdered his boss. True, his expression appeared angered, but he looked troubled too. He may not admit it, may not even realize, but he needed her. She couldn't leave. Not yet.

"I'm saving your ass again," Gracie snapped.

Ethan turned away and peered through the bushes, gazing at his house, as if he debated to return inside. "I guess you are. Where did you park?"

"Across the street. In the tree-lined inlay."

"Let's go."

"Where?"

"To your truck." He grabbed her hand, urging her to her feet, then he released her and took off in a run. "Hurry," he shouted over his shoulder. They sprinted across open field, jogging against the hot wind. The uneven land made running difficult and dangerous. Great for an ankle sprain or twisted knee.

Ethan slid to a halt, a palm behind him.

Gracie stopped. Overheated from the sprint, she raked her fingers through her hair, holding the strands into a makeshift ponytail. The arid breeze did little to cool the back of her perspiring neck.

"What's wrong?"

The sound of an engine roared down the main road, coming their way.

Ethan dove to the ground and rolled for a crevice. "Get down."

Gracie dropped to the dirt and trailed Ethan, spinning her body into the cranny. They peered over the gap's edge as a strange vehicle turned into the driveway and swayed down the rocky drive, passing them without slowing.

"The same guys?"

"Someone else."

"Cops?"

"Don't think so." He jumped to his feet. "Let's get out of here before they realize no one's inside the house and come searching."

Gracie scrambled out of the ditch and hurried to catch up with a jogging Ethan. He'd cleared the fence without effort and rushed across the road, disappearing into the hidden outlet before she made it to the barrier. She made it to the barbed wire and hunkered down. A rumble of an engine growled from the short distance.

"Hurry, Ms. D.," he shouted. "Enemy's coming your way."

Gracie didn't bother to try and find him. She scuttled underneath and in a full run, headed for the cluster of trees. She crossed the asphalt with ease. The second her foot hit dirt, she lost her balance. A hand appeared from out of nowhere and grabbed her arm pulling her into a safe hideaway the moment Ethan's uninvited guest sped by. She plunged against him. They tumbled into a pile of rotten leaves.

She lay on top of him, her fingers clutching his muscled biceps, her face buried into his powerfully built chest. She inhaled deep, relishing his musk scent.

He smelled like sweat, dirt and…oh so male.

The guy may or may not have done anything against the law but what he did to her should be illegal.

"That's one."

She raised her head. "What's one?"

A corner of his mouth lifted, his eyes twinkled. "I owe you. The list of you saving me is ever growing, and it'll take me a lifetime to catch up, but at least I have a start."

Gracie rolled off him, and slowly rose to her feet. She flinched and nearly fell, sitting back down. Ethan eyed her with a frown. "Hurt yourself?"

"Maybe." She touched her ankle that now stung. She hissed. "I think I twisted it."

He rolled to stand, and swept her up in his arms, drawing her close to him. "What are you doing?" she cried, though not fighting him.

"Another payback. Where're your keys?"

"Back pocket."

He maneuvered around the trees, carefully carrying her to the waiting pickup. "Get ready. I'm setting you down."

He gently placed her on her heels. She grabbed the edge of the truck's bed, balancing on one leg, holding her wounded foot off the ground. A hand slid across her rump, gliding into her short's pocket, then out again.

"What are you doing?"

Ethan held up her keychain.

She snatched the dangling metal from his fingers. "I can drive." She glanced around. "Where is your pickup?"

"Safely hidden." He held out a flattened palm, his expression irritated. "Give me." Reluctantly, she handed her set of keys to him. He helped her inside, buckling her into the seat, speeding around to the driver's side, started the truck and backed onto the road.

"Where are we going?"

He remained quiet for several seconds. "Your place?"

She slid down into her seat. She'd regret this, but she was too involved now. "You just cancelled out your paybacks."

****

The ride to her house was silent. Neither spoke a word after he turned over her vehicle. The only sound was the blowing of cool air through the vents. Ethan appeared lost in his own thoughts, and Gracie teetered between concentrating on her swollen ankle and wondered again who the hell Ethan McCarthy was.

She needed to find out. "Why are you so secretive?"

"What?"

"How come you won't reveal anything about yourself? We've been close, right?"

"We had sex." He hesitated. "I hate to sound heartless because being naked with you was out of this world, but that's all it was supposed to be."

She swallowed, doing her best to ignore the implication they were nothing but unpremeditated, except when everything was stripped down, that's exactly what they were. Casual.

"Yes, except now things are different. I'm helping you, and I deserve to know about you."

"I didn't ask for your help."

"You didn't refuse it either."

A long silence settled. Gracie feared the conversation was over, and she wouldn't learn any more than she already had.

"Some things I can answer, there are others I can't, but go ahead." He stretched to adjust an air vent. "You're going to anyways."

"Why aren't you talking to the police?"

"I got a feeling they want to arrest me."

"Wouldn't it be better if you tackled this situation head on?"

"No."

Gracie waited for him to elaborate, but he stayed quiet. His discreetness didn't stop her. She was determined to discover something about him.

"What company do you work for?"

"Institute of Management Consultants. Original, I get it. We're based out of Canada."

"Are you from Canada?"

"Born there, and I've lived in the area for my first two years, but I grew up in Corpus Christi, which I consider my hometown. As an adult, I've traveled quite a bit. I served in the military, Army for six years. I believe I mentioned I was in Afghanistan. Anything else?"

"Ever married?"

"Nope. My work keeps me away a lot. In case you're wondering, I don't have a place I call home, so it wouldn't be fair to do that to any woman."

"Where do you keep your stuff?"

"I don't have a lot, but most goes with me. The rest—" he shrugged "—stays at my brother's."

"Do you think about settling down?"

He stared out the windshield, seemingly lost at the sun reflection bouncing off the truck's hood. "I'm not good for any woman."

"Why?"

"Bad home life growing up. My parents stayed together, still are. They fight like crazy. We never had calm. Our situation was volatile. My brothers and I either ducked to avoid flying vases or hid in our rooms to stay out of the line of fire. I refuse to put anyone through that."

"You don't have to. You can learn from their mistakes."

"Did you learn from yours?"

"From my divorce? I'm trying to, but—"

"Not what I'm talking about, Gracie," he interrupted. "You're not the kind of woman who sleeps around, therefore, I suggest you be more selective to whom you bring home."

"You mean I should be careful of you?"

"You need to be wary of everyone."

"So you're a mistake?"

"Yet to be determined."

"Do you know who killed Mike?"

There was a slight pause before he answered, "No." After another hesitation, he asked. "Any more questions?"

"Just one. How old are you."

"Thirty." He grinned. "And you?"

"I'm done."

"You're forty."

Gracie gazed at him through narrowed eyes. "How did you know?"

"Did my research." His grin widened. "Krystal told me."

"Wait till I see her."

"It's only a number, Gracie. Now, my turn." He stopped. "What's your story?"

"My parents are Eleanor and Max Desoto. I'm named after my mother but go by our middle name. They're wonderful. They retired and live on a golf course. I also have a perfect younger sister, Kylie."

He shot her a side glance. "No malice there."

"I'm speaking the truth. She's one of those people that can do no wrong. My folks are good people who think she's great. They view me as more of a screw up, but in an affectionate way."

"How can that be? You've started and run a very successful business. You can hold your own with anyone."

"My parents don't relate my work success to being victorious. Kylie married a CEO of a huge insurance company. She's a stay at home, soccer mom with four awesome kids. My folks see me as a failure because my marriage didn't work, and my son Mason acted out a bit during our breakup period. They believe the reason my domesticated life didn't do well was because I chose to work outside the home."

"That's crazy."

She lifted a shoulder. "Just how they are."

"Okay. Then let's discuss your big imperfection. Your ex. He's not still pining after you, is he? The last thing I need is some crazy former spouse wanting to kick my ass for messing around with his ex-wife."

She held up a palm with a grimace. "Trust me, not an issue."

"Okay. How come? Guys gotta be a fool to let you get away."

"Thanks." She blushed and dipped her chin. "I married my high school sweetheart. Thought it was a forever thing. We went through a rough patch. He decided I didn't love him anymore, didn't want our marriage. He even went as far as to accuse me of finding someone else."

"Any of it true?"

"Not from my perspective. His on the other hand…"

"So in other words he was projecting his feelings on you as a way to leave the marriage."

"Exactly. For a while, I think he managed to convince some, but as always, the truth comes to light."

"Did he ever admit his transgression?"

"Nope. He still claims it was all me. Although I've barely left the house since our break up. Him, on the other hand, well let's just say he hasn't been lonely."

"You're better without him."

"I think so. I just wish things were easier on our son. He's in college now, but he was home when this all went down, and he got to see the worst of both of us. It makes me sad."

"You and your son survived. My gut tells me you're better for what you've experienced. I'm betting your son sees that, too."

"He's stated he doesn't want to be like his father. He wants to be a good man."

"That's great. You deserve a good man, too."

She turned to him. "Are you a good man, Ethan?"

"How's the ankle?"

Once they arrived at her house, he drove the truck

127

into her garage, the door shut tight before he shut off the motor. "Stay put," he told her as he stepped out.

He rushed to her. She already had her side opened. He scooped her in his arms, carefully maneuvering her crowded garage to carry her inside. Once in, he sat her on the sofa and removed her shoe. He lowered next to her on the couch, sitting by her elevated leg, placing it on a sofa pillow and inspected the wound.

"You do have some swelling, but I don't think it's anything serious. No bruising. Ice ought to bring the puffiness down. You'll be as good as new tomorrow." He rose. "Where do you keep your ice bag?"

Her brows knitted.

He gave her a disbelieving look. "Don't tell me you don't own one as accident prone as you are."

"I did. But I lost it in the divorce."

"Your ex got the ice bag when your marriage broke-up? Did you put up a fight for it?"

"Stewart's a doctor. All medical stuff went with him. He even took a half filled aspirin bottle."

"What have you used since he left?"

"A plastic sandwich bag."

"If I wasn't in trouble, I'd go to the pharmacy and buy you a new pack."

Gracie shuffled uneasily in her spot. "What kind of trouble are you in?"

"The kind as in the less you know the better." He paused. "Where do you keep your sandwich bags?"

"You're not involved in Mike's death, are you?" she blurted.

"You're not answering my question."

"Neither are you."

"Never mind, I'll find them."

He clomped into the kitchen leaving Gracie more confused. If he didn't know anything about Mike murder, why not come out and say so. But then again if he did, would he tell her? So that would mean…what? He had information; he was protecting someone. He did it?

She didn't want to consider the final alternative. While she couldn't say she knew him, she did understand a part of him. She just wished she believed in her instincts, because they told her he was a good man. Since the Stewart fiasco, her trust radar tilted off kilter, therefore she doubted she'd ever rely on blind faith again.

She stretched across the end table for the remote and flipped on the TV, muting the volume. A recent picture of Mike filled the screen. Gracie gasped, a palm slapped over her mouth. The next slide showed a younger photo of Ethan dressed in his military uniform. Though the sound was turned down, the implication screamed.

A rattling noise startled her. She spun around. Ethan stood beside her, holding a plastic bag loaded with ice. He grimaced at the television.

"Mystery solved now, eh, Ms. D?" He bent to remove the remote from her hand. "Mind if we check the baseball scores?"

Chapter 13

Ethan flinched at the sight of his image displayed on the television screen. He glanced at Gracie. "I guess it's official," he said dryly. "I'm a wanted man."

"You can't be sure. I don't have the sound on."

Ethan stared at her. He gestured at the TV. "My picture's posted because I'm a suspect. Why are you making excuses? You should throw me out or call the cops."

"I can't do either." She pointed at her swollen ankle she'd propped onto a sofa pillow. "Thought you wanted to check the ball scores."

He pressed the remote and switched off the television, happy to not see his photo splashed over the screen. He stood beyond her and studied the blank monitor, trying to disregard that he'd just been outed as a possible murder suspect. A missing, possible murder suspect.

"How are things coming with the ice?"

He glanced at the cold plastic sandwiched between his hands. "Oh," then strolled to where she lay. He placed a kitchen towel he'd found on the counter over her ankle, and easily situated the frozen bag across the swollen area. She jerked.

He smiled. "Cold?"

"It's ice. What do you think?"

"Here." He tossed a bag of chocolate into her lap.

"Thought this might help."

"Thanks." Gracie raised her chin as she removed a bit of candy from the bag. "I don't believe you killed anyone."

Ethan's eyes narrowed. "You hardly know me."

"I trust my instincts."

"Of course you do."

She made a face, then popped the candy into her mouth. "Okay, that's not exactly the truth. You don't behave like a murderer."

"You've met enough killers to understand how they act."

Perhaps he should accept her belief in him, but he couldn't allow her to let him off the hook so easily. A stout nip of remorse seeped through him. He'd essentially used her for his personal gratification, and while she did the same with him, it didn't relieve him of the guilt. Or his disgrace for utilizing her as a means of escape and her home to hideout from the authorities.

"I refuse to accept that I've slept with somebody who killed another person."

A corner of his mouth lifted. "So this is more about your moral center as opposed to me offing my boss."

She had the decency to seem embarrassed. Her hands folded, she gazed at her lap without a word.

"Not that I blame you. Just about everyone's had sex with someone they wished they hadn't."

She lifted her head, her eyes bore into his. "That's not the way I feel at all."

"What if I did kill Mike?"

"Are you confessing?"

"I'm playing devil's advocate."

"I can't live with regrets," she said evenly as she

unwrapped another candy bite. "What's done is done. All I can do is move on. Make sure to not repeat my mistakes."

"So you made a mistake sleeping with me." His heart almost stopped. In most instances he wouldn't care if a woman considered being carnal with him a lapse in judgment. Yet, for some odd reason, he hoped she'd never view him as a gaffe.

"You sort of implied it earlier."

"Not from my perspective. I'm talking about yours." He smiled at the comforted look on her face as the candy melted in her mouth. "Let's say I'm not a murderer. I'm curious as to your opinion regarding our weekend beyond the 'what's done is done' attitude."

He couldn't believe he'd gone there. Why did he care what she thought?

They fucked. It was good. Move on. Yet, here he was, holding his breath, hoping for a positive response. He sat down on the sofa next to her, snitching a piece of candy while he waited for her answer, glad she didn't slap his hand away from her bag of sweets.

She hesitated, as if considering her reply. "We're consenting adults. We didn't do anything wrong, so I don't view our time together as a mistake." She stopped and stared at him in the eye. Her tongue slowly traced her upper lip. "Nor do I feel any regret for helping you today, even if I've stepped outside the law."

He briefly wondered again why she'd shown up at his house. He quickly dismissed the thought and focused on the sudden urge to kiss her hard, and then allow nature to take its course.

"So do you want to talk about it?" she asked.

"Sex?"

"Sex?" she squealed. "Where did that come from?"

"I don't—we've been debating if our sleeping together was in error. You seemed to want to elaborate."

"You thought I'd be interested in discussing a play by play of our bedroom antics? Compare point scores maybe?"

"I'm off topic?"

"Way, way off."

God, he should keep his mouth shut. Better yet, why he hadn't bypassed her when he'd noticed her nosing around his property. He knew the land well, and he could've easily slipped by her, even hotwired her truck, to use as an escape. Yeah, she may have gotten caught by the county Mounties, or worst case scenario by his other unwelcomed guest, but he'd been careful to keep her knowledge of him limited. Unless she confessed, they wouldn't even be aware she'd trespassed. She'd be in the clear, and he'd be rid of her.

So why didn't he just leave her alone?

"You men." She gave her head a solid shake. "I'm offering to talk about your current situation. The one where you're hiding from the police."

"The less you know the better," he told her again in a quiet voice. "I would like an explanation, though. Why did you help me?"

Her clasped hands visibly gripped tighter.

"Gracie? I'm guessing you showed up at my home because you suspected I might be in trouble, though I doubt you thought this through."

She raised her chin to meet his gaze.

"So what's your reason for helping me? Things would have been a lot easier on you if you'd yelled for the police."

"I considered it."

A little ting of disappointed trickled through him.

"Two attempts have been made on your life in the past week, correct?"

"One I consider inadvertent and lame, because really? I'd like to believe anyone paying attention would escape a runaway tractor." He grinned. "Present company excluded. Still, my gut tells me the effort was aimed at me. Or at least invoked to send me a message."

"What kind of message?"

"I think someone wants me out of dodge."

"My point. If the killer is after you, why would you murder Mike? Doesn't make sense."

He hoped the police bought into her argument. In the beginning he'd agreed with Mike to not bring in the authorities, but certain things couldn't be ignored. He didn't believe Sheriff Bud, Mike's good buddy would be a source of aid, seeing as he doubted the life-threatening endeavors were fully discussed, if at all.

"I hope once this is over you'll be as understanding," he said.

"If you're honest with me. Why does someone want you out of the way, or worse have you killed?"

Good question. One he needed to set aside some time to figure that out. He must get his head on straight to do that and find a way out of this mess. Being around her only incited turmoil. His normally cool interior rotated like a cyclone of chaos in her presents.

Ethan pushed off the sofa, glanced at his filthy clothes, then looked back at her white couch. He released a quiet sigh, glad he hadn't left any dirt on the cushions. He wished he had a place to clean up. She'd allow him to use her shower, except he'd be unable to go into the stall alone. As much as the idea appealed, sex with her again was off the table. Literally.

He hooked his thumbs into his jean pockets. "I should go."

Her body jerked as if he'd punched her in the stomach.

"I don't want to draw you anymore into this. I shouldn't have come here in the first place." He strolled to a window facing the front of the house and peeked through the blinds.

Twilight had settled, but the neighborhood appeared busy. Like most people who lived in Texas, residents took advantage of the later, summer hours to mow their laws, take evening walks, or just enjoy the outdoors after the heat had tapered to tolerable. He turned to Gracie, taking in the comforts of the tranquil room and the lovely woman in the middle of it all. He wished he didn't have to leave—but he needed to be realistic. He'd never be able to stay with her.

"How nosey are the neighbors?"

"Some are real snoops. Plus we've had several break-in's lately, so everyone is on high alert."

"Glad we parked in the garage. The last thing either of us needs is someone seeing me on the news and then seeing me here."

"True. The lady next door came by the other day for me to show her how to work the camera on her phone. I've also heard a lot of people are installing video recorders around their houses, and of course, many are getting their concealed handgun license."

"Great. A bunch of Special Forces wannabes."

"Everyone has worked hard for what they have, and they want to protect their stuff." She gazed at him. "You realize your hiding only makes you look guilty."

Ethan didn't respond. How could he, when she was right on?

He returned to her, standing several feet from the sofa. She watched him, as if waiting for him to explain. "There are worse things to worry about as opposed to the perception of others. Even if the law is concerned." He took a moment to process his thoughts. "Thanks for your help today, by the way. One day, when all of this is over, you can tell me why you showed up at my house."

Gracie continued to look at him. "As soon as you explain your involvement."

A fierce heat smoldered in her eyes. The green in her irises deepened. She wanted something from him. Something he shouldn't consider. Without thinking, he marched to her, kneeling down beside her. His mouth captured hers. She pressed her lips into his in return, her palms slid over his chest and settled around his neck. The kiss slowly deepened, his tongue firmly inside her mouth, devouring her sweet taste. He inhaled her scent, feminine, fresh like the summer air. Intoxicating. How easy it would be to get lost in her, letting his lives roadblocks disappear. Another night of skin on skin would alleviate him from everything, if only for a short time.

His hand slipped under her shirt, working his way past her bra to find her breast. He rubbed and pulled. His fingers caught her nipple and twisted the tip molding the mound into a wonderful, tight point. A heated throb pulsated between his legs. He was almost a goner. If he didn't stop now, it'd be too late. He had to end this.

Breathless, he abruptly removed his hand and pushed her away. "Sorry."

Her expression looked confused and hurt.

He placed his palms on her shoulders and squeezed. "We can't." He nodded toward the dining room. "But if that were possible, I'd have you naked and on that table in a heartbeat."

Ethan swiped his lips across hers, the back of his hand brushed against her protruding nipple as he stood. Reluctantly, he moved further away.

"I really need to leave, Gracie."

"Where will you go?"

"Haven't figured that out yet." His lips twisted, both knew full well he wouldn't reveal his intended location. "Can I borrow your cell phone? I've turned mine off and removed the battery so I can't be traced. I'd rather not reconnect it, especially if someone can track me here."

"I keep it in my purse. And my bag is still inside my truck, in the backseat on the floorboard."

"Thought business owners were never without their phones."

"I'm usually not." Then she grinned. "Not true, actually. I keep it with me during work hours, but it stays out of reach when I'm home. More peaceful that way. But I wouldn't mind having it near now that my mobility is limited."

"I'll bring everything to you when I'm finished."

He left her and walked through the kitchen and into the garage. Inside, he wiggled past an assortment of lawn equipment and bags of fertilizers and such, trying to manipulate his body to her vehicle without knocking things over or injuring himself.

Evidently she used the enclosure as an extension for business storage, leaving only enough space for her pickup. Because of his size, he had a difficult time wedging between the mass, but movement wasn't as hard as when he'd arrived, carrying Gracie.

He opened the backdoor and sat on the warm, leather seat. Going through her handbag was a different journey altogether. How she found anything in the multitude of what he was certain she'd claim as necessities was beyond him. He searched until almost to the point of dumping the whole thing in the seat, finally discovering her cell in a side pocket, the most logical choice to keep it, although obvious didn't seemed to fit her.

He pushed seven buttons, and then put the cell to his ear. It rang only once.

"Yeah?"

"It's me," Ethan said.

"I figured. Confiscated someone else's phone?"

"In a manner of speaking. You saw the news?"

"I saw."

"Deputies showed up at my place." Ethan glanced at the house. "Along with another unwelcome visitor."

"Shit."

"Only a matter of time before they send out the big guns. I need you to come get me and help me find a place to lay low since the powers that be refuse to let me leave town."

"I've already got a hideout set up. I was just waiting for your call so I can come get you."

"Good. But wait till it's a little darker before you

do. Too many people outside."

"Of course. Wouldn't want to be too noticeable. Where are you?"

He swiped his tongue across his mouth. Gracie's sweetness still lingered on his lips. "You know."

"Yeah." There was a huge sigh. "So much for not getting involved."

Ethan pushed the off button and deleted the number before he collapsed into the seat. "So much."

Chapter 14

The next day, Gracie slowly mounted her office steps, trying to disregard the sense of dread she'd been feeling since she and Ethan separated. For most of the night, she stayed glued to the media outlets, hoping for good news, but thus far all reports had been non-informative, speculative, or negative.

She entered the main area making sure she hid her slight limp. She'd kept ice on the ankle all night. The swelling had gone down, just as Ethan had said it would. For precaution, she took a handful of ibuprofen in case, but if she miss-stepped, she felt a bit a twang.

"Morning, Betty."

Her secretary shoved her tablet away, and studied Gracie as she walked further inside. "Oh, honey, how are you?"

"I'm okay," she replied, knowing her answer wouldn't reassure.

The local news had plastered Ethan's photo all over the television. They'd also splashed his picture across the front page of the newspaper, and the article had even hit the internet and gone viral.

"You are?" Betty rose to follow Gracie into her office. "Suspicions about your boyfriend are being broadcasts from here to Jupiter and beyond. The police want to talk to him." She eyed Gracie. "Except he's disappeared."

"I've seen the coverage too, Betty." She hurried behind her desk, standing motionless. A stack of folders lay in front of her. She picked up the pile and moved them to another spot for something to do while she suffered through Betty's interrogation.

"What part did you play in his vanishing act?"

"None." Gracie glanced away to avoid eye contact. "I don't know where he is."

Betty frowned, her expression showed she didn't believe her. "Do you suppose he murdered Mike?"

"I'm unsure what to think." Gracie sighed. "Wait. I'm certain he didn't kill anyone, but is he mixed up somehow?" She lifted a shoulder.

Betty lowered into a chair, still watching her. "Your association could be bad for business."

"We're not involved, per say." Gracie dropped to her seat. "Our relationship is new. I shouldn't be too caught up in his mess."

"I'm not talking about your weekend of delight, missy." Betty leaned forward, lowering her voice. "No one saw you with him yesterday, did they?"

Gracie's eyes widened. The woman was telepathic or she had spies. Either way she was spooky.

"Don't bother denying it."

"Fine. I went to his place." She did more, but she wouldn't go there. She'd never hear the end of it. Plus she ran the risk of Betty telling her mother, and all hell would break loose. The fact she was forty didn't sway Betty or her mom from holding back their opinions on anything, especially concerning her love life. "We spoke, but he left soon after. I have no idea where he went once we separated."

"You need to stay away from that young man. You

may be wrong about him. He might hurt you."

"He won't," Gracie insisted with exaggerated confidence.

Ethan hadn't done anything to harm her physically, and she doubted he would, even after his nightmare diabolical. On an emotional level the man was killing her. Yet, she couldn't make herself walk away from him.

The buzz of her cell phone saved her from anymore of Betty's cross-examination.

"Hi Krystal."

Betty rose from her chair to leave, shutting the door behind her.

"Hey girl." Krystal sighed from the other end. "Got some news about Mike's murder. Thought I'd give you a heads up."

"What now?"

"I'm assuming you caught the media avalanche about Ethan missing and him being a suspect in Mike's death."

"How could I not?"

"Right. Some semi-good news. He turned himself into the police last night."

"He did?"

"They're holding him. I don't know for how long."

Gracie's heart sank. "He didn't do this, Krystal."

"Yeah, that's what I thought at first." Krystal paused. "Except some new details surfaced."

Gracie gripped the phone to keep her hand from trembling. "What kind of details?"

"I can't say right now. We're at the nursery. Why don't you swing by after work? We'll talk and maybe come up with some answers."

"I'll leave early."

****

Gracie stepped inside the nursery office using the backdoor. Heated murmurs came from the main work place. It sounded like people arguing. She walked to the doorway and stood. Krystal, Quinn, and Vivian sat at the lunch table, heads together, speaking in an animated low-toned conversation.

She strolled into the room. "Am I interrupting?"

Krystal jumped from her chair, while the others stared, surprised by her appearance. Her friend ran to her, and threw her arms around her shoulders and squeezed. "Hey girl. How are you?"

Gracie gave her a tight smile. "I'm…here."

"As we all are." Krystal waved a hand at a chair at the break table where Quinn and Vivian remained seated. "Sit."

Gracie pulled out an ancient, lime green, vinyl chair, allowing her sudden wobbly legs to collapse. "You're open?"

"Not yet." Vivian wiped her eyes and sniffed. "Mike's will hasn't been read. We assume Mickey will inherit the business since he's worked here forever."

"Work is a loose term, unless something changed," Gracie said, dryly.

"You've got that right." Vivian adjusted the half-filled box of tissue in front of her. "Mike thought he was a frickin' genius. Mickey seems to presume the nursery will be his too since his brother never bothered with the place."

"He's sure he's the beneficiary. He's asked us to come in to answer phones, take care of the plants, and keep up with the paper work while we're shut down,"

Krystal explained.

Gracie glanced at her friend. "At least you won't be out of a job."

"True. But I'll be more comfortable being here after Mike's killer is behind bars." Krystal picked up a pen and tapped the end against a legal pad lying in front of her.

"Ethan's in jail." Quinn's tone sounded satisfied. "The murderer is where he belongs as far as I'm concerned."

Gracie lifted her chin a smidgen higher. "Ethan didn't do it."

Vivian's brows shot up.

"Oh Gracie." Quinn shook her head, wearing a pitied expression. "One night with him, and he's gotten to you, hasn't he?"

Gracie squelched her sudden rising anger, realizing Quinn's attitude could be spun from jealously. Still, she found it difficult to keep her temper in check.

"Nothing of the kind, Quinn," she lied. "Instincts tell me he isn't the killer. I trust my gut. This man is not the murderer." She suspected her friends believed otherwise, but she was almost sure Ethan wasn't guilty.

Quinn lips turned upward. Her smile didn't quite reach her eyes. "He must be a hell of a lay."

"Zip it, Quinn." Vivian flapped a wet tissue in her direction. "You were hot for the guy, and he never showed any interest in you. You're just pissed."

Quinn opened her mouth, then twisted her lips. "I'm saying what the police believe."

"Really?" Vivian's brows rose. "You sure are quick to pin this on Ethan. He rejected you, and you could be setting him up. Mike was awfully upset over

Ethan's fumigation diabolical. He even talked about firing you. Are the cops aware you have *good* reasons to be considered a suspect?"

Quinn shot out of her seat, pushing the chair so hard it fell backward, crashing to the floor with a bang. "All right." She balled a fist, throwing her thumb over her shoulder. "You and me. Outside."

"Such violent tendencies." Vivian shook her head as she slowly rose to her feet. "But I can kick your sorry ass with one boot."

Gracie leaned closer to Krystal. "I thought they were friends."

"It's a loathe, hate kind of relationship. We're in hate mode at the moment. All right," Krystal interrupted. "This isn't why we're here. Arguing over stupid stuff won't solve anything. Both of you sit down."

Quinn stopped, bending to pick up her chair. Her glare remained glued to Vivian as she scooted her seat underneath the table.

"Thank you," Krystal said, though she sounded annoyed. "This whole situation saddens me. Mike's death, an employee possibly accused of killing him, and now this." She looked at Gracie. "Do you remember what the approximate times you were with Ethan over the weekend?"

"Um, all night Friday, and we were together up until about four on Saturday. We separated for a few hours, and he returned about ten." She frowned at Krystal. "Why do you ask?"

"Because I hoped you'd be his alibi." Krystal's gaze dropped to her pad.

"Ethan told the police he met with Mike around

seven-thirty at the nursery and stayed for an hour before he left. He also admitted their discussion was heated, although he denies the disagreement turned physical." She raised her head and gazed at the group. "Homicide pinpointed Mike's death around nine. Ethan can't produce anyone to substantiate his whereabouts during that time."

Quinn's eyes narrowed at Gracie. "What do you think of your boyfriend now?"

"Don't start, Quinn," Krystal said sharply.

Ethan was agitated when he arrived at her place, but she thought the reason was because she knocked him into the rose bushes.

He claimed he fell in the mud changing a flat tire, but it hadn't rained in weeks. Greenhouses' irrigations created sludge. He admitted being at the nursery where he could've gotten dirty.

Then there was the nightmare, which possibly would've turned darker if he hadn't woken up.

Still, his behavior wasn't so odd as if he'd done something horrendous, like kill someone.

Krystal kept reading from her pad, "Mike died from a gunshot wound." She stopped to swallow, her voice quivered. "He'd also been hit numerous times in the head before the killer drove and parked the tractor over his lower extremities."

Vivian covered her mouth with a palm.

"So sad," Gracie murmured.

"Yeah," Quinn agreed. "Somebody really wanted to make sure he was dead."

"So vicious, but very personal." Vivian's eyes watered. "They need to look at people who knew him."

Krystal continued, "Ethan McCarthy enlisted in the

army right after junior college. An excellent soldier, he rose among the ranks, later joining the Special Forces unit as a sergeant. His primary mission in the faction was to train and lead indigenous guerrilla forces, and he did that until he left two years ago, discharged honorably." Krystal laid the pen down and looked up. "Although the report doesn't state his reason for leaving the military, rumors circulated later and suggest a particular incident pushed him over the edge. He spent some time under a doctor's care."

"Did the rumor say what his issues were?" Vivian twisted her wet tissue between her hands. "I'm assuming they're mental?"

"Confidential."

The room became still. Implications hung in the air. Gracie remained motionless, but her thoughts churned. The near-violent attack against her remained fresh in her mind. Did he lose it during an argument with Mike and do the unthinkable? She shook away the notion, refusing to believe he could murder anyone in cold blood. He seemed to have a difficult time recalling his dream the other night. Maybe he didn't remember killing him.

Quinn gave her a questioning glance. "Did he reveal any of this to you?"

"He told me he'd served in the military, but he didn't elaborate."

"You sleep with the guy, and you don't know what happened to him in the army?"

"No Quinn. Our careers, past or present didn't come up when we were in bed. We were busy doing *other* things." Gracie tucked her bottom lip beneath her teeth, wishing she could snatch back her words the instant they'd left her mouth. She didn't mean to let Quinn get to her and hated she'd stooped to her level.

"Quinn," Krystal scolded. "Enough. If you can't act any better then you need to go home."

Vivian dabbed away another flow of tears and sniffed. "You possess a lot of information about this murder, Krystal, who's your source?"

Krystal retrieved her pen and nervously clicked the end. "Charlie's friend, Phil works at the police department. He was over last night, and after a few beers, he shared a little too much." She shook a finger at Quinn. "Don't go blabbing."

"I don't blab, Krystal."

Gracie sidestepped that landmine and kept her focus straight ahead, her mind worked in overdrive. "Have they located the weapon?"

"I'm guessing no."

"He probably stashed it somewhere, or he's thrown it in the river," Quinn said.

"If we could figure out where to locate it…"

"Gracie, we don't agree on who killed Mike, but either way, you need to stay out of this." Quinn stabbed a forefinger in her direction. "Anyone who kills once will kill again, especially if it means saving his ass."

"I can't, Quinn. I believe in Ethan. I'm going to find a way to help him. Two attempts were made on his life this week, correct?"

Krystal's eyes brightened. "Yes, that's right. The first one, the one you saved him, was serious. The second was no laughing matter either."

"Exactly." Gracie gave Quinn a satisfied glimpse.

"He could have set the whole thing up to throw suspicion off him." Quinn snatched a nearby magazine and flipped the pages without looking at them. "He'd planned on killing Mike all along."

"He was in pretty bad shape after the first incident," Krystal said.

"I rescued him, Quinn. I was inside that greenhouse; it was filled with chemical. He would've died had Reed and I not shown up." She turned to Krystal. "Have you considered Mike's death might be connected to the disappearing plants?"

"Crossed my mind. I gave the information to police. But they didn't do anything with it. They'll probably use it against Ethan. Make the thefts a motive."

Quinn turned her attention back to the conversation. "What missing plants?"

"Are you talking about the hundreds marked diseased?" Vivian wanted to know. "I thought there was something strange about that. They weren't sick, were they? What's happening to them?"

"Someone is ripping Mike off," Krystal said. "For what purpose I have no idea. The detective I spoke with speculated Mike stole his own product and used the robberies as a tax-break, expanding the materials worth and pocketed the overages."

"A rumor in town claims Ethan tried to blackmail Mike. The missing plant angle would fit the scenario." Vivian tossed her soggy tissue and fluffed another to wipe her leaky eyes. "We all know Mike wouldn't give in to extortion. If it's true, the situation may've gotten out of hand to the point to where Ethan killed him."

"Blackmail." Quinn raised a fist. "That's it."

"That can't be just 'it'." Gracie argued.

"I don't believe Mike destroyed his own plants for

profit, and I hate anyone would think that." Krystal tossed her pen onto the pad. "I'm betting the lost material is the key. The police are blowing the whole thing off. Things aren't good for Ethan, but if Gracie believes in him, then I trust her instincts. We should help."

"Thank you," Gracie said softly.

"I'm in," Vivian agreed. "What's the plan?"

"We need to do some investigating of our own. We could meet for the next few nights. Find out if anything happens."

"Come here after dark?" Quinn stared at Krystal like she'd lost her mind. Even Gracie gave her a funny look, but Vivian nodded.

"How will doing that help Ethan?" Gracie asked.

"Mike's gone. No reason for the burglaries to continue if he was having them pilfered for profit. If they disappear while Ethan is locked up, then we have something to take to the police. He can't be blackmailing. We can possibly prove his innocence."

"Or his guilt," Quinn said snidely.

Gracie frowned at Quinn, refusing to be drawn in.

Krystal lifted a shoulder and turned to face Gracie. "It's a risk, but at least we'll know one way or the other."

"Are we allowed here after hours? Won't we get in trouble?" Gracie asked.

"If we ask I'm sure the answer is no, but if we don't…" Krystal raised her brows with a smile. "This place is located in the middle of nowhere. Who'll tell? The police are almost finished with their investigation, and they believe they have their man, so nothings stopping us."

Gracie refused to consider the consequences. Clear Ethan, clear her mind. "I'm in."

Chapter 15

Ethan gulped the last drop of beer as he stared at the water below. The moons subdued spark radiated over the river's ripple. His growing issues drifted through his head. Mike's death, the possibility of murder charges, which transferred into a wrecked reputation even if he was proven innocent.

His fucked up life in general.

Gracie.

The drained can crushed easily in his fist.

The woman somehow managed to slip into his heart, and she'd stayed there. His mind couldn't find any escape from thinking about her despite his dismal circumstances. His impulses bounced from blame to out of control erotic daydreams that drove him wild. Both had him wanting to rush to her and do—something.

He shifted his gaze into the darkened sky.

And she's the reason he'd ended up here. He squeezed the flattened tin between his fingers and gave it a toss into the rushing water. Time to go. Except he didn't want to. He hadn't been to his house since the police released him, and going to an empty home was just sad. Eyes closed, he sucked in a load of air in an effort to keep his panic at bay. His lids lifted as he stood in the twilight, alone. So very alone. Hard to believe it'd come to this. After following a bunch of last ditch orders that stressed him to the point to where he'd imbibed way too much, he was done.

Thoughts in a whirl, he scrambled to his feet, and stood on the edge of the pier.

An odd sound made him freeze.

Subdued.

Behind him.

He did a half turn and gazed into the darkness.

Other than the frogs harmonizing with the river's flow, he couldn't make out anything unusual.

Just his imagination. He'd drunk several beers, and he wasn't used to so much alcohol, one being his usual limit. Probably an animal getting a drink down the way. He jammed a hand in his pocket, hoping he hadn't locked his keys inside his truck. Relieved, they jingled between his fingers as he took a step.

He stopped.

He heard it again.

The strange soft bump. Didn't sound like anything wild, and the thud was definitely in back of him. "Who's out there?"

A jolt hit him from the rear. In a split second, an attacker was on him. His body swayed above the rushing stream below. He grabbed for something to latch onto while trying to wrestle away from his assailant. They tipped sideways, toward the water. Their weight propelled them over the dock's edge, tumbling into the murkiness beneath.

His capturer released him the second they crashed into the river. Ethan sank into the muddy depths until his butt bumped the spongy bottom. Holding his breath, he pushed from the base, thrusting his body upward. After a few moments, he broke the plane, releasing a gush of air.

His feet found the sodden floor.

Good, this area was shallow enough that he could stand and keep his head above the surface. He looked around. His attacker seemed to have disappeared.

On alert, he combed the darkened surroundings. Treading water, he used his arms to explore alongside the dock, beside the supports, and beneath the shifty river's rim, searching.

Nothing.

He gauged the length to the top of the pier, ready to hoist up and get the hell out of there.

A palm clutched his shoulder. He snatched his attacker's wrist and whirled around. He tensed his other hand, tightening it into a ball, his fist set to lay this pest out in the mud.

They both gasped.

"Ms. Desoto." He released her and stared. Gracie Desoto stood in front of him, bouncing in the current. A small, solid log was positioned above her head.

"Ethan?" She dropped her weapon, shoving her wet tresses away from her eyes.

"Either my savior or my opponent. By the looks of things, the latter appears to be this case." He gestured at the wooden dock, then to the water. "I'm assuming you're the cause for our eleventh-hour dip?"

She clutched the log and glared at him. "Why are you on my pier?"

She sounded angry. Obviously, she wasn't happy to find him on her property. With good reason. He'd essentially walked out on her, again, and now he was a person of interest in the death of her former boss, ending with him semi-intoxicated at her home late at night.

"Technically I'm no longer on your pier."

She shot him a death glare.

A hand raked through his damp hair. He'd have to tell her something, anything. Except the real reason, he wanted to be with her. "Hard to explain."

"Please try."

"I was upset. The police held me for twenty-four hours. They had nothing, I mean, nothing. No evidence, other than my being with Mike before he died and my military background. Because of this proof, I'm a person of interest." He spat out the words as if they were poison. "After they freed me, I decided to get drunk."

She gazed at him without a stitch of remorse on her face. Not that he deserved any, but hell, a smidgen of sympathy on her part would make things a lot easier.

She opened her mouth. Reflections from the moonlight displayed a blaze in eyes that showed she was about to set him on fire.

He shot out a palm triggering a slew of water to trickle down his arm. "Before you start, I'm aware drinking won't solve anything, but at the moment it seemed like a good idea. I picked up some beer, actually I bought a lot of beer, and for the last hour I spent my time driving past your house."

Gracie's eyebrows rose as she crossed her arms over her chest. "Alcohol and behind a wheel?"

"I know. But I wanted to see you, and I was afraid you wouldn't want to be around me, which under the circumstances is probably for the best."

"You wanted to see me?" she repeated, dropping her arms, her voice high and squeaky. The moon had disappeared behind a cloud, therefore, she was only an outline in the shadows but he could hear the smile in her tone.

Ethan groaned. He must still be a little drunk. "Yes. I missed you. I parked across the street and drank some more." He paused. "I suddenly felt suffocated. I needed fresh air, so I decided to go for a walk and ended up on the dock." He stopped and peeked at her. "I was about to leave when you came up behind." He hesitated and backed further from her. "Why did you shove me into the river?"

She clasped her hands in front of her. The cloud had moved away from the moon so he had full view of her wide smile. "And you missed me."

He ignored her, bothered she only caught the mushy parts and totally disregarded the fact she'd been ready to take him out. Again. "Do you want to hurt me? I mean the other night you took a swing at me with that heavy ass flashlight, and tonight you pushed me off your pier, and were ready to cold cock me with a hunk of wood."

She wadded to him, sliding her hands across his shoulders, moving in close. Way too close. Gently, he disengaged her embrace, and gripped her wrists. "Gracie. We're going to draw some unwanted attention."

She jerked free, snapped around, and splashed toward the pier.

He fanned into the water, performing an easy breast stroke to follow her. "Gracie."

"Ms. Desoto."

Damn this woman. He shouldn't have come here. Common sense told him to go straight home. The consumption of a few beers almost had him professing his feelings for her, which would've been crazy. He needed to get away, leave, before he did something completely stupid.

She paddled to a ladder he somehow missed and scaled the steps onto the dock. Ethan trailed close behind.

He'd made it to the top rung when she whirled to him, standing in the moonlights glow and pointed a finger in his face. "You frightened me."

Her white t-shirt clung to her body, giving him a clear view of her lovely tits underneath. A corner of his mouth lifted as her breasts delightfully jiggled. Ethan totally lost focus.

"Okay, but—"

"Don't you 'but' me." She placed her hands on her waist. The shirt tightened. Saliva filled his mouth as he fought to restrain himself. "I'm willing to forgive and forget. And you're being nothing but difficult, as usual."

"Please keep your voice down." He stepped onto the pier and patted the air with his palms. "People nearby may not like the noise. They might call the cops."

"Really? You've been sitting in a jail cell under a murder suspicion, and you're worried about the neighbors calling the police because we're loud?"

"They never locked me up. I sat in the detective's office the whole time."

"Whatever." She turned and stomped away, her bare feet echoing against the dock's wood.

Ethan sighed and smiled at the moon's radiance shimmering on her tight, round butt. He hurried to catch up, slipping an arm around her waist. He tugged her to him. "I'm sorry I upset you, Ms. Desoto. I'm overwhelmed from past few days, and I'm disturbed by you shoving me into the water."

Gracie answered with glare.

"Okay, maybe you'll explain later." He bent forward and brushed his lips against her temple. "Forgive me, please?"

She snuggled into him, tilting her chin up. He couldn't resist. His insides burned, on fire from need. Her hands stroked across his chest; her fingers caressed his arms. He twirled her to face him, mashing their saturated bodies together, crushing his mouth into hers.

Without breaking the kiss, Gracie rose up onto her toes. Her body trembled. He positioned his hand under her butt and hoisted her up. Her legs wrapped around his waist and situated herself into his throbbing erection. She clenched, his hardness nearly burst into the middle of her thinly covered thighs.

He licked her bottom lip, and set her to the ground. "Lay down." he commanded in a low growl.

Gracie's eyes grew round. "You want to do it here? On my dock?"

His hand lightly skimmed over her breasts, past her belly, under the elastic of her bottoms. Fingers glided between her legs. Heat, wet, and swollen. Her body yielded against his.

He released an easy chuckle. "Why not? No one will know. We'll have to be quiet, though."

"I'll do my best," she mumbled breathlessly, as they lowered. "But I won't make any promises."

Thirty minutes later, Ethan lay on his back, his arms pillowed his head.

"I'm not sure if this is a revision of my teenage

years or if we've sunk to a new low."

Gracie giggled. "It is bad, huh?"

Ethan was almost positive her entire body blushed. He was a little stunned, too. While he was always one for an adventure, this was over the top, even for him. Yet, this ride was so good.

"We probably shouldn't stay out here like this. Let's go inside and get out of these soggy clothes."

He stood, tugging at his wet boxers. "Um, I don't know if you've noticed, but we are almost out of them."

She followed suit, dragging her pajamas over her firm thighs. She gazed at him with an expression of guilt. "I bet you believe I have no self-control."

"You're not the only one who wants to have sex everywhere." Ethan chuckled. "The chemistry between us makes us crazy."

"Think so?"

"I am a man, and while men are not known for restraint where the entity between our legs are concerned, I've maintained scruples since I've become an adult. With you, I just lose it."

Gracie's face broke into a huge smile.

Ethan wanted to throw himself back into the river, and not come up until the alcohol was out of his system. He searched his mind for a save. "This is one for the record books."

"You're sure to get extra points."

Ethan stood and offered her a hand. "I will."

"Do you maintain a point system on all of your sexual encounters?"

"Only a joke, Gracie." He smiled at the positive end to the day from hell.

They entered the house. He drew her close, taking

her hands, fingers interlocked. "I know we've played around, and had some fun, but I need you to understand something."

She looked at him, her eyes anxious.

"I didn't kill Mike. It's important you believe that."

"I do." She gave him a half grin. "You don't seem like the blackmailing type."

"Ah, you've heard the gossip."

"I have, but it doesn't make sense. Attempts were made on your life, too. I don't understand why the detectives aren't taking that into consideration."

"My attorney posed the same question to them when they were interrogating me. Basically, they blew off both incidents, but the fact is, somebody went from trying to kill me to making me the murderer."

"That's crazy." She shook her head, her damp strands snapping into her face. She combed a hand through her hair, then jiggled the drops from her fingers. "We're soaked," she said as if this was the first time she'd noticed their wetness. "Hang on a minute; let me get us some towels so we can dry off."

Ethan grinned wickedly as he watched her leave. The low lights gave him even a better view of the deliciousness underneath her flimsy pajamas. The material clung to her like plastic wrap, outlining her small body perfectly.

He remained in the doorway after she left, not wanting to tread any more river water onto her hardwoods. He hadn't given it much notice to her home when he was here before, but now he took it all in.

The living area walls were painted a dark blue, decorated with vintage prints, combined with white furniture and subtler, pine woods. Knick knacks and light fixtures also antiquated, along with a mixture of family photos, sans the ex, were spread about to give the room a homey but classic feel. Something he was unfamiliar with and the hominess made him uneasy, but he knew he'd get used to this comfortable decor, and even come to like it after a while, especially if she came with the package.

"I dug out some beach towels." Gracie held a large, thick, fluffy towel to him. "If you want I can put your clothes in the dryer."

"I'm going to have to start paying you for doing my laundry." He took the wrap and patted his face, then unfolded it to wipe away as much moisture as he could. "Now let me ask you something concerning tonight's events. And I want the truth."

Her expression was cautious, which made him wonder if she'd give him a direct answer.

"Is someone harassing you? Is that why you're so jumpy anytime something odd comes around your home, and the reason you're constantly trying to de-brain me?"

She let out a long sigh. "It's stupid for me to be afraid, but we've had several burglaries in the area."

"You'd mentioned that the other day. And I don't think anything is wrong with being scared. Caution can be a good thing." He rubbed the small knot on his forehead from the other night's flashlight attack. "To a point."

Her expression darkened. "I tend to get a little overcautious. I had an incident in my past."

"Care to share?"

"When I was a young girl, my parents left me home alone for the first time. Someone broke in.

Nothing happened to me. I hid in my closet until they left with a load of our stuff, but I could identify them to the police. Neighbor boys from across the street. The family held a grudge against me and my family for the longest time until they moved. They intimidated me to where I didn't want to leave my home. The incident still causes me to be jittery whenever I hear a strange noise around my house."

He wrapped his arms around her, and brought her close. "I'm sorry. How 'bout I do a check outside. Just to make sure." He gently pushed her away. "Fetch me the flashlight you tried to kill me with the other night.

Twenty minutes Ethan returned. "I checked the house's perimeter. No strange footprints, broken shrubs, or paint chipped away around the windows. Everything looks fine."

"Awesome. Now I can sleep better."

"No sleeping until I've checked one more place." He snatched her hand.

She frowned. "Where?"

He grinned, leading her up the stairwell. "Your bedroom."

Chapter 16

Something was off.

Haywire.

Ethan sensed the strangeness in the atmosphere, in the still of the darkness.

A loud whoosh from behind startled him. He rose to his elbow, instantly alert. Another blow up, an ominous tweet followed the wiz, trailed by an explosive blast. The discharge was fierce, so brutal he thought his eardrums would splinter from the noise.

He stiffened.

The earth shook as the detonation struck the ground.

His body lifted. Arms flailed, he hurled through the air, his torso twisted, turning the opposite direction of his lower extremities. He landed in a throbbing heap several hundred feet away. Pain riddled over him. His limbs seared from the heat, his entire body burned, as if on fire while flames rained around him. Bits of ash pierced his skin, leaving singeing whelps wherever they touched. The smoldering odor combined with flesh…the distinctive, metallic scent of blood saturated the surroundings. Bodies were scattered, many with limbs barely hanging on or missing. Some moaned, while others lay motionless, their lives stopped in a mere instant.

He tried to move, to leave, but his legs were so

heavy, like they'd turned into blocks of wood. Unable to budge from his charred site, he panicked. Something was wrong. Why couldn't he lift his legs?

People ran past him, yelling in fear, but he wasn't able to understand them, only catching a word or two. They vanished into the darkness, away from the pouring smoke surrounding them.

Where was he?

His heart hammered into his chest. He held an arm out to the escaping crowd, tried to shout for help, but the words strangled in his throat. Smolders from fires, death, and the smell of danger lingered. He needed to getaway. No one would lend him a hand. He had to save himself.

He flipped over and raised his chest, balancing on his hands. A cluster of brush—brambles the fire had yet to destroy—was located about a hundred yards ahead. If he could make it to the mass, he'd be safe for the time being. He stretched an arm in front of him to crawl toward his target, dragging his useless legs behind him.

Every muscle in his body tensed. He stopped.

Warm hands seized his shoulder blades. His stomach plunged. He'd been captured. Someone spoke to him, but their words sounded foreign. He didn't detect any threats in their tone, though they might be trying to trick him.

Trust no one.

Instincts told him that he must escape or this would be his end.

He only had one shot.

He braced, ready to pounce.

Swiftly, he whirled around, trunk first. His hands expertly went for the throat. Surprised, they released him. He pressed down on their neckline and squeezed, constricted, weakening his adversary. Tighter, his fingers gripped into the flesh, ready to snap his enemy's neck as he sensed their life evaporate beneath his touch.

He heard the rumble before viewed the helicopter blades drifting above. A relieved breath escaped. He was saved. His grip slackened as he glared at his prisoner. And so was this guy.

He lowered his head, his face placed close, nose to nose with his foe. "Who are you?" he growled.

A gurgled "Ethan," replied in a rigid, anxious voice.

Thick fog swirled before his eyes. His mind reverberated into an out of control carousal, whirling backward until it fell off its axes. His head throbbed as his heart rate raced out of control. His skin felt like it'd been stripped from his bones, leaving every exposed nerve to scream from agony. The contents inside his stomach lurched, threating to exit at any second.

After several minutes, the heaviness began to subside.

Gracie's frightened features hovered lucid in front of him.

He jerked his loosened hand from her throat. "My god, Gracie."

She sat up in the bed, scooting away, cowering into a mound of pillows piled against the headboard. Her fingers clutched her neck. Her large eyes brimmed with tears from the horror.

He ran a palm across his rough, shadowed jaw. His body shook, sweat poured from his brow. The nightmare happened again. Something had set it off. Only the dream had never been this bad, never gone this far.

He glanced at a terrified Gracie, still gazing at him with a shocked expression. His eyes watered as he held in floods of emotion he couldn't recognize. How would he explain?

"I'm sorry," he whispered, stretching to her. His trembling fingertips grazed her arm. She winced, jerking from his contact. Reluctantly, he pulled away. He sniffed and swiped the back of his hand across his eyes, brushing a seeping drop from his whiskered cheek.

"You, you tried to kill me?"

How should he answer? That was exactly his intent. He checked his legs, to make sure they worked before he rolled out of bed. He rushed to the bathroom.

Standing over the sink, he turned on the faucet and splashed cold water over his face, soaking his skin, hoping to wash away the bitter reality. He snatched a towel and dried before he gazed at his reflection in the mirror. Sleepy streetlights peered through the small window, combined with the darkness distorting his image to show him precisely as he viewed himself. A monster.

The expression on her face—he'd tried to kill her. He hadn't realized his hands had been wrapped around her neck, but still.

His insides churned. He hurried to the toilet and lifted the lid, heaving the contents of his stomach into the commode. He flushed, and then sank to the floor, resting his forehead on the cool porcine. His abdomen lurched again, but he had nothing left to throw up. He was empty. Totally empty.

"Ethan?" The soft click of a switch lit the room

with a dim glow.

He raised his head but didn't bother to look at her. How could he?

Her robe tightly knotted, she stepped further into the bathroom, and although he caught that she stayed clear of his reach.

"Can you tell me what happened, why?"

He swallowed searching for the right thing to say. The exact words to make this go away. "I would never hurt you intentionally…a bad dream. I had a nightmare."

She seemed to relax a little, but he wasn't sure she believed him. "Except this one was worse than last Saturday's."

He gulped to moisten his arid mouth. "I have these, these dreams. Horrible—something sets them off. I can't control…" He wiped away another onslaught of perspiration. "I'm sorry." His voice sounded dry and raspy.

What else could he tell her? He had no explanation, because there wasn't one. Silence strained between them. What little trust she had in him faded before his eyes.

"Did I do something to bring on the dream?" she asked, her voice still packed with fear.

"Of course not." Appalled she would even think she was the reason the damn thing erupted, he shook his head quickly. "I don't know why they happen. It's been a long time since…" He stared at her. "Do you want me to leave?"

She waited as if to consider his offer. "You can stay. I don't know if I'll sleep, though."

She was only being kind. She didn't want to be

with him.

"No, I should go."

He struggled to get to his feet, though his legs felt unsteady, rubbery. He tried to regain his balance, couldn't. He collapsed in a heap on her bathroom floor.

"Ethan." Gracie raced to him, her hands outstretched. "What is happening?"

He gazed at her worried expression. "I can't—my legs. They won't move."

"We should call for help."

He shot out an arm. "No. I'll be fine. Just takes a few minutes."

Her forehead wrinkled as she motioned to his dissolved body fused to the floor. "This has also happened before."

He bobbed his head. Ethan remained on in place, hiding his face into his hands. A small twitch in his right thigh made him glance up. Feelings were returning. He glanced at Gracie, who'd gone back to the safety of the doorway.

She continued to watch him worriedly. "Can I do something?"

"Get my clothes."

"They're in the dryer, but they should be finished this time." She turned and left, leaving him alone for several minutes.

Thankfully, the sensations in his legs returned. He used the bathroom vanity to hoist to his feet. He clutched the counter until everything felt normal again.

Gracie reappeared, holding his neatly folded clothes. She carefully walked to him, to hand him his things. He tried not to notice how quick she pulled away once he took them, but the action was too obvious to overlook.

"You're okay now?"

"Better." He slid on his boxers and reached for his jeans.

"Tell me more about these dreams."

"I haven't had them in a long time. They weren't this bad before. Something, I assume my current situation, has triggered them again."

"You keep saying again. You're not telling me everything."

"I can't recall one thing. All I know is it's too disturbing." He heaved a sigh and he slipped an arm through his warm shirt. "I don't want to talk anymore, Gracie."

"That's fair." She folded her arms across her chest and glared at him. "Except your little episode almost cost me my life. I think I'm owed more than you not wanting to discuss the problem."

"I'm sorry." He stretched to her, but once more she jerked from his reach, only this time, she turned away. He blew out a stream of air. She was right; he did owe her more of an explanation. That meant revealing a dark secret few were aware of.

"I suffer from post-traumatic stress disorder. PTSD." She pivoted back to him with a look of shock. "It's been under control for a while, but..." He shrugged. "These attempts on my life and Mike's violent death seemed to have set them off again."

"You've been treated for this?"

"Therapy."

"Then you need to go back."

"I will. As soon as this thing with Mike is over."

"Sooner, Ethan. Tomorrow. I'll go with you. I

don't understand anything about this disorder, but I want to help you."

"You can't help me, Gracie. As a matter of fact, I should stay away from you."

"Why?"

"Because I almost—hurt you, and I don't want to ever harm you. Besides that, I'm the person of interest in a murder of one of the most prominent citizens in the area. You don't need to be seen with me. You're a mother and a successful businesswoman. You have a reputation to uphold." He attempted to smile. "Don't want to give your parents any more ammunition. They'd really think you were a screw up if you're hanging out with a murder suspect."

"We could prove you didn't do it. And get you the help you need."

"No we can't. Think about it. The combination of my problem and Mike's death make a great fit. I have to fight this alone." He made his voice cold. "You're not to get involved." The last thing he needed was Gracie Desoto mixed up any more in his mess. He was guilt ridden enough. It was his fault she'd been drawn in this far. "From now on, you need to stay out of my business." He moved to her and placed his hands onto her shoulders. Although her body stiffened from his touch, he kept his palms glued to her. "For your own safety. If you have any problems with break-ins, then call the police immediately." He tried to give her another small smile. "Although I'm confident you can take care of yourself, one day it may not be me you're attacking."

He released her and headed toward the bedroom door. He hurried down the stairs, glad his legs now were sturdy and able to carry him. Gracie followed him silently.

He swiped up his wet shoes, electing to leave them off. They walked outside and onto the street to where his truck waited.

"Will I see you again? After you get help?"

He didn't answer.

"Ethan?"

He unlocked the cab door and slipped inside. "It depends on how things go."

"The police?"

"If someone bothers you, they'll do a search of your property. They'll perform a more thorough inspection than what I did."

"That's not what I'm talking about."

Ethan wrestled for tolerance. Guilt overwhelmed him from what he'd done to her—or what he could've done. He needed to get away from her, to think, to purge the past memories swirling in his head.

"You're a person of interest in Mike's murder. I was with you the night he was killed. Surely the authorities are going to want to question me."

His jaw tightened. "No one will contact you. They're unaware you exist."

"So you, you didn't tell anyone about me?"

"No. And if you care for me, please keep it that way. Again, keep our relationship quiet."

He grasped the handle and shut the door with a slam. Eyes forward, he started the engine. Without as much as a glance in her direction, he sped off into the night, leaving her at the curb.

Chapter 17

Ethan stomped on the accelerator. An inadvertent glimpse in his rearview mirror had him fighting the desire to hit the brake and turn around. Gracie stood in the middle of the road, her silhouette immersed in the streetlight's glimmer as she watched him leave. Thank God he couldn't see her face.

Fuck. He should've followed through with his original intentions and not see her again. Yet he somehow ended up on her dock.

Who was he kidding? Chance wasn't a factor in his appearance tonight. He'd purposely sought her out. He needed her. His life had turned to shit in the matter of seconds, and he wanted their connection. To feel human again. And she made that happen.

How did he repay her?

By trying to kill her. Unconsciously, yes, though awake or not, the end results would've been the same if she hadn't managed to rouse him. A lot of things going down in his life he may easily dismiss, even this bogus murder inanity, but no way could he justify hurting her.

The distressing memory flooded his thoughts.

The look of disappointment, her loss of faith in him. The fear in her eyes would haunt him forever.

He glanced in the mirror one last time to view her fading image. She needn't worry about him messing up her life any more. Their moment had ended. He was out of her hair for good.

And he was miserable.

He turned onto the empty stretch of interstate and forced the pedal to the floorboard, not bothering to search the area for the local police or highway patrol. A speeding ticket would be a mere raindrop in a hurricane after what he'd experienced.

At the moment, he didn't care if they captured him, threw him in a barren jail, and tossed away the key. Solitary confinement would suit his disposition perfectly.

Within minutes he arrived at the lonely, dark turnoff to take him home. God, he didn't want to spend the rest of the night by himself. The fact he was dead tired was futile. His horrifying nightmares would replace sleep.

The buzz of his phone hailed him away from his melancholy mood. He yanked the gadget from the side pocket of his truck, glancing at the caller ID before he pushed the "on" button. "Yeah?"

"You okay?"

Ethan sighed before he answered. "If spending twenty-four hours with the police hounding me because they believe I bashed someone's head in before I shot 'em at point blank is okay, then sure, I'm great."

"Talk about a twist." His caller gave a humorless chuckle. "I've been trying to reach you since your release. Where've you been?"

"Having a party." He braked for a dark curve as he continued to travel at high speed on the lengthy, zigzagged, country road leading to his cabin. "A pity one."

"By yourself?"

"Kinda late for you to be on the phone. Thought mama gave you a curfew."

"Ah, so you had some company to help you descend into your weltered disgrace."

Ethan wasn't going there. He'd get scolded for being with Gracie, but no one could make him feel any worse than he already did.

"Past your bedtime, isn't it?" he goaded.

"Okay, I'll let the subject drop—for now. I'm calling about some stuff concerning Mike's murder anyway."

"What kind of stuff." Ethan's tone was guarded.

"Rumors are spreading like wildfire. The cops have discovered the missing plant saga. They're speculating Mike stole his own product to write off for profit."

"Our cities finest. A cracker jack team of misfits."

"Make your wiseass jokes. They're also guessing that you uncovered his little scheme and tried to blackmail him. The story is Mike refused to pay, an altercation occurred, and you killed him."

"Yeah, that's what happened."

"You need to take this seriously."

"I'm trying," Ethan said dully. He couldn't even think about the homicide investigation or any other trouble he may be facing at the moment. The only thing on his mind was Gracie and what he'd done to her. "Mike was a prominent citizen and did a lot for the community. The cops are pressed to make a quick arrest, and their grasping at nothing, trying to turn nil into something. Which is where I fit in. This isn't news to me."

"What makes the situation worse is this is a small town. Murders don't occur every day, hell, they rarely have one a year, and those usually stem from domestic disputes or bar brawls. Open and shut cases. These circumstances are way beyond the local law enforcement's capabilities."

"Tell me. They're disregarding the attempts on my life."

"How are they explaining that away?"

"They're not. They just ignore the fails." Ethan sighed. "This whole thing would be over if Mike would've kept his nose out of our business. And he'd still be alive."

"Yes, but it is what it is. His death has fucked everything up and put us back at square one."

Several moments of silence passed. Ethan's fingers tensed around the steering wheel, sensing the next subject would be a topic he didn't care to discuss.

"What about you and Gracie Desoto?" his caller asked timidly. "Is your little romance still ongoing or did you end things?"

And there it was.

"What's to end?" He didn't need another reminder of Gracie. He refused to talk about the situation because the usefulness no longer existed. They were done. "Why do you keep harping on the woman? She was a minor distraction, that's all. No romance."

"Good. You can't afford any diversions. Even small ones."

"No shit," Ethan barked, then more calmly asked, "So what's the next move? Or am I excluded from new information since I'm generating a ton of unwanted attention?"

"We meet tomorrow night, ten-thirty. Haven't heard a word about you being ousted so I'm guessing you're still in. You should be careful, though. I don't need to tell you our fearless leader is less than happy with your involvement with the cops."

"As if I had a choice." Ethan slowed, guiding the truck toward his extended drive. He flipped to his high beams. The bright lights bounced, fronting his pickup over the bumpy pathway. "This whole thing smells like rotted meat. I'm being set up. I'd sure like to find out who pointed the police in my direction."

"Probably the same person who tried to kill you."

"My thinking exactly. Someone wants me out, one way or another. Shouldn't be hard to figure out the scum. Only a handful of people were aware of my meeting with Mike." Ethan swallowed. "I thought everyone was trustworthy."

"Apparently someone isn't."

"I want a few minutes alone with whoever is trying to ruin or end my life." Ethan put the gear in park and switched the key to off. "Let's get together before we meet with everyone else."

"Got some ideas?"

"Call it a hunch."

****

Gracie struggled through the office entrance, her arms packed with the usual amount of work she'd taken home, plus a wardrobe change and accessories.

Betty peered over her glasses. She leaped from her chair, triggering it to roll backward, the wheels rotated with a high squeal. She rushed to her. "Why didn't you holler for me, missy?" She yanked the door wider, relieving her of a pair of heals Gracie had crooked between two fingers. "What's with the duds?"

Gracie carried a hanging bag to a coat rack and

hooked her suit over the peg. She dropped her make-up kit then she took her shoes from Betty and set them next to the stand. "Mike's service is today."

"That's right. I heard the funeral is this afternoon." Betty picked up her cup and scuffled to the coffee pot for a refill. "I'm bettin' there'll be a huge turnout. You better leave early."

"I plan to."

Mug overflowing, Betty carefully maneuvered behind her desk. "Is your man going?"

"Don't know, don't care."

Betty's eyebrows rose. "Trouble in paradise?"

"We're over," she said as if having her heart broke happened all the time.

"Tell me everything."

Gracie had realized she and Ethan were nothing except sex. He used her. These past few days taught her something. She couldn't do just the physical. She'd developed feelings despite his secrecy, his constant disappearing, and his episodes.

Nevertheless, she wouldn't dwell on this. She would allow herself to sting for a while. Then she was on a mission to forget this man. Betty was about to be disappointed.

Gracie lifted a shoulder. "Nothing to tell."

"Your break up came from somewhere."

"We had a fling." She averted her eyes. "We're done and yes, I'm a little upset because I thought things would last longer." She shrugged again. "Wasn't in the cards. I'll be fine. I made sure I didn't get attached."

Betty glared. "Eleanor Grace Hays Desoto."

Gracie's head shot up.

"You did not have a casual hook up, and you're not

a little upset nor will you be fine anytime soon."

When the woman spewed full names, she meant business. She released a reluctant sigh. Gracie may as well spill, though Betty probably already figured the situation out.

"I don't understand. He shows up at my house last night, unannounced, saying he wanted to see me and he missed me. We talked a while and then we…"

"Had sex." Betty finished.

"Right. After he had a nightmare. Not the first one." She stopped to choose her words. "His dreams are—violent." She gazed at Betty, fighting an assault of tears she'd been holding back since he'd left her. "I woke up with his fingers clutched around my neck."

"Oh, Gracie." Her voice sounded distressed, although her expression revealed something else. "This is so terrible, but I warned you to stay away from him."

Gracie ignored her "I told you so" comment. "He was in the military, Special Forces, stationed in Afghanistan. He didn't clue me in on the details, though he did tell me he suffers from post-traumatic stress disorder. He's had treatment and was fine for a while, but Mike's murder has set his illness off again."

"Poor man." Betty's cloud of gray hair shook. "How horrible for both of you. Does he plan on returning to the doctor?"

"I'm not sure." A sudden foreboded sensation tightened in Gracie's chest at the memory of his evident distress. His eyes holding painful memories that would never fade, haunted her. "Betty, I'm concerned. I want to help, but he, he won't let me."

"You can't press the man. They aren't like us women. They scare easy, and he's definitely frightened with these awful things hanging over his head. He's in no position to be with you. As a matter of fact, the boy didn't have any business coming to you last night. I've said this already, but you don't need to be involved with this young man, at least until Mike's death is solved."

Gracie shut her eyes, massaging her temples with her fingertips. "There is something else." She raised her lids and stared at Betty. "If he's suffering from PTSD, then what if he did lose control during a confrontation with Mike." She halted. "What if…"

Her secretary shook her head as she picked up a package of sugar from a small bowl she kept on her desk. "What's your gut tell you? Do you really believe him a killer?"

"I don't think so. The bottom line is he probably doesn't want to be with a woman whose ten year's older than him, and he's trying to blow me off nicely."

"That's your excuse." She jiggled the packet, tore it open, and dumped the white granules into her cup. "He said he missed you and wanted to see you. He showed up to be with you. He needed you. Plain and simple. Watch what he does instead of listening to his words. Appreciate he was honest enough to share with you what he's going through. That should help you decide."

"He left me, remember? The actions make everything clear."

"You're right. While he might want you, hopefully he cares enough for you not to drag you into his mess." Betty picked up a plastic spoon placed nearby and stirred her coffee. "With any luck the police will have the same impression and keep you out of it."

Gracie fidgeted. "I asked him about that. He assures me the authorities aren't aware we were together on the night of the murder, so they won't be bothering me."

Betty's expression turned grave as she observed Gracie for a long time. "That changes things."

"Why?"

"On the surface that looks all well and fine. But you be on your guard. If he were so innocent why wouldn't he tell them about you?"

"He says he didn't kill Mike," Gracie said almost defensively. "Two attempts were made on his life, too. The police are ignoring that little factor."

"Gracie, I don't know if your man murdered anyone, or anything about someone trying to kill him, but something doesn't ring right. The man's hiding more than he's sharing. He's up to something. Probably something no good."

Chapter 18

Mike's service was nothing short of a mob. Even though she'd left early, Gracie was forced to park several blocks over and hike on foot in one hundred plus degree heat and in high heels no less, to get to the chapel.

Thankfully, Krystal had saved her a spot or she would've been stuck in the crammed standing room only section on the second floor. She maneuvered past Quinn to squeeze in between Krystal and Vivian, lowering into her seat with a thankful sigh.

Eyes swollen and nose red, Vivian plucked several tissues from a box in her lap and passed them to Gracie. "In case you get overly emotional."

Gracie murmured thanks, needing the tissue more to mop her brow still covered with perspiration from her trek over rather than for tears.

"Glad you made it," Krystal whispered.

"I thought I wasn't going to." She combed the crowd, spotting numerous familiar faces. "I knew there'd be a lot of people, but this is ridiculous."

"Mike was a popular guy," Krystal said.

Quinn stuck her head around Krystal. "Plus the fact he's the first person in this town whose murder is," she raised both hands using her front two fingers for air quotes, "unsolved". Got a few folks curious."

"Why do you say it like that, Quinn?" Krystal

adjusted Gracie's collar, which evidently had gone cockeyed when she'd hurriedly slipped it on walking into the chapel.

Gracie knew what Quinn referred but chose to let the remark pass.

After last night, she was in no mood for a confrontation with anyone, especially this annoying woman. She searched the swarm again, taking in the hordes of mourners. Mike was a pillar of the community, but she had no idea he had this many admirers.

Quinn leaned forward and gave her a sly smile. "He's not here, Gracie."

Gracie frowned, again knowing full well to whom Quinn referred and not liking the implication one bit. "Who's not here?"

"Ethan."

"I didn't expect him to be." Gracie placed a palm over her heart. "Not under the circumstances." Her fingers skimmed up her chest, and lightly stroked her neck as she shoved the memories of the previous evening from her thoughts.

"Heard the DA is taking the evidence police collected to the grand jury," Quinn continued. "Your sweetie is about to be arrested for Mike's murder."

Gracie's heart squeezed, her body tensed. Quinn caught her frames visible rigidness and flashed a shrewd smile, aware she'd gotten to Gracie. "Unless he's disappeared again." Her grin grew as she thrust the verbal blade in deeper.

"Quinn, this is not the time or place," Krystal scolded.

Vivian patted Gracie's arm. "Ignore her. She's

green because Ethan wanted to be with you, and he never once noticed her."

Though Vivian had a point, she couldn't close her eyes to Quinn's insinuation. Talk about surreal. The man she'd slept with last night may've killed the man whose funeral she was attending today.

The possibility of Ethan being arrested played on her mind throughout the entire service, and she wondered if the evidence they had against him was solid. She didn't want to believe he was capable of killing anyone, but after what happened the evening before, how could she not consider the possibility? She had to be realistic. Except, she'd also experienced a tender side of him. His violence only transpired during his sleep, so, did that mean…she didn't understand any of this.

After the minister said the final prayer, the mass of people gathered in the aisles. Every exit passage was clogged as grievers pushed to extend their condolences to Mike's two sons.

Krystal snatched Gracie by the arm and dragged her through a less crowded side door. "Hope you didn't want to pay your respects to the family," Krystal remarked, as they walked outside with Quinn and Vivian trailing them. "I'm past ready to vacate."

Gracie released a wry chuckle. "I'm always willing to leave a funeral."

"Me too, unless it's my own. Then I'm not sure I'll want to get out so fast."

"This place is worse than a circus," Quinn said. "I wonder if these funeral goers are actually acquainted with Mike or if they're here to gawk."

"Mike was well-known." Vivian sniffed, wiping

her eyes. "Those who didn't know him in life want to get close to him in death. It's not uncommon."

"Is anyone going to the cemetery?" Krystal asked.

"Yes, I need to tell him goodbye one more time." Vivian wadded another soaked tissue.

Vivian had wept incessantly since Mike's death. She'd been infatuated with the man for many years, making her feelings known once his wife died after a long illness. Though her sentiments were unreciprocated, she remained a loyal, trusted employee, and friend to the family. Hopefully she'd move on now.

"Why don't we meet at the gravesite? Afterward let's celebrate Mike's life with dinner and a drink in his honor," Krystal suggested. "I'm thinking maybe we ought to check out the nursery tonight, too, so we can do that after we eat."

"I'm all for food and a toast to Mike; hell, I'm good to go to the grave now," Quinn said. "I don't get the point hanging out at the plant farm at night, especially since the police already got their man insight. We might be asking for trouble if we messed with any evidence."

Gracie hated to agree with Quinn, yet she wasn't sure about going to the nursery after dark either. The homicide occurred in the evening hours, and since she didn't want to believe Ethan a killer, then whoever did commit the murder remained on the loose.

Krystal's nose wrinkled, squinting against the sun "Don't we want to find out if Ethan's the actual killer? Or if thieves are still taking the plants? It'd be nice to clear Mike's name and prove he wasn't stealing his own stuff for cash."

Despite what happened with Ethan, Gracie would

also love to establish his innocence, too. Not so much for him, or for the time they'd spent together, but for her peace of mind.

Quinn folded her arms over her chest wearing a defiant expression on her face. "If the district attorney thinks they got the proof to prosecute Ethan, then that's good enough for me."

"The DA is human." Vivian sounded annoyed, like she was tired of Quinn's constant harping on Ethan's potential apprehension. "Humans make mistakes."

Quinn gave her a sharp look. "Not this time."

"He hasn't been arrested yet," Gracie put in, aggravated at Quinn's constant goading.

"The more I think about it, the more I question Ethan's guilt." Krystal smiled at Gracie. "I mean, yeah, he could be responsible on paper, but the police seemed to have tied this case up in a neat, giant bow. Something's off. I don't believe for a second Mike tried to commit fraud by stealing his own inventory. Those missing plants played a part in his death. Homicide isn't going to dig any deeper. We should explore other options as opposed to accepting Ethan's to blame."

"Krystal's right," Vivian put in. "We need to get to the bottom of this. Mike deserves to have his real killer locked away for good."

Krystal's gaze jumped from Gracie to Quinn. "We're in agreement? Cemetery, dinner, and then we scope out the nursery."

Gracie bit into her bottom lip, giving her friend an uncertain nod, while Quinn watched the swarms of people passing them by.

"Quinn?" Krystal's brows rose. "Will you be joining us?"

She huffed. "I guess. But I'm only going to show you all I'm right. Ethan McCarthy is a cold blooded killer."

"Whatever, Quinn." Krystal rolled her eyes. "We can make a game plan for tonight while we eat." She gazed at the line of vehicles that had already formed, snaking around the building and moving at a crawl. The traffic on the street had congested and was at a standstill. "We better get going if we want to make it out of the parking lot."

"Don't think that'll happen anytime soon." Vivian tossed her damp tissue into the stifling breeze as she turned and strolled toward her car parked nearby. "But we can give it a shot."

The women split in different directions. Gracie did her best to hurry on her extended trek to her pickup. Her shoes squeezed her feet and slowed her down. The heat intensified since the beginning of the funeral, the temperature soared to higher levels making her trip even more grueling.

She picked up her pace about half a block from her truck. She seriously needed to sit down and get rid of these heels. If her feet were too swollen, and she couldn't get them back on by the time she reached the cemetery, she'd pay her last respects barefooted.

Mike would understand. If he didn't, then he could take it up with her in another realm.

She neared her truck. An unshaven, disheveled man stood close by her vehicle, lingering. Great. All she needed was to encounter some homeless guy. Not that she wasn't sympathetic to plight of the poor, but she didn't carry cash, and she hated to disregard anyone in need. She reduced her stride as she got closer. She looked harder at the man. Something seemed familiar about him. She stopped. The guy resembled Ethan.

Her heart rate exploded and rammed against her ribcage.

Was that…yes, Ethan was waiting for her.

Shoving her achy feet and the heat aside, she hurried to meet him, stopping a few feet away. Their eyes met as pure betrayal brimmed over in her chest. Ethan wasn't alone.

Chapter 19

Gracie gaped at the intimate scene playing out in front of her.

The woman, the blonde she'd seen Ethan dancing with at Mike's party, the one who Ethan reassured her wasn't his girlfriend, had her arms wrapped around his neck, and his hands were placed securely on her waist.

She snapped to what she was staring at. No longer able to view this cozy little picture, Gracie spun on her heel and broke into an awkward sprint. The spike of her high heel jammed into a crack of the uneven concrete. Gravity jerked her to the sidewalk. The damaged shoe flew over her head, landing in the grass beyond her. Her body vaulted, then skidded forward, ripping the skin from her palms, elbows, and knees.

She didn't allow herself to wallow in the pain. She bounced up, continuing her clumsy dash to her truck, leaving her errant footwear behind. Key turned, the engine rumbled, she shoved her vehicle in gear, guiding it into traffic, ignoring the honks and angry fists from drivers she'd cut off. She sped down the road, weaving in and out of lanes.

Almost instinctively, she steered toward her office, screeching her tires as she parked. The lot was empty, the building dark. She kicked off her remaining shoe and rushed to let herself in.

She stopped in the middle of the room. For a brief

moment, she was lost.

The afternoon sun glimmered through the one small window, a cone pattern shined across the tiles. The lone desk was cleared, empty. Good. Betty had left for the day.

She stepped further inside to her private office and onto the fridge to grab a soda, then she collapsed into her chair, throwing her drawer open. She dumped the bag of chocolates in the middle of the desk. The candy spread over her work, but she didn't care.

Once the top was popped, she took a long swallow as she peeled back the sweet's paper. The chocolate melted in her mouth. She held her legs supine to study her bloodied knees, then her feet sagged to the floor, too distraught to care about the throbbing scrapes or the aches.

Was she more disappointed or surprised? Maybe a little of both. She had no desire to analyze her feelings. She wanted to wipe her mind clean and forget every moment since she'd met Ethan McCarthy.

She stood, ready to change back into her work clothes, and then remembered Krystal. She'd rather not speak with anyone, but her friend was probably worried when she didn't make it to the graveside. She leaned for her phone, lifted the receiver, and pointed a finger to punch the dial.

A soft click came from the outer area followed by footsteps tapping on the floor.

Damn. She forgot to lock the door.

She returned the phone to its cradle and tiptoed to the doorway and peeked around the edge. She backed against the wall. After several more deep inhalations through her mouth, she stepped fully into the room.

She glared at her guest, her voice frostier than an iceberg. "Why are you here?"

Ethan held up a shoe. "You lost this."

She crossed her arms, her frown deepened.

He laid her broken heel in the middle of Betty's bare desk. "Quite a spill you took." He indicated to the blood running down her knees. "You're bleeding. Are you all right?"

"You want to explain what's going on back there?"

His chin dropped to his chest. A quiet fell between them. He raised his head, giving it a significant shake before he finally spoke. "I can't tell you anything." His lips tightened as he raked a hand though his hair. "There's a lot you don't know about me."

"I'm nothing but a big fool. An old fool, since I actually believed someone ten years younger than me could be interested in me." Her anger grew with each word.

"You're nothing of the sort. And our ages made no difference to me, you know that. This is my fault. I never planned for any of this to happen."

"I got it."

His head fell, he stared past his feet onto the shiny floor. At least he had the decency to appear ashamed.

"You mean you never intended for us to happen, right?" Without waiting for his reply, she continued, "You came after me and used me. Somebody else was in the picture all along."

Ethan spun away so his back was to her. "You're a good woman, and you deserve the best life can give you." He returned to her. "You're beautiful, funny, and smart. The past few days have been great, despite a possible murder wrap hanging over my head. But I've always known this, us, we could never work." He hesitated. "I'm sorry."

Gracie barely listened. He was attempting to let her down easy. No point. He could go on about how wonderful he thought she was, or apologize over and again. The bottom line, he didn't want her. He preferred someone else. He could save his guilt speech and leave.

"So what you're telling me is you followed me here to dump me. Formally." Gracie's mouth flattened. "You've been trying to do that all along, but I refused to see it. I was nothing but a good time to you."

Ethan shoved his hands into his jean pockets.

"Okay. It's official. We're done. You can go now."

He nodded once then swung toward the exit. "You're an amazing woman, Gracie. But this is too complicated."

"What is?" She ought to let this go. Let him go, except she wanted him to witness the pain, to see the hurt in her eyes. She didn't want him to forget her face. "You owe me more than too complicated."

"I do, but that's all I have to say."

She flung a hand at him. "Then leave. I don't want to ever see you or hear from you again."

His chin dropped to his chest as he opened the door. He stepped outside and paused to watch a car whiz by on the highway in front.

Gracie followed him, standing in the doorframe. Ethan hiked to his truck and was inside, without giving her a second glance. The engine roared as he backed out and then sped away. A cloud of dust swirled in the recently vacated spot.

She reeled around to go in. Another pickup turned into the lot. Tires screeched as it skated to a halt. The door flew open. Krystal bolted out, running to Gracie.

"What happened to you?" She stopped to take in Gracie's appearance. "You're hurt?"

Gracie clutched her hands together, her focus on the direction to where Ethan's truck had disappeared. "I had a small accident." She sighed. "Heel of my shoe broke."

"You're bleeding." She hurried up the steps and took Gracie's arm. "Let's get you cleaned you up." She guided Gracie indoors and into her private office.

"I want to get out of these clothes first." She gathered her work duds and went into a postage stamp size bathroom. "Help yourself to a soda."

It didn't take long for her to change. Krystal had gotten her drink and was digging around in the top drawer of a tall file cabinet sitting in the corner, bringing out alcohol, antiseptic, and bandages. She carried the goods to the desk. "Sit."

Gracie did as she was told, snatching her soda on her way down.

Krystal squatted beside her and began to clean her wounds. "So what was Ethan doing here?"

Gracie tucked her bottom lip under her teeth. She'd hoped Krystal hadn't noticed his truck speeding away. "He came to break up with me. Officially."

Krystal's brows rose, but she kept the rest of her expression passive. "I know you don't want to hear this, but it's probably for the best considering his circumstances. Did he say anything about that? His possible arrest?"

Gracie hissed as her friend cleaned a particularly deep scrape.

"Sorry."

"To answer your question, no. He basically clarified where our relationship is—or isn't, then I told him to leave. Besides, I was more interested in the blonde he held in his arms as opposed to his upcoming arrest record."

Krystal stopped dabbing and stared at her. "Where did you see this?"

"After Mike's funeral. It was the same woman he danced with at the party. They were together, not too far from my truck." She gave an abbreviated version explaining last night to until he'd left moments before Krystal arrived.

"Okay, we're done here." Krystal screwed the cap back onto the alcohol. "I can't fix your heart or your relationship. He's a jerk and not worth the time. We're meeting Vivian and Quinn at Los Amigos, so let's go have some good food, then we're going to solve Mike's murder."

"Krystal, I don't—"

"No excuses," Krystal interrupted. "Doing this will get your mind off Ethan. You'll have plenty of time to go through the anger, denial, grief, and whatever the other emotions you need to deal with. But for tonight you're going to put him behind you."

****

Gracie groaned as she made her entrance into the eatery. Only Quinn waited at the table.

Quinn spotted her too and gave her a feeble wave. Since there was no way for Gracie to backtrack and go outside to wait until the others showed up, she returned her gesture and strolled to where Quinn sat. She put on her best smile and gave Quinn a super polite greeting as she approached, but only after ordering a margarita with a sidebar from the waiter.

"Make it quick." She glanced in Quinn's direction.

Quinn had two small glasses of clear something in front of her. She downed each in one gulp and held up the empties. "Bring me another too." She gazed at Gracie. "You missed the graveside service."

Gracie smiled, unwilling to reveal a smidgen of her afternoon once she'd left the funeral. "Traffic."

Quinn gave her a disbelieving look. "Uh huh."

"Everything going okay?" Krystal pulled out a chair to join them, Vivian not far behind to Gracie's relief.

The night turned out to be good for Gracie. She put her sorrows behind her, at least for the time being. Good food, friends support, and a strong drink did wonders for her ailing heart. After several spiked beverages she even found Quinn tolerable.

At the end of the evening, Krystal raised her glass. "We need to toast Mike and his life."

Everyone cheered and clinked before taking a drink.

"He did a lot for so many people." Krystal dabbed her eyes with her napkin.

"No one was better," Vivian agreed. "I hope they catch the bastard who did this soon."

"The killer is Ethan McCarthy." Quinn lifted her shot glass and downed her drink, then wiped her mouth on her sleeve. "I'm sure of it."

Krystal scowled at Quinn. "Why would you even say something like that? No information has been released, and he's yet to be arrested."

Vivian looked at Gracie. "I'm iffy on the whole Ethan thing, too. Things seem bad, but I have trouble getting on board with his guilt. I bet you don't even want to think about him being a murderer, considering how the two of you are." She grinned. "I'd hate to give up a man so delicious.

Everyone at the table focused on Gracie, who felt like someone splashed icy water in her face.

Quinn's eyes narrowed but twinkled, a trace of a smile played at her lips. "You and Ethan break-up?"

No use denying it. Her heartache must be written all over her.

Krystal gave Gracie a sympathetic glance. "I don't think she wants to talk about it."

"It's okay. Ours was a causal relationship. We've gone back and forth all week, he tends to run hot and cold and then—" She paused to sigh. "This afternoon, after the funeral, I caught him with the blonde he was dancing with at Mike's party. They looked...close."

"They were really into each other that night," Quinn said. "They seemed awful chummy. I'm surprised he didn't go home with her."

Gracie gave a sad chuckle. "I suppose they're doing more than the foxtrot."

A murmur of sympathy went around the table.

"Did you talk to him?" Vivian questioned. "Ask him what's going on."

"We did speak afterward." Gracie's mouth twisted. "I didn't get much. Well, I officially got dumped. After that I threw him out of my office. Told him to leave me alone." She raised her glass to drain the contents. "Tired of his indecisiveness."

"Lame," Vivian said.

Everyone went quiet. Krystal held up her hand for the waiter's attention and made a circle motion to each of them for another round. They remained silent until their drinks arrived.

Quinn spooned a mound of her dessert and pointed her utensil at Gracie. "You know what I'd do if I was you?"

Gracie was afraid to ask, but did anyway. "No, Quinn, I don't."

"I'd go over to his house and tell him you want the truth. You deserve a real reason. Make him explain what's going on between him and that woman and why he did you this way. Not right to leave somebody like that. Even if you haven't known him a long time."

Amazement charged through Gracie. She almost believed Quinn felt sorry for her. "It's not that I don't agree, Quinn, but what's the point? This was nothing more than a weekend. A crazy fairytale."

"Every woman wants a fairytale, Gracie, and their happily ever after." Quinn replied softly. "All women are worthy of one, too. And when it doesn't happen, we should at least be told why."

"Oh, Gracie, I'm not a fan of this idea," Krystal said. "Do you even know where he lives?"

"I've visited him a couple of times."

"Then tonight, after our meeting at the nursery, you go find him, girl," Vivian instructed, "and get some answers."

Okay the idea was crazy, but she did want closure. Yeah, she'd be paying Ethan McCarthy one more little visit. Damn the breakup, she wouldn't leave until he explained everything to her, including his involvement with Mike's death.

Chapter 20

After they finished their meal, the women discussed traveling arrangements for their late night excursion to the nursery. They voted to take one car instead of four, since so many would be conspicuous. Quinn drove the smallest vehicle, the easiest to hide.

With the ladies piled in her compact, they left town. Quinn increased her speed, driving at a high rate down the dark, winding roads. Gracie and Krystal sat in the tiny back, gripped the seat in front of them so not to be thrown into each other or the side doors.

Krystal leaned over to Gracie. "If I knew we'd be riding a rollercoaster, I wouldn't have eaten so much. Her driving makes me queasy."

"Seriously. At least you only had one glass of wine. Anymore and you might be in some major trouble."

They reached the nursery in half the usual time, Quinn screeched the tires to a halt at the security gates. She punched in the code, then curved around to look at Krystal. "Gate opened or closed?"

"Probably should leave them open in case we need to make a quick getaway."

Vivian twisted toward the backseat. "You don't think someone may get suspicious if they drove by and noticed?"

"This road isn't that busy in the daylight hours

unless it's customers coming to shop with us," Krystal reasoned. "I can't imagine any traffic this far out after dark."

Quinn gunned the accelerator. The car lurched before she zipped through the entrance, driving to the other side of the building to park. The woman exited the vehicle and gathered in a tight circle next to the office.

"So now what?" Quinn asked loudly.

Vivian whipped in the direction of Quinn with a forefinger pressed to her lips. "We must be quiet."

"Why? Nobody's here."

Krystal gazed into the darkness. "We don't know that for sure, Quinn."

Gracie eyed the bleakness surrounding them, eyeing a group of live oaks. Clusters of Spanish moss dangled from the limbs. Other than an occasional light flurry to toss the sprigs, the nursery appeared vacant. Everything was eerily still, the air humid and sticky. Like a huge storm was about to roll in. During the day, the nursery was peaceful and in a weird way, lovely. Night was totally different. In the darkness, the place held almost a sinister aura.

"Did anyone think to bring flashlights?"

"I brought two, but they're small." Krystal opened the car door, reached into her purse, and took out the miniature penlights. She flipped the switches on then off, and nodded before she handed one to Quinn, stuffing the second into her back pocket.

Vivian held up her phone. "My cell has a decent light."

Gracie stuck a hand into her jeans and brought her cell out. "I think mine has a flashlight as well." She turned on the light, satisfied with the appearance of the beam. "Yes, this works."

"I say we split up. Gracie and I can explore the west side, and Quinn and Vivian can take the east."

Vivian walked a few steps away from the group and shined her light at the sealed greenhouse where Mike's body had been discovered. Yellow tape surrounded the enclosure and rattled from the near non-existent breeze. "What exactly are we looking for?"

"We're trying to discover if plants are still being taken," Krystal explained.

Vivian returned to the party and gazed at Krystal. "You've been taking care of them. Surely you'd noticed blank spaces."

"There hasn't been any missing since Mike's death." Krystal's expression turned solemn as she scrutinized the darkness once more. "But that doesn't mean someone isn't going to show up tonight. If nothing else, maybe we can discover how they're getting them out without anyone spotting them."

"And if we find another exit, then what?"

"I don't know." Krystal sounded frustrated. "I just want to prove Mike wasn't robbing his business for money."

"I'm all for clearing Mike's name," Vivian said. "But you think we're going to find anything roaming around?"

"Doubtful, because we didn't plan this very well," Quinn pointed out. "We were supposed to talk about details at dinner, but we forgot."

Krystal released a discouraged moan. "You're right. This idea blows."

"We can at least walk the fence line," Gracie

suggested, hoping to make Krystal feel better. "If we find where they're breaking in, we'd have a start."

Quinn swished her light down gravel road as she strolled into the night. "Yeah, we might as well do something since we're here. I hate to waste a tank of gas."

Vivian lifted a shoulder before she followed Quinn into the gloom. "Her concern is beyond touching, isn't it?"

Krystal tugged at Gracie's upper arm, urging her to move the other way. "Come on, let's make this quick."

They trudged deep into the blackness, following the dimly lit path, their small rays offering the only light. A muggy wind had risen and whistled through the trees bordering the nursery's boundaries. Insects and night crawlers remained mum. Almost as if they understood the edgy atmosphere and chose not to participate. Even the stars elected to take the evening off.

Flowery scents intoxicated the air. Smells reminiscent of a distant past usually pacified, but instead of a calming, the odors made the evening seem more ominous.

"Krystal." Gracie's soft voice ricocheted into the nothingness. "I don't know if the thefts are still going on, but it's dead here tonight."

Krystal flitted her shaft from the fence, to the trail, returning to the fence. "I was thinking the same thing."

"We ought to call it a night. We'll come back when we're more organized. Bring some protection in case we encounter whatever or whoever we're looking for."

"We should have postponed in the first place. I've been so focused on exonerating Mike, my mind hasn't been straight. I'll call Vivian and tell her and Quinn to meet us up front." Krystal stopped and slid a hand into her pocket for her cell phone. She pressed the "on" button. "Damn. My battery is dead." She returned the device to her jeans and looked at Gracie. "Do you have Vivian's number programed?"

"No. We were work friends, but our friendship never made it to the point of exchanging personal stuff."

"I won't even ask if you've stored Quinn's information."

Gracie chuckled. "That'd be the dumbest question ever. Let's go to the car and wait for them."

The two women turned around and retraced their steps. Neither spoke as they made their short journey back passing rows of greenhouses. Doors had been left ajar to ventilate. From inside, silhouettes of oversized leaves vaulted within the dimness, giving the eerie impression of darkened demons flying over the mutedly lit floors. Plastic coverings rattled adding to the night's peculiarity.

"I keep a set of office keys in my purse," Krystal said as they approached the building. "We'll sneak inside, and I'll call Vivian from there."

"Do you know the alarm code?"

"Yes. Mike changed it every—"

A loud crack exploding from the other side of the nursery interrupted her.

Several short screams trailed. Both women stopped in their tracks. Krystal switched off her flashlight.

"What was that?" Gracie stretched her neck, her gaze searching the dark.

"No clue, but it can't be good." Krystal jerked

Gracie's arm, dragging her in the direction the sound came from. "We need to find Quinn and Vivian."

"Wait." Gracie yanked her back. "That sounded like a gun. We need to stay here." The inside of her mouth became instantly parched. Someone lurked within the darkness, and her gut indicated that person wanted to do them harm. She scanned the ground for something to use as a weapon.

An alarmed Krystal considered her suggestion. "We can't leave them if someone is out here firing a gun."

"What if whoever is shooting is Mike's killer?"

"Our friends need our help," Krystal argued.

"We should call the police first."

"That'd be Sheriff Bud, and he's already downed a twelve pack of his favorite brew by now. We may all be dead by the time he gets here."

Another blast boomed, trailed by several more shots.

Chills peppered across Gracie's neck, traveling over her arms. "We need someone to find our bodies." She looked at her friend and held out her phone. "Call Bud, Krystal. He's better than nothing."

Krystal carefully opened the car door and extinguished the interior lights.

"Damn it." Quinn's intonation vibrated through the obscurity.

"They're okay." Krystal murmured, relieved, then she shouted, "Quinn! Hey Qui—"

"Krystal." Gracie grabbed her arm and yanked her down as she squatted. "Krystal, think. We can't yell. Someone might be roaming the nursery with a gun."

"Krystal," Quinn hollered. "Where are you?"

"Over here." Krystal flashed the light for a split second to give Quinn their location. "Be quiet though. We don't need to draw any added attention."

Quinn hurried to them, panting, her complexion ghostly white.

"Are you all right?" Gracie came to her feet. "What happened?"

Quinn motioned over the top of her head. "A bullet. Whizzed right by me just as I tripped on a rock," she rushed in between pants. "I jumped up and started to run. Another shot ripped past my ear."

Gracie and Krystal exchanged a worried glance. The fears Gracie hoped were an overactive imagination ignited and caught on fire. "You're sure someone was shooting at you?"

Quinn held up her left hand. "I swear."

"Did you see anyone?" Gracie asked. "Where did the shots come from?"

"I don't know on both counts."

A low engine rumbled from the rear of the nursery. White flashes glinted though the trees' thickness. The noise increased, growing closer. A pickup's shadow materialized in the distance, heading toward the exit.

"Hide," Krystal cried in a whispered shout.

They scattered and crouched behind the front of Quinn's car, peeking above the hood. Gracie's insides shuddered as she watched the truck. Something was all too familiar about that vehicle. Her teeth sank into her bottom lip, glancing at her companions, hoping they weren't getting the same vibe.

The three ducked lower as the truck passed them, then it flew through the opened gates.

The ladies rose, their gazes glued to the sinking

taillights.

"Did anyone get a good look?" Gracie elevated to her tippy-toes for a better view of the disappearing red dots. "I couldn't see a thing." This was almost the truth. She really couldn't make out the truck, though instincts told her exactly who it belonged to.

"Me either." Krystal brushed the dirt from her jeans. "I wonder if that was our shooter."

"We should follow them." Quinn sprinted to the driver's side and yanked the door open.

"They're gone." Gracie's gaze remained on the now empty road, her interiors still churning. The last thing she wanted was a confirmation on her suspicions. Sometimes it was better not to know. "I doubt if we'd catch them, even as fast as you drive."

"Quinn?" Krystal brow furrowed as she glanced at the other woman as she slammed the car door. "Where's Vivian?"

"We got separated when all the ruckus began."

Krystal flipped her flashlight's switch. "We need to find her, then we should get the hell out of here."

"We ought to bring in the police." Quinn planted her feet. "Some serious crap is going on. I almost died back there."

"You're right and we will. As soon as we know what to call them for."

"Someone was shooting at me, Krystal."

"I don't doubt you; I heard the gunfire. Except the only thing we have is you tripping over a rock and you're not hurt. No proof of anything. The nursery is located in the middle of nowhere. Gunshots are common out here. People hunt wild hogs or get drunk and shoot just because."

"Krystal's right," Gracie agreed. "And we'll need to make sure we're not involved."

Quinn motioned toward the opened gate and pointed. "What 'bout the truck?"

"Okay," Krystal reasoned. "Trespassers. So are we. We could get into trouble for being here without permission."

"Vivian's disappeared?" Quinn raised her chin and placed her fists on her hips. "We might want to call them to find her."

"Let's search for her before we do that." Krystal positioned the light to shine ahead, wandering into the night. "She's probably hidden and is waiting until she's sure the coast is clear before she makes an appearance."

The women traveled over the nursery shining lights into crevices and culverts, calling Vivian softly. They stood in doorways of the greenhouses, directing their soft glimmers insides. No sign of Vivian. Curving to the rear, they approached the last rows of houses.

Spears stabbed the back of Gracie's neck, her hair stood on end as she hurried past a field of decorative statuary for sale. Instead of ornamental, now they resembled headstones in the waning twilight.

Quinn sped to the next to the last house and gestured to a spot in the dirt. "This is where I fell. I bet that house is riddled with bullet holes."

"Riddled from a couple of shots?" Krystal laughed as she shined her light around the area. Gracie stood at the entrance of the nearest house, positioning her phone to comb the insides. Nothing appeared out of the ordinary.

Krystal spun to Quinn. "Do you remember where you lost Vivian?"

"When I tripped."

"Was she ahead of you, or behind you?" Gracie carefully guided the bright stream across the house one more time.

"Behind me."

Gracie stepped away from the doorway and swept the ray over the row. "She might be on the far side of the nursery looking for us."

"Or," Quinn's voice quivered. "Whoever was in that truck took her?"

Gracie and Krystal stared at each other. The possibility seemed farfetched, but there didn't appear to be another explanation.

Gracie scanned the night again. "It's so dark out. I'm betting we missed her, and she's up front waiting for us. One of us should go back to the car while the others keep looking."

"Alone?" Quinn asked in a high-pitch squeak. "I'm not going anywhere else by myself out here. Truthfully, I don't feel safe with us together."

"I'm uneasy about a split, too," Krystal said. "We've already lost one person. Separating isn't a good idea."

"We have our phones." Gracie pulled hers out of her jeans. "Well, almost. Krystal's battery is dead."

"Mine works. I can call Vivian." Quinn reached inside her shirt pocket for her cell and pushed a button. She put the devise to her ear. "It's ringing." There was a long silence. "No answer." She tapped "end" on her screen. "Voicemail."

Gracie returned to the threshold of the greenhouse. Krystal moved behind her and shined a light inside. The brightness reflected spectral outlines of large palms

206

springing in the feathery breeze.

Gracie held out a hand. "Over there. On the floor." She directed her beam to the center.

Krystal leaned forward. "What is that?"

Quinn wiggled between them and squinted. "It isn't a plant." She took a step inside.

Gracie snatched the edge of Quinn's shirt and yanked her back. "Don't go in." Gracie gulped twice and choked. "I think that's a body."

Chapter 21

The three women stood stunned, their gazes fixated on the lifeless individual.

Krystal adjusted her shoulders, leaned forward, and squinted, shining her light inside. "That certainly looks like a dead person. There are legs and a torso, and it doesn't appear to be breathing. The head is hidden by the big pots of geraniums, so I can't see who it is."

Gracie let her flashlight drop to her side and twisted toward the others. "We should call Sheriff Bud now. Drunk or not, he needs to be notified." She glanced at Quinn. "Do you want to dial 911, or would you prefer me to?"

Quinn stood motionless, her eyes wide as she gaped into the greenhouse. Out of the blue, she released an earsplitting screech and pointed. "That's Vivian. Vivian's dead." Then she bolted, running down the pathway.

"Crap." Krystal faced in the direction Quinn sprinted. "Come back, Quinn. We need to wait for the authorities." But her pleas fell on deaf ears. Quinn continued her run, disappearing into the darkness. Hands on her hips, Krystal stared after her a long time. She spun around and walked past Gracie to the doorway, gazing at the deceased in question.

Gracie thrust out a hand. "Don't disturb anything."

Krystal gestured at the corpse. "Do you think that

could be Vivian?"

"She wore a dark shirt, similar—she's disappeared." She gazed at Krystal. "I can't tell if it's a man or a woman the way the body is positioned."

"How will we find out who that is without going inside?"

"The person might be shot in the head, like Mike. Do we want to be up close and personal?"

"What if they're not dead, and just hurt?"

"None of us are trained to help. We need to round up Quinn, and get the hell out of here the minute after we phone the police."

"Vivian was my friend, Gracie. Yours too." Krystal sniveled and wiped her eyes. "If that's her, we're not leaving." She stepped closer to the threshold.

Gracie grabbed her forearm and yanked. "Krystal don't."

She stopped and turned to Gracie. "We've known her for years. We spent most of the day with her and shared a meal with her less than an hour ago."

"I understand, Krystal." The memory of the pickup driving through the nursery only a few minutes before swept through her mind. Ethan's truck. She was almost sure. Except she didn't want to believe he did something so horrendous. "The pickup. Whoever is inside might've done this. But Krystal, what *if* they were here for another reason. The killer may still be on the grounds. Waiting—for us."

Krystal seemed to consider the theory. "Gracie, I'm sure whoever was in the truck is responsible for all the weird stuff happening recently."

"I'm betting several people are involved in this plant stealing scheme, and maybe the vehicle is connected. We believe Mike's death is tied to stolen material. Most likely he died because he interfered. We're snooping too. Vivian is possibly dead, missing for sure. Someone shot at Quinn. They may not want us here. That person might be hiding anywhere, listening to our every word. It's so dark, we wouldn't have a clue." Gracie tugged Krystal's arm. "We're not safe. A deserted area is ideal for getting rid of people. Killers would be long gone before anyone found us."

Krystal remained still.

"Come on. Let the authorities handle this." Gracie gazed out into the night. "I hope Quinn didn't go off the deep end more than usual and leave without us."

"You're right. We do need to get out of here." Krystal took a step then stopped, clutching her abdomen. "I'm not sure I can make it though. My stomach is upset."

Gracie slanted closer to her friend. Krystal's brow was wet from sweat, her complexion pale under her tanned skin. "Yeah, you don't look so good."

"I don't feel so good."

"Probably from stress." Gracie looped her arm though Krystal's. "I'll help you."

Krystal nodded. Gracie guided her down the graveled path. "If you want to stop, or anything else, just say so."

They moved at a slow pace, traveling in silence, jumping at every sound. Thankfully, the wind had picked up, and the air wasn't as sticky as before. The warm breeze would've been comfortable if the circumstances were different.

The massive area was well laid out. During the daylight, the nursery was easy to maneuver, but at night the place appeared distorted. Eerie. It seemed like they walked forever before they caught sight of Quinn's vehicle.

"Good," Gracie said relieved as they approached. "She's still here."

"The car is, but Quinn's not." Krystal wandered to the front of the vehicle, catching her second wind. "We've got to find her. Especially if someone's out to kill us. They'll shoot Quinn first, for sure."

Gracie stooped to peer through the window. "You're overreacting."

"No, I don't think I am. If someone wants the three of us dead, Quinn will be next. Many times if I had a gun, I would've shot her myself."

Gracie straightened. "A lot of people feel that way."

"So you understand my point."

A distant low guttural moan pierced the darkness.

Krystal froze. "Did you hear that?"

It became quiet for a moment, then another series of groans followed.

"That must to be Quinn." Krystal's voice held a hint of relief. She walked further away and stopped again.

Gracie remained by the car. "Are you sure? Sounds more like a wounded animal."

"It's Quinn." Krystal hurried in the direction of the noise.

Gracie rushed to catch up. "Slow down. Might be a trap."

"I don't think so. That's Quinn."

Even with Krystal's assurance, the two treaded carefully across the trail toward the peculiar sound.

They circled the building. The groans grew louder, coming from the other side of the office.

"Anything?" Gracie whispered as they advanced to the steps leading to the back entrance.

"Not yet."

The women lifted their lights and shined them onto a small deck. Amongst the shadows, a small form curled up against the door at the top stairs. Quinn scrambled to her feet, leaped from the edge, and threw herself into Gracie. She buried her face into her shoulder and wept loudly.

Gracie looked at Krystal helplessly.

"Quinn?" Krystal dislodged her away from Gracie, giving her a solid shake. "Get a grip. Now's not the time to lose it. We need to stay in control."

Quinn lifted her head. She wiped her wet face with a shirtsleeve. "She was my best friend. She saved my life, and now she's dead."

"Best friend?" Gracie and Krystal exchanged confused glances. "I thought all they did is fight."

"Their way of relating."

"How did she take care of you, Quinn?" Gracie flipped her phone light off and slipped the device back into her pocket.

"The killer pointed a gun at me, and she shoved me down. My good friend took a bullet meant for me. She died in my place."

Gracie frowned at Krystal.

Krystal shrugged. "You said you fell when you stumbled on a rock."

"I did," Quinn insisted. "I tripped because she pushed me into the ground."

"You didn't say anything about being shoved

earlier."

Quinn divided a glare between Gracie and Krystal. "This has been very traumatic. I may be having some delayed reactions or repressed memories or something."

Krystal opened her mouth but apparently decided against getting into an argument. "You're right, Quinn, this situation is upsetting. We'll do better if we're not here, so let's go home."

"We're going to leave her?" Quinn gestured out into the gloom. "We can't. She's a hero."

"We're not sure if the victim is Vivian. We're speculating at this point."

"Krystal's right. If we've discovered a murder, the police need to be called. We shouldn't mess with any evidence and spoil a chance to discover who killed her."

"We already know, Gracie," Quinn exploded. "Your damn boyfriend pulled the trigger."

Arms crossed across her middle, Quinn glared at Gracie waiting for her to challenge. Quinn's words stung, more than if Gracie had been shot herself. Ethan may be a jerk, a user, or just a plain sorry ass, but she still couldn't accept the guy was a cold blooded killer.

She stepped in front of Quinn. "You're talking out your butt. You have no proof to support your claim."

Krystal quickly maneuvered between the two, holding up her hands, a palm facing toward each of them. "Okay, okay, this is not the time for a fight. We've got too many things happening, and we need to stick together." She raised her brows at Quinn. "Quinn?"

Quinn's chin fell to her chest. "I'm sorry Gracie. I'm a little crazy."

More so than usual. Gracie nodded as an acceptance to her apology although she didn't fully forgive her yet. "We need to leave. This place has us jittery."

"I agree." Krystal walked to the vehicle. "Let's go. Once we're far away, I'll borrow Gracie's phone to call Bud and report. I'll explain we were scared the murderer is still on the property and so we left."

Quinn shook her head. "We shouldn't leave her."

"Hey," came a shout from behind. "Y'all aren't going without me, are you?"

The three woman froze and gaped at the shadow strolling toward them.

Krystal was the first to discover her voice. "Vivian?"

Vivian walked to the group. "Yeah, it's me, what gives?"

"We heard shots, and we couldn't find you." Gracie was still in shock, but happy to find her friend alive and well. "We found a body, we thought—"

"A body?" She whirled around. "Where?"

Krystal indicated the direction. "In a greenhouse. Next to the last house on the back row."

"You were with me when the gun was firing." Quinn seemed bewildered. "You pushed me down, right? You saved me."

Vivian shook her head. "A strange noise was coming from the potting barn. I stepped inside to check things out while you walked ahead. I hid after the blasting started and stayed till the coast was clear."

Quinn held up her cell. "I tried to call you when we couldn't find you. Why didn't you answer?"

"Turned my ringer off." She smiled guiltily.

"Sorry."

"Doesn't matter now," Krystal said, relieved. "We're glad you're okay."

Gracie pointed out into the darkness. "There's still a dead person lying in the back of the nursery."

"Then let's go find out who the newly deceased is," Vivian said. "After, we can call Bud, though I'm sure he's about seven sheets to the wind by now and will be no help at all."

Krystal glanced behind at Gracie with a meaningful look. "The pickup earlier probably was our bad guy, but there is a chance it wasn't. The person or people who were shooting could still be here."

Vivian's expression showed surprise. "What pickup?"

Krystal explained the occurrences that'd happened up until they'd met up again.

"The shooter had to be in the truck," Quinn insisted.

"Maybe. I'm convinced the plant thieves have something to do with Mike's death." Krystal glanced at Gracie. "And I agree with Gracie. More than one person is involved. Someone could be here, and we wouldn't even know. We may be viewed as a threat. They might come after us."

Quinn broke into a run to her car, flinging the door open. She motioned to the others. "Let's go. I think I'll trade my car off tomorrow. The murderer probably saw it and could run the license plates on the Internet to track me down. I'll end up dead, too. He may think I know something."

"I doubt it, Quinn." Vivian followed Quinn and opened the car door. "Everyone knows you don't know anything."

"The killer doesn't."

"I saw the killer, so no worries there."

The group kept their eyes on Vivian who nodded with a deliberate smile. "I cracked one of the potting barn's doors to peek out after the shots were fired. He walked right past me." She looked at Gracie. "I'm sorry. But it was Ethan. And he had a gun."

Chapter 22

This assignment fit him to a tee. Ethan glanced at the gun lying on the seat next to him as he disregarded the lingering odor of cordite that still tickled his nostrils. He zipped down the desolate, snaky road, driving away from the chaos. Away from another nightmarish memory. He snatched his phone and pressed the direct dial with added force.

"Are you still inside?" he asked when his connection answered.

"Yeah, where the hell are you?"

"I had to leave. Too many people hanging around. What the fuck's going on?"

The sound of a throat clearing came from the other end. "I'm in the sales office, looking out the window." There was a pause. "Vivian, Krystal, Quinn, and your *girlfriend*, Gracie Desoto are outside."

Ethan chose to ignore the jab about Gracie. "I thought I caught a glimpse of Vivian snooping around the potting barn."

"Did she catch you?"

"Not sure." Ethan swiped a hand over his face to wipe a burst of perspiration from his forehead. He forced his concentration from the incident, keeping his focus on the drive and conversation. "What are they doing now?"

"Seems like they're having a serious discussion."

Another hesitation followed. "I can't do anything with them here. Any ideas?"

"Not at the moment. Unless you want to call the good Sheriff Bud and report them for trespassing. Anonymously, of course."

"Too risky. We may end up running into each other."

"Doubtful. After he's drank his evening meal, he wouldn't notice if you stood right in front of him. He's not that great of investigator when he's sober." Ethan gave a dry chuckle. "He's probably sleeping off his liquid dinner anyway."

"He needs his imbibes. Guy's got a rough job. Not to change the subject, but were those your gunshots I heard coming from the nursery?"

"One of them," Ethan answered wryly. "Not sure where the others came from."

"You found the mole? Who's setting you up?"

"Yep and he is no more. It came down to him or me.

"Who we suspected?"

"Ortiz."

"Damn. You're sure?"

"Yeah. We had a little conversation before he drew on me. I'd hoped I was wrong. I'm pretty sure he was taking orders from the big boss." Ethan sighed. "'Bout to put in a call. Get a group out there to clear away the mess before anyone finds him. We don't need any more locals getting involved."

"True that. Just be sure to report in sooner than you normally do. I'd already clued the boss lady in on suspicions if that helps."

"I plan to." Ethan turned onto his drive, rotating the

knob to his headlights to off. Using only his senses, he guided his truck over the twining, graveled path. "Hopefully she'll allow me to disappear now."

"Don't count on it. Sounds like she wants you in on this till the end."

"That's my vibe, too. I can always hope." He veered away from the main drive and circled around the grassy land, dodging trees and wild scrubs until he faced the front of the house.

"In the meantime, watch your back. Your terminating Ortiz is bound to open another can of worms."

"I'm aware," Ethan said. "Get creative and run those women off so you can finish your work. They need to stop nosing around in our business, especially Gracie."

"I think they're about to go. They're getting in the car."

"Good." He punched the off button with his thumb.

He maneuvered his truck into a clove a trees then killed the engine. His alert gaze remained fixated onto the small cabin he'd called home for the past few weeks. He stayed inside, watching his house. He didn't need anyone to tell him to be careful. His instincts screamed. A threat lingered close by. A glint of light flickered through the front window. Hair on the back of his neck stood, raising to full height.

With a sigh, he stretched across the seat and picked up his gun. Time for another showdown. He quietly pulled the latch on his truck door and slipped outside. He crept across the grass, hiding behind the surrounding brush, keeping an eye out for anything out of the ordinary.

A blanket of clouds circled low. Quick flashes of light danced from one vapor to the other as deep rumbles from above indicated a storm was moving in quickly. The encircled live oaks rustled and swayed around him. Strong winds whistled a foreboding tune, carrying the scent of danger within its gusts.

His adrenaline kicked up a notch and seeped through every channel of his body, each nerve ending going into high alert. Expertly, he sidled to the door and twisted the knob. Just as he expected. His uninvited company left it unlocked.

First mistake. He pushed it open with the tip of his boot.

Quietly, it slowly swung ajar.

He slinked around the edge. He aimed his pistol into the darkness, cocking the striker, his finger ready to pull the trigger at any oddness.

The storm had progressed. Lightning flashed through the opened blinds, his furniture eerily silhouetted against the flares. A sound from behind made him flinch. His gut gave him a solid nudge. He spun toward the bedroom, catching a slight movement. An earsplitting blast came from the doorway. Ethan dove behind the couch, just as a spark of heat zipped past his ear.

Close. His heart pounded. Too close.

All these attempts on his life pissed him off royally. Time to finish this. He peered from behind the sofa, waiting. His trigger finger itched.

Ready.

Nothing.

His opponent was doing the same as him. Hoping he'd make the first move. He removed a cushion and raised the edge barely above the top of the sofa's surface.

Another explosion zoomed his way.

He raised and fired. One more shot followed. His foe had discharged again.

Several thunder rolls boomed above as Ethan hit the ground, revolving across the floor, halting near the big screen. He rose to his knees and knuckled the floor to steady himself. A solid blow from behind smashed into his head. A rough groan ripped from his throat. Pain exploded throughout his entire body. His hands covered his forehead. Warm liquid saturated his palms, trickling down his jawline.

He lay still, his face bloodied and body feeling broken. But he didn't hear anything. Maybe this is what they came to do.

Beat the shit out of him.

He brushed the blood from his eyes, managing to open one. He attempted to lift his head. Unbearable pain crashed against his brain as another moan escaped.

Somewhere in the distance, he swore somebody chuckled. Evil. A dark figure—a mere shadow stood above him holding something small in their hand.

A flash of lightning sketched over a cruel, twisted smile.

In slow motion, the second hand raised, followed by a decisive click.

****

Gracie drove down the unlit roads at a steady speed, her headlights reflected against the pavements' blackness. She forced her thoughts to remain blank. If she deliberated too much of what she was about to do, she'd turn around and forget this crazy idea. She should. Ethan ended their so-called relationship, and she ought to let things go. Keep everything in perspective and not come off like a half-crazed, half-desperate woman she's sure he'd believe her to be after this final encounter.

But she needed to know.

She didn't even understand why. Had she fallen in love with him, as Betty insisted? Or was it because this was the first real relationship she'd experienced since her marriage ended. Or maybe the combination of too much alcohol and the prodding of her friends made her contemplate then make this impulsive journey.

Whatever the reason, she was determined to see it through.

Clouds swirled as lightning flickered across the night sky. The wind had picked up. The heavy gusts seized her truck, shifting the vehicle off to the side. She held the steering wheel steady, careful to keep it on the road.

Thoughts of tonight's events at the nursery circled in her mind, too. What was going on at that place? Whose body was inside the greenhouse? Had to be Ethan's truck passing through since Vivian saw him—with a gun. Quinn will add his armed presents to her guilty arsenal, and for sure let the authorities in on the information.

She drove to the hidden cove across from Ethan's property, turned in and parked, cutting her engine. She gazed into the blackness, observing the storm as it reeled though the darkness. Tall pines gathered around the spot, bent; their flexed trunks ready to snap at the wind's strong will.

Really, she must have lost her mind. To say this

was a bad idea was an understatement. Yet, she opened her door and stepped outside. The cool gales shoved her into the truck's side. Rapid flashes projected ominous shadows against the haziness. Low rumbles growled, seemingly at her.

Gracie ignored the drama and sprinted across the open field, hurrying to the cluster of brush. She reached into her pocket for her phone, snapping on the light to guide her into the thicket. She fought her way through the undergrowth, trekking the dimmed outlined path until she faced Ethan's backdoor. She turned off her flashlight.

No lights were on inside. He wasn't home. Bravely, she stepped from her hideout, hiked to the house, and peeked in the bedroom. Everything remained dark. How could she find out anything if she couldn't see? She sneaked to the other set of windows. Nothing. No real clue as to where Ethan was or what he was up to.

This whole idea was a bust from the get go. She doubted he'd give her any information if he had been here, and *if* she'd summoned enough nerve to knock on the door.

She may as well head back to her truck. Tiny drops pelted her skin. The storm was almost over the house. If she didn't hurry, she'd be drenched within seconds.

On a whim, she touched the doorknob and gave it a twist.

The door slowly drifted open. Gracie froze and surveyed the murky innards of Ethan's house. She allowed her eyes to adjust as she mounted the rear step, standing in the pitch-black opening. Nothing stuck out, yet something was off. She sniffed the air. A strange smell saturated the space. Her phone was still in her hand. She flipped the light back to on and carefully scanned the room, walking inside to the center.

Rain tapped on the roof, spattering across the windows. The storm had blown in and was raging in full force. Didn't matter. Time for her to get out and return to her truck. She'd just have to get wet.

She took a step toward the opened door. A huge flash of lightning brightened the insides. A slight crack in Ethan's bedroom caught her attention. She stopped in her tracks.

One peek and then she would go.

She walked to the room and pushed the door open all the way. She moved further inside and stood at the foot of his bed, her back to the wall. Crashes of thunder vibrated through the house, lightning popped past the windows.

Gracie should leave, but she could think of a lot of things she'd rather do than go out into this weather.

On the other hand, she didn't want Ethan to show up and catch her at his house after he'd dumped her. Again. If she had a choice of fighting hurricane force winds or getting caught at Ethan's home, the storm would win.

She rushed toward the exit. She stopped, swallowing a scream. Panic seared through her. Her gut twisted. A glint of her light captured a movement on the further side of the bed. She remained motionless as she stared at a shadowed outline.

Gracie silently inhaled and took a small step, keeping her eyes on the darkened silhouette. The figure moved, too. Something hit against her knees. She stumbled and fell sideways, landing in the middle of

Ethan's soft mattress. She instantly rose to her feet, shuffling toward the door, fearing the person in the room would be upon her in the matter of seconds.

Nothing happened. Gracie waved her light. The profile mimicked her. She released a chuckle. Only her image in the mirrored closet.

She walked to her reflection and put her hands on the closet and cracked the door open. Flashes surged, roars rattled louder. She became still, starring at the mirror. Her heart hammered into her chest.

Something behind her had moved.

She wasn't alone. And the other person wasn't there for a social visit. Instincts told her to run. Get out. Now.

Chapter 23

Gracie ran for the door. Large hands grabbed her shoulders and yanked her backward. Massive arms encased her upper torso, securing her wrists between big, rough palms, rendering her nearly immobile. She swung a leg to the rear, driving her heel into a shin.

Her assailant released a raw groan and threw her down onto the bed, bending her arms behind her. Her phone was still clutched between her fingers. The attacker knocked it away, bouncing the device off the floor, as a sharp heaviness pushed into the small of her back. He anchored her feet with one leg, and tightened her wrists together behind her.

The only thing that could move was her heart, thrashing into her ribcage.

He bent to press harder into her. Stale breath brushed against her cheek. An angry, voice whispered in her ear. "Who are you and why are you here?"

Screams wedged in her throat as fear gripped her insides. She buried her face into the wad of sheets. She needed to calm down. Think. She wouldn't be able to overpower this guy. If she wanted to escape, she'd have to use her brains.

He clutched a chunk of her hair and jerked her head backward, still keeping a firm hold over the rest of her. "I asked you a question."

Gracie inhaled. A loud crack echoed from behind,

followed by a fainting moan. He let go and rolled off her as a thump connected with the floor.

She was free.

For a moment.

Strong fingers grasped her upper arm and spun her with added force. A beam of light shined into her face.

"Gracie," he deadpanned.

Gracie squinted into the brightness, then relaxed into the mattress. "Ethan."

He glared at her. "What are you doing here?" He heaved her into a sitting position and snapped off the flashlight. "Don't say a word."

"Then how come you're asking me questions?"

"We'll discuss this later. Right now, be quiet." He nearly jerked her off the bed. "We need to leave."

Gracie wrestled away, tumbling back onto the mattress determined not to go anywhere until he answered her questions.

He snatched her wrist again and pulled her to her feet, bringing her close to him. "I'm not kidding, we have to get out of here. Now."

"Seriously. The rain is pouring down. I'm sure the water is almost up to the house. We'd be smart to stay put until this lets up."

"Seriously. Staying is not an option. Where did you park your pick-up?"

"Same place as the other day. Ethan, I need some explanations before we do anything."

"I could use a couple of answers myself." Flashes of lightning showed his stern look. "But now's not the time." Keeping a firm hold on her, he led her into the living room.

"Wait." She stopped, twisting her arm from his

grip. "My cell phone is on your bedroom floor."

"You can get it later." He took her hand and tugged, lifting a leg to take a large step. "Watch out."

Her foot hit against something hard. She stumbled forward. Ethan squeezed his grasp to keep her upright. She pointed at the roadblock and gave the object a curious stare. "What is that?"

He picked up a duffle sitting near the exit. "Let's go."

Gracie wrenched away and gaped at the dark, large obstacle covering the hardwood. Another spurt of light illuminated the room.

A shriek escaped. She gestured at the mound. "That's a body." She stared at Ethan. "A dead person."

"Persons."

For the first time, she noticed a huge, fresh gash on the side of his head.

Blood oozed from the wound and streamed down his face. The lack of lighting made it difficult to judge how bad the cut was, though the slash didn't look good.

"As in two. A second is on the other side of the bed. He had a hold of you before I took him out. Don't understand how you missed either of them. Now quit yelling, better yet, stop talking. Let's get out of here before we run into any more trouble."

"You're bleeding, too. What happened to you?" She pointed to the man on the floor. "Did he do that to you or the other one?"

Ethan nodded at the guy at their feet. "Him." He walked to the doorway and scanned the outside. "Might be more waiting for us. They'll do much worse if they catch us."

Gracie followed him and peered around him. The

rain blew sideways, although the worst of the storm seemed to have passed.

"Perfect." He snatched her hand and pulled her into downpour.

Cold drops stung her skin as wet winds swirled about. Keeping low, Ethan guided her through the prickliest brush, puddles of rising water, and sloshy mud.

By the time they reached her truck, they were breathless, soaked, and filthy.

Ethan opened the passenger door and gently shoved Gracie inside before he threw his duffle into the backseat. Then he hurried to the driver's side. Once settled, he turned the engine and drove out of the cove.

He guided the truck onto a hidden road, which went undetected unless someone was aware of it. Neither spoke. Ethan focused on fighting the reeling wind and heavy rains. Gracie glanced at the enigmatic man beside her and shivered, unsure if the quiver was from her being cold, angry, or if she was scared. Maybe a little of each. Whatever the cause, she needed to strategize a way out of this mess.

"You shouldn't leave your keys inside your vehicle. Your truck might've been stolen."

"I was thinking the same thing." She paused and swallowed hard. "I left them in the ignition in case I needed a quick getaway." She gave him a side glance. "Who knew?"

"I want to understand this. Explain to me why you broke into my house."

Gracie flinched. And there it was. She was hoping the nasty weather might prolong this conversation because she had no desire to reply. Yet, she had questions of her own, and her nerves may burst unless she got answers.

"I liked to understand things, too. Who were those men inside your house?"

"Let's try this again." Ethan took his eyes off the rutted highway to glance at her. "Why were you inside of my home? This is the second time this week you've come over uninvited. I'm beginning to get some uneasy vibes about you."

"Yeah, I'm not the only one giving off uneasy vibes." She crossed her arms across her chest and turned away. "Since I've saved you a couple of times, and slept with you, I think I deserve a pass on this one."

"The first time maybe, but not tonight. I made myself clear today. We're done."

"Exactly. And I need resolution." She blew out a stream of air, doing her best to keep the shakiness out of her voice. "We were fine. We had a good time together. As quick as we started, everything stopped. I understand up to a point. You never intended for this relationship to happen. For that matter, neither did I. But it did. You ended us. I'm guessing because of your involvement in this Mike situation. Then I see you with someone else." She took another deep breath. "That's not fair, Ethan. When you sleep with a woman and leave her after, be a decent guy and explain the reason."

Ethan turned onto a smoother road and pressed the floor-peddle, but didn't say a word.

"Okay. And you're the first guy that I've...you know..."

"Had sex with?"

"Right. You're the first I've slept with since the divorce. Maybe I'm a little crazy because I need to know I'm not. That I can make a good choice, even if it's not forever. I've come to realize I didn't make a great decision when I married Stewart. I suppose I've come off a bit needy in the process."

He remained silent. So much for confessions. Figures. In retrospect why did it matter? He'd already ended their relationship anyway.

"So much for resolution on either side. Where are we going or do you plan to keep me in the dark about that too?"

"I have someplace to be."

"Of course. Shouldn't I get a little more information since I'm along for the ride?"

"Doesn't concern you."

The tires caught on a slippery groove. The truck slid sideways, heading for the overflowing gulley. Gracie's teeth sank into her bottom lip as she grabbed the dashboard. Ethan pumped the brake and turned into the skid until the vehicle was back onto the roadway.

"Ahhh, safe," he said, as if he were impressed with his driving skills.

"I don't feel safe."

"Why don't you?"

"Um, two dead guys in your house is enough. Tell me what you're up to. You owe me that much."

He slanted a second side glance at her. "Okay, I'm going to say this. You had no business at my home. Also, you and your buddies shouldn't have been hanging around at the nursery tonight. Any one of you could get hurt or worse. That's a dangerous place, and you need to stay away."

"So that was you. I thought so."

Ethan kept his eyes glued ahead.

"Gunshots. Body in a greenhouse. Then the two men inside your house." She shook her head. "You're mixed up in some kind of mess, aren't you?"

"What are you babbling about?" Ethan pulled the truck to the side of the road, threw the gear into neutral, and spun to her. "You want an explanation, so I'll explain a small bit, but once I do, no more questions." He coughed dryly and then cleared his throat. "When I got home, I discovered my front door was unlocked. After things that have been happening, I was suspicious, and rightly so. Two men were inside. One waited in the main area and the other held you down on the bed. The first guy—let's just say he almost got me, and the second—it was you or him. So I did what I had to do to save you."

"Thank-you," she said in a small voice. "I suppose you won't explain why they're after you."

"No."

"Are you going to notify someone about those men in your house?"

"Taken care of."

Ethan put the gear back into drive and manipulated the vehicle back onto the highway. The rain had let up. Sputters of lightning revealed tall stalks on either side of the road. Gracie glanced at Ethan's blood stained profile.

"Will you at least tell me where are you taking me?"

"I've already told you. To an appointment. And the only reason you're going is because you crashed my home and placed yourself in danger." His tone was soft but clear. "You've given me no choice."

"Where is this meeting?"

"At a motel."

Gracie's head snapped. "At a what?"

He may as well kill her too, because after everything they'd been through, she would go to a motel with him over her dead body.

"You heard me."

"I did. Either I'm delusional or I misunderstood you."

He stayed quiet.

"Unbelievable. I don't know what kind of ideas you're entertaining, but after this afternoon, our sex days are over. For good for me since I'm constantly fooled by men. Anyway, you can drop me off here, or kill me, or whatever you plan on doing with me. But we won't be sleeping together. Nope." She shook her head. "Not happening."

"Calm down. No hidden motives here, that's where I need to be."

"Your meeting is at a motel. Oh wait your appointment is at a motel. Rather late for a rendezvous. Does it involve a woman? Like the blonde I saw you with this afternoon?"

His attention deviated to focus as he steadily guided the truck through a water-filled slope. "We're going to wait."

"What exactly are we waiting for?"

"You ask a lot of questions."

"You could try answering some of them."

"I did. I told you where we're going. One more answer than I intended to give you."

"How charming," she quipped, tired of his vague attitude. "You should calculate charm into your point's column. It doesn't have anything to do with sex so this would be a different kind of points, although I'm sure you can diversify the point data. Is that doable?"

"I sense hostility."

"Do you? You've concealed a lot about yourself. I don't even know you." Gracie made a frustrated noise. "Why can't you be honest? If we can't be truthful and trust one another—" She flung a hand. "Never mind. Our weekend together was only about the sex anyway."

"Gracie."

"This is what I think. You like me." She twisted and poked a forefinger into his shoulder. "You want more with me, but that can't happen. Do you know why?"

"No." Ethan sighed. "I suppose you're going to tell me."

"You're a liar."

"A fair assessment," he said sarcastically. "Didn't you say you don't know me?"

"Okay, I don't know you, but I know you."

"That makes no sense."

"It makes perfect sense. You just don't understand."

"You got me there."

They remained silent as he turned off onto a paved two-lane highway. The rain began to come down again. After what seemed like hundreds of miles of driving, Ethan was forced to slow up. A semi-truck surrounded by police cars' flashing lights blocked the traffic. People stood in the rain, lined up in the wet ditch.

Gracie pointed to the scene, her head spun as they passed. "What's going on?"

"Border patrol. Looks like they've intercepted a smuggling operation, probably from Mexico or further into South America. The coyotes running the setup will be pissed at the driver for getting caught. From what I hear, human contraband is a lucrative business."

She turned for one last look at the group as they faded into the distance. "I understand they've come here illegally, but I can't help but feel bad for those people. They must be terrified."

"I'm sure. Unfortunately, the authorities have a job to do, and it's not always pleasant."

Gracie laid her head back into the seat. After the day she had, she was exhausted. Her eyelids dropped. She drifted into a comfortable dose. It seemed like she'd just fallen asleep when an unexpected lurch woke her. She raised and blinked several times. The storm had moved on, with only sparks of light in the distant clouds provided evidence that it occurred.

They'd parked in the lot of a rundown motel. A blue neon sign flashed in front. A harshly-lit bare window indicated vacancies available.

Gracie took in the Deluxe Inn logo plastered over the doorway. "Looks like a classy place."

"Nothing but the best. Wait while I go check in."

He got out, taking the keys, and strolled into the office. Minutes later he returned. He restarted the engine and guided the vehicle past a short line of rooms to the back, then pulled into a space near the rear center of the building.

"We're staying here?"

"What? You don't like this place?" he asked with playfulness in his voice. A first for the evening. "You hoped for a five star resort with a butler, personal chef, and, turn down service with mints on the pillow, oh no wait, you'd prefer chocolate."

She bit her bottom lip. The single story, brick building appeared old and dirty, even in the dark. A small, dingy light bulb hung over each door revealing a need of a coat of paint.

"I hoped for at least clean sheets."

He pulled the handle up and glanced at her. "Think of the adventure. Something to tell the grandkids one day."

Ethan snatched the bag from the back and stepped outside. Gracie followed him into the humid night air. He reached into his pocket bringing out an old-fashioned motel room key with a number five taped on one side. He opened the door and moved aside for her to enter.

She walked inside and took in the surroundings. The place smelled damp and musty. "You're sure your appointment's here?"

Ethan turned on the solitary lamp. A cheerless low wattage bulb lit the room. He placed his duffle on the single bed, then stepped to a window unit and flipped a button. The air conditioner clanked three times, then blew a warm draft.

"It's late and I'm beat." Ethan yawned. "I'm ready for some sleep."

"I'm not sleeping with you."

"Sleep standing up, the floor, the bed. Your choice." He unzipped the duffle, drew out a large t-shirt, and threw it at her. "Wherever you chose, you'll want to clean up and change into something dry."

An arm flew out to snatch the shirt. "You need to ditch this attitude. I may have crossed a line or two—"

"May have?"

"I might be just a weekend fling to you, but I'm

more than that." She shook the shirt at him. "I deserved to be treated better than this."

Ethan raked a hand through his hair. "You're right, you do."

"You agree with me?"

"I do. I truly wish I could be worthy of you." He stared at her, his gaze unwavering. "But I'm not."

Chapter 24

Ethan glanced at the closed bathroom door before he pulled his damp shirt over his head. Why couldn't Gracie Desoto stay out of his business? He'd done his best to keep to her at bay, to push her away, even. Yet, she kept barging back into his life like a herd of cattle storming across the range.

As if she knew.

He didn't want to be rid of her. As hard as he tried, he couldn't stay angry with her for continuous invasions in his life. Somehow, between all of the mayhem and craziness, she'd gotten to him and into his heart. A feisty little rebel, she managed to land on her feet after she was dealt a disheartening blow, and he admired her for her perseverance. He desired to get closer to her on a cerebral level and even more so on a physical one.

He looked at the closed door again.

Who was he kidding, he wanted all that she would give and more. And now he'd practically confessed.

Except they couldn't happen. For one thing, he doubted she'd agree to allow anything between them after this afternoon. Her libido may be forgiving, but her heart wouldn't, and her heart ruled her actions. Besides, his choice was already made. He had to leave. A murder wrap hung over his head to the point his situation had reached code red. For her safety and his own, she needed to stay away from him and vice versa.

Which led to another problem. How would he keep away from her tonight?

He stared at the bed as his mouth formed into a straight line. The *only* bed. His gaze transferred to the aged, cracked linoleum. Although she'd been adamant about them not sleeping together, they'd either have to share because neither would want to sleep on this floor. At least he preferred not to, and he'd be the one doing the gentlemanly honors if it came to that. But being in bed with her, sleeping so close without touching her would definitely test his restraints.

He unzipped his jeans and fought his way out of the soaked denim, then he wrangled his cell phone from his pocket, checking if the thing was as waterlogged as the rest of him. By some miracle, everything still seemed to be working. He released a relieved sigh as he dropped his sodden pants on the floor.

The bathroom door opened. Gracie exited and stopped. Her mouth fell as she stared at him. He returned her gaze; his heart battered against his breastbone at the sight of her. Wet hair slicked back, wearing only his shirt, she never looked sexier. Tonight would be difficult for him to behave, no matter where he slept.

"You're naked," she sputtered, her voice hoarse.

"What?"

"You don't have any clothes on."

Ethan glanced downward as a sudden cool draft breezed over his damp skin.

"Yeah, um." He bent to snatch a pair of running shorts out of his duffle, then he quickly stepped into and slid them over his legs to cover his lower extremities. "I need to wash off and a towel." Two long strides, he sidestepped her to go into the bathroom. "Extras are in here, right?"

She merely nodded, still looking at him. He snatched a towel from the rack and patted away the excess moisture. He caught his reflection in the mirror, and leaned in to inspect the newest lump protruding onto his forehead. The rain had washed away the blood, leaving him with only the swelling. He glanced at Gracie, who still stood beyond the doorway. "My new bump covers the little nick you gave me quite nicely."

"What are you mixed up in, Ethan?"

He stepped around her and walked to the bed, lifting the blankets to crawl under. "You decide where you're sleeping?" He smiled as he settled into the thin, yet lumpy mattress. "Desk looks a little rickety, and I'm guessing the floor hasn't been cleaned in about ten years. Probably creepy crawlers hiding under the bed, too. And they only come out after dark."

She made a face. "I could always sleep in my truck."

Ethan laughed. "Shitty as this place is inside, I wouldn't advise going out in this neighborhood. Especially for sleeping."

She glanced around the room, her expression soured, as if she realized her choices. "Fine." She marched to the opposite side of the mattress and stood. "I'll stay with you." She held up a forefinger. "Only with some ground rules."

"You're aware I only play by my own rules."

"Right." She planted her hands on her hips and glared at him. "I caught you in the middle of the street cuddled with another woman, and you've yet to explain the situation. You followed up by coming to my office to dump me. So, yeah, I'm mindful of how you operate."

"I doubt that."

"Of course you do, but I don't. Let's not forget you kidnapped me, and you weren't gentle about it."

Ethan sprang up in bed. "I what?" His shoulders stiffened as his gaze locked with hers, not believing she was going there. "Did you just accuse me of kidnapping you?"

"You forced me to come here with you." Her cheeks reddened as she looked away. "That's kidnapping."

"Excuse me?" Ethan's tone held a strained edginess. "You were inside of my house, uninvited. Technically, you broke in."

"Technically, your door was unlocked. Nothing was broken into."

Ethan ran a hand over his face. This woman frustrated him on so many levels. "Gracie, when you walk into someone's house without an invitation or without their knowledge, it's considered breaking in, unlocked or otherwise."

She stole a glance in his direction. "I was waiting for you."

"Waiting for me." He released a humorless chuckle. "Inside my house. In the dark."

"I didn't see your car in the drive, so I assumed you weren't home. I wanted to check and see if I could find out when you'd be back."

"How can you verify anything with the lights off?"

"Lights draw attention."

"To who? The police, maybe? Because you broke

into my house?"

She bit her lip. "You were the one lurking around with two guys waiting for you. That doesn't happen to normal people. I'd have called the cops if you'd let me get my phone."

"Fine." He stretched across the bed. He grabbed his cell from the nightstand and held it out to her. "If you believe you are in danger, then by all means, call the police."

She stared at the device for a long second before she pushed his hand away. "This isn't necessary."

"Oh, I think so." He thrust the phone at her. "Go ahead, call someone. Tell them you're with me. A liar, kidnapper, or whatever else you want to brand me. If something happens to you, they'll know I'm the one who harmed you."

"We don't need to do this."

"Fine." He tucked the phone away. "If you're lied to, kidnapped, or anything else, you have no one else to blame but yourself. You had your chance."

"You're being charming again, aren't you?"

"Gracie—I understand you're angry at me, which is why I'm overlooking your nutty behavior."

"Nutty behavior?"

He patted the air with one hand. "Calm down, neither of us is acting normal, especially after all that's happened the past couple of days. Admit it."

She physically relaxed. "I suppose."

"I'll make you a deal. If you'll be patient, I will explain everything—later. I can't give out any information at the moment. In return, I do need you to tell me something now," he hedged, hoping she trusted him enough to buy into his offer.

Her brows rose.

"What exactly went on at the nursery tonight?"

"You should know. You admitted you were there."

"I'm aware of my whereabouts, but I need you to describe what you saw. Your perspective, so to speak."

At first, she seemed reluctant to answer, but after she contemplated for a few minutes, she began to talk, giving him details of her and her friends' evening. He listened patiently as she explained.

"You've been busy showing up in places you shouldn't be. Mike's murder, random gunshots, and a possible body are many reasons for you and your friends to stay away from the nursery." He tugged at the sheet blanket and sank deep under the covers. "What did you guys hope to find, anyway?"

"We're hoping to find out who killed Mike. Krystal wants to prove the police's theory is wrong."

"Which is?"

"Mike was destroying his plants for profit."

"So you're playing detective."

"Trying to. We seemed to come up with more questions than answers."

He watched her through narrowed eyes. She was mulling over something. "What's on your mind, Gracie?"

"Those smugglers we passed by on the way got me to thinking. Someone's been stealing plants, right? Suppose they're using the material as a cover. Like drugs or something. Mike found out, confronted them, and that's why he was killed."

"You're suggesting the nursery has an internal smuggling operation."

"Makes sense, don't you think?"

Ethan shook his head.

"What?" She frowned. "What else could it be, Ethan."

"Mike destroyed his material for profit."

"Mike may've had faults, but he wasn't dishonest. He'd never do that."

"You and I knew two different Mike Manzels." Ethan paused. "Were you aware that the business was in trouble? Financially?"

The shock in her expression told him she was surprised.

"The place had been run so inefficiently for a long time. Mike had lost a ton of money and stood to lose a lot more, if things were permitted to go on the way they were."

"Most of his hires were low waged laborers. Many illegals, coming from south of the border. How could he be in the red?"

"Can't say. I've only been with the operation for a few weeks. I can tell you his bringing me in was his last resort to saving the place."

"You've revamped the running systems?"

"I made several recommendations before his death." Ethan raised a shoulder. "Mike wasn't keen on any of them."

"What will you do now? Give Mickey your suggestions."

"I don't think Mickey is interested in any of my ideas," he replied dryly. "I suspect once I'm cleared of killing Mike—" he stopped and looked directly into her eyes "—and I will be. I'll be heading to my next assignment." At least he'd hoped to get his new orders soon. He expected to be instructed to get out of town and disappear any second now. Everything here was getting too hot.

"So you're saying my idea sucks."

"Not at all. In most instances, your scenario is sound, but in this case not so logical." He lay back into the stiff pillow with a grin. "Would it make any difference if I told you I think you're really cute when you're crime solving?"

She bit into her bottom lip. "Don't get flirty. Nothing's going to happen. You dumped me remember?"

"Gracie. Sometimes doing the right thing isn't what we want to do."

She picked up the corner of the sheet and twisted the ends around her fingers. "You're saying you didn't want to break things off with me?"

God, no. He wanted to tell her the truth. He wanted to be with her, but if he did, everything in his life would alter. Change wasn't in the cards for him. "Let's just say, you were right earlier. I like you a lot. But I have too much confusion going on to be the kind of man you need me to be. You deserve to have someone cherish you."

"Confusion. You're talking about your PTSD?"

"The disorder is a huge problem." He gazed at her still standing at the edge of the bed. He frowned and nodded toward her.

"Is that why you're there instead of lying with me? You're afraid, aren't you? You're scared of me."

"One reason."

"One?"

"You did break up with me earlier." She remained silent for several seconds. "I do care about you, Ethan, more than you could ever know. But yes, I'm frightened of you, too." She stared at him. "Not only because of your disorder. I'm terrified of you and for you."

Although what she said didn't surprise him, her words still stung. He was at war with himself, wanting to make things right with her, but he must follow through and meet his obligations. But he had to try and be honorable, even if it was just for tonight.

"Would it help if I told you I can go without sleep for several days? I'll force myself to stay awake; I can't have any nightmares. I won't hurt you if I'm awake."

She gazed at him, her eyes round. "What happened to you? When you were in Afghanistan. What brought on these horrible dreams?"

He stayed quiet for several seconds, debating whether to answer.

"It was a combination of many events." He blew out a stream of air, deciding what he could reveal and what needed to stay buried. "You see a lot of awful stuff…and you do some bad things. Sometimes it's deserved, but other times it isn't. At the end of the day, you put everything away. You don't think about it. You can't remember or you won't emotionally survive. So you keep moving. Do your job." He ran a hand over his face. "But eventually everything that's been bottled-up comes out. It has to, or you'll explode." His gaze settled on Gracie. "Happened one evening—we were doing training exercises. A rocket was lobbed from an unsophisticated launch site, just inside the wire where we were located. The detonation was huge. People…they were hurt, many dead. Friends, comrades. I was nearby. The explosion lifted me off the ground.

When I landed, I couldn't feel my legs."

She gasped.

"Someone came up behind me. Yanked my head back. Put a knife to my throat." Ethan almost went into a trance as the images formed before him, almost real. "Even though I couldn't move, my training took over. Without thinking, I rolled around and easily overtook him. I snapped his neck. He died instantly." He swallowed. "Just a kid. Maybe sixteen."

The room went silent, the only sound was the sporadic motor of the air conditioner.

"It was him or you," Gracie finally said.

"Helicopters came in just after. Took me to the hospital. They ran tests, but other than a bruised disk, I was fine. No reason for the paralysis. But the dreams started. So they took me to the head doctor, and that's when I was diagnosed with PTSD."

"Taking a sixteen year old's life would do that."

"I went into treatment for several months and after I was declared "cured", I left the army. Went into civilian work, and have been fine for several years. All this crap with Mike has stirred everything up again."

"I'm sorry," she whispered.

"Not your fault." He lifted a corner of his mouth. "Now you know all of my secrets."

"Not all of them."

His brows lifted. "What haven't I told you?"

"The woman you were with earlier today." Gracie stared at him. "Who is she, Ethan?"

Chapter 25

Gracie propped to her elbow, her mind foggy. She held up a palm to block out annoying rays that shined though a large gap in the worn drapes. For a moment she struggled to remember where she was before the memories returned in a rush.

She was in some dump Ethan dragged her to after he discovered her inside his house. With two dead guys. Or at least she thought they'd been killed, and since one's intent seemed on ending her life, Ethan's bold move was probably for the best. She shuttered and pushed the idea aside, not allowing her mind to go there. She didn't want to think about who Ethan McCarthy actually was, especially after what he'd revealed to her last night.

Sluggish, she rose from the—she hesitated to call what they'd slept on a mattress. The cushion was more like a foam pad covered with a sheet. She made her way into the bathroom, fighting the craving for a soda. And a toothbrush. Maybe Ethan had one in his bag she might borrow.

She stopped. Ethan.

She peeked around the corner. No sign of him. She walked to the bed and placed her hand on the spot where he'd slept. Cold. Even the indention where his body lay had faded. And his duffle was missing. She looked at the edge of the nightstand as a chill ran through her. Her keys had also disappeared.

"Don't tell me he took my truck and left me stranded." She hurried to the door, grabbed the knob and twisted, yanking it open. Her stomach curled as she stared at the empty parking space.

The bastard had stolen her pickup.

She gave the door an extra shove and went back inside to dress. How would she escape this awful place? Her mind shifted into overdrive. First, she needed a plan. Outline her pros and cons. Cons were easy. Her purse was in her truck, under the seat. Therefore, she had no identification or cash. Her cell phone lay somewhere on Ethan's bedroom floor, hopefully not busted into pieces. Of course, the lack of transportation was obvious.

What about pros? An even shorter list. She had none. She supposed after everything she should feel lucky to be alive. Lucky. That's right. Ethan abandoned her in the middle of nowhere without food, money, or a means to get out of here. She waded up his t-shirt and threw it on the bed.

Yeah. This was so much better than being dead. She gazed at the nightstand again. A phone.

The room had a phone. She rushed to pick up the receiver and pressed nine. Silence. She pushed down harder, repeatedly, only to get the same results. She slammed the earpiece back into the cradle, staring at the useless piece of junk. This dive probably shut down their landlines with everyone having mobiles these days. Economics. Still, they should remove the damn thing and not get people's hopes up.

Then again, the motel may have had nothing to do with the phone not working. Sneaky Ethan probably found a way to disconnect the wires.

A thunderous hammering from the outside interrupted her annoyance.

"Gracie? Are you in there?"

Gracie rushed to the door and threw it open. "Krystal." She flung her arms round her friend's neck. "Thank you, thank you, and thank you."

Krystal squeezed her shoulders as she stepped inside, her nose wrinkled. "Why in the world are you here?"

"I'll explain everything later. Please, let's leave now."

She pointed to the rim of the building. "My pickup is parked in the front." Krystal looked past Gracie and into the room, her expression still disgusted. "Did you bring anything, like an overnight bag or a purse or something?"

Gracie snatched up Ethan's shirt twisted on the bed and held her arms out her sides. "I'm packed."

****

"Thanks for coming all this way," Gracie said, once they settled inside Krystal's vehicle and were headed out of the lot.

"That's what friends are for. Although the drive isn't too far. I was at the nursery when I got the message. We're only ten minutes away."

"How'd you know where to find me?"

Krystal gave her an odd look. "You texted me."

"How can that be? I don't have my phone."

"Don't know. Tell me how you ended up at the Deluxe Inn."

"I need a soda first." Gracie shot a final glance at the dreary building as they sped away. "I thought I knew the area, and although old, this place is new to me."

Krystal gave her another side-glance. "It's a hideout."

"For?"

"All sorts of things. Mainly the motel's reputation is where extra marital activities happen." She paused. "I assume you need to go to your office." Krystal didn't wait for her to reply but made the turn toward Gracie's work.

"I'm not sure how I'll operate today. I'm without a truck or a cell. I don't even have my ID."

Krystal reached behind for a white bag, sitting it on the console between them. "Donuts will make your day better."

"Always." Gracie opened the sack and sniffed the fresh baked pastries.

"Okay, I can't wait for you to have your soda fix. So tell me, what the hell happened after we spilt up?"

"I'll give you a brief rundown and fill in the blanks later. Betty's going to want every detail, and I'd rather relive my humiliation just once."

****

Krystal drove her vehicle around to the rear of the Gracie's small building.

The two women glanced at each other and back to her personal parking space—where her truck sat. Gracie opened the door, jumped from Krystal's pickup, and rushed to her own. She tugged at the handle, but it didn't budge.

"At least he didn't keep it." Krystal had followed her. "Can't get in?"

"Locked. No worries. I keep a spare set of keys in

my desk."

Relieved, she led Krystal into her office.

Betty leaped from her chair the moment they entered. "I thought you two might be together." Hands on her hips, she gave Gracie a stern going-over. "You could've at least let me know where you were so I could tell your customers something." She shuffled her desk and picked up her empty coffee cup for a refill. "Been lying to them all morning," she muttered, then louder asked. "Why in the world didn't you take your stuff with you?"

"Stuff?"

"Your purse and keys are on your desk. You left your phone. I didn't snoop, but your bag kept ringing, so I'm assuming your cell is inside somewhere. You never do that." Betty's eyes narrowed as she spun to Gracie, carefully holding her full cup. "You've been with him, haven't you?"

"If you give me a second, I'll tell you everything."

She stepped around Betty, hurried to her office and onto her fridge, snatching two drinks from inside. She handed one to Krystal, who'd trailed behind, with Betty in the rear. Gracie popped the top of her soda can and took a lengthy sip.

Krystal and Betty were already seated across from her desk, Betty's filled coffee cup balanced on the chair's wooden armrest.

Gracie lowered into her chair, checked her purse for keys and her phone, not even wondering how Ethan got her things inside. He obviously had his ways. Once reassured her possessions were intact, she proceeded to tell what had transpired after the group broke up the evening before, incorporating some of the particulars for Betty's benefit, and to avoid sticky questions later.

Betty gave her a sharp glare. "Goodness, girl, where's your mind these days?" She shook her head. "People dying, goons trying to kill you, spending the night at the Deluxe Inn of all places. I hope your mama never finds out."

"You're the one who told me I needed to find a guy and have some fun."

"I created a monster." Betty adjusted her glasses. "Krystal and I may need to do an intervention to get this man out of your system. You're acting downright irresponsible. If I had any idea you'd behave so foolish over a fellow, I'd left you alone."

"Fat chance," Gracie mumbled.

"So did you discover who the blonde is?" Krystal asked.

"No, he claims that's not open for discussion at this time." She gave her friend a grim look. "What's going on at the nursery and the body? Did Bud sober up enough to come investigate?"

"Nothing. There isn't anyone, dead or otherwise."

Gracie frowned. "How can that be?"

"We were mistaken. An allusion, perhaps? Our mind playing tricks with all of the craziness around us?"

"I know what I saw," Gracie insisted. "There was a corpse in that greenhouse."

"Someone was possibly knocked out," Krystal suggested. "Then they got up and left after they came to."

Gracie tucked her bottom lip under her teeth. She refused to argue, since she had no concrete evidence to support her theory. But after what she'd witnessed at

Ethan's, she was sure the person in the greenhouse was dead and was probably killed by those gunshots.

"I felt like a complete fool bringing Sheriff Bud out last night," Krystal said.

Betty chuckled. "Bet he wasn't happy. He'd already settled in with his toddies."

"No, I had to go back and meet with him, and he was none too pleased. He accused me of being overexcited and said it was probably a neighbor shooting wild hogs. I went to where we thought we saw the body this morning. The plants haven't been disturbed, no blood, or shell casings." Krystal's brows dropped. "As a matter of fact, the ground cloth looked swept clean."

Betty let go a loud sigh. "This whole thing keeps getting weirder by the second. I wouldn't be surprised at anything that happens now. Use to be such a nice town."

Gracie circled the half-empty can with both hands, turning it slowly on her desks surface.

"So how did Krystal get a text from you if you didn't have your phone?" Betty asked.

"Ethan must've sent it," Krystal said.

Gracie's thought also. She glanced at her friend. Her complexion had paled, and she looked like she was going to be sick. "Are you okay? You don't look well."

"I'm a bit queasy. I think the excitement plus the extra running around has run me down. After Mike's death is solved, I'm going to sleep for a week. How about you? What are your plans for the day?"

"A hot shower and a toothbrush." Her stomach rumbled. She rolled her chair away from the desk and stood. "And some real food."

Krystal rose to her feet. "Stop by the nursery on your way after you get cleaned up. I'll get lunch, and we can talk more about this. Maybe we can piece together some of this puzzle."

****

Clean and much better overall, Gracie entered the plant farm office's main room. Krystal sat at the table studying a short stack of papers. She looked up as Gracie walked in, her eyes as big as serving platters.

"What's wrong?" Gracie seated herself across from her friend. Krystal pushed an opened folder toward her. "What is this?"

"Mike's will."

"How did you get a copy of his will?" Gracie didn't wait for an answer but picked up the document to read a highlighted area. She lifted her gaze and stared at Krystal. "Wow."

"Crazy, right?"

"Where'd you get this?"

A huge bang came from behind. Gracie flinched and turned toward the front door. Quinn burst inside, her arms loaded.

"Oh yeah," Krystal said. "Quinn's bringing lunch. I told her you were starved and to bring a lot."

Quinn dumped five sacks on the table in front of them, and onto the scattered pages.

Gracie looked at Krystal "How hungry did you tell her I was?"

"Careful, Quinn." Krystal pushed the packaged food away from the paperwork. "These documents are important. We can't afford to have them covered in grease."

"Sorrrry," Quinn disregarded Krystal's papers and

dug into the bags and doled out burgers and fries to each one. "Where's Vivian?"

"Don't know." Krystal opened a packet of ketchup and squirted it onto a piece of butcher paper. "She should be here by now."

Quinn grunted. "What's the important papers?"

"Mike's will."

Quinn sat and peeled back the wrapper on her cheeseburger, disinterested.

Krystal slid the folder to Quinn. "Mike's lawyer messengered it to me a while ago. It's the beginning phase, I'm sure, but...I'm overwhelmed."

Quinn opened the file and silently lip read. "What the hell?" She gazed at Krystal. "Mike left you the nursery?"

"That's what it says." Krystal pushed her food away and rubbed her temples. "I'm so exhausted that I can't even think. And I don't have a clue how to run this place."

"You've run it all along." Gracie smiled. "You'll have no problem once everything is settled. Focus now on getting Mike's murder solved and his name cleared because if his death is connected with this place, then your life could be in danger. Ethan might be right. All of our lives may be at stake."

"You're correct, Gracie."

"What?" Gracie turned toward the voice, in mid bite. She stopped. An imposing barrel of a gun was positioned nearly eye level. And aimed at her forehead.

Chapter 26

"Well, this is a surprise." Gracie feigned calm although her heart had leaped from her chest and lodged inside her throat. She did her best to remain still so as not to provoke the finger on the trigger to twitch as much as half a centimeter. "What's with the gun?"

"Should be obvious."

Gracie glanced at her friends. Krystal's eyeballs were round. She stared at Vivian and the pistol pointed at Gracie's temple while Quinn continued to munch on her meal.

"You're here to kill us?" Krystal asked.

"I hoped to avoid doing anything to you because you're my friends." Vivian dipped her head toward the document lying in front of Krystal. "Things have become too complicated."

"Mike's will caused you problems?"

Vivian glared at Krystal. "He left the nursery to you, right?" Her fingers constricted around Gracie's forearm as she pressed the gun's barrel further into her head.

Krystal returned Vivian's look, her expression horrified.

"Then yes, you inheriting the plant farm is a huge problem for me. I also take issue with the three of you snooping into my business, although up until seconds ago, I wasn't too worried."

"You were the one blasting the gun last night?" Gracie already knew the answer, but she wanted Vivian to confirm.

Vivian smiled. "That was me."

"Who were you shooting at?"

"Quinn."

Quinn gagged, and coughed.

Vivian's face reddened. "Lucky for her she fell down when I pulled the trigger," she said through clenched teeth.

"I didn't fall." Quinn unblocked her throat. "Somebody pushed me."

"What exactly is going on, Vivian?" Krystal asked.

"This is not the time for revelations, Krystal. Gracie. I want the details Ethan told you during your little pillow talk sessions."

Tiny needles pricked every inch of Gracie's skin. Vivian's concern over what Ethan had said could only mean one thing. He was involved.

"Ethan didn't tell me anything."

Vivian eyed her. "I don't believe you."

"We rarely talked about his work. And I can't remember an iota of what we did discuss with a gun pointed at my head."

Vivian slowly drew the hammer back. "I bet you would with a little extra persuasion."

"Gracie," Krystal choked.

"Vivian, this is crazy." Gracie jerked from the woman's grasp and shoved the barrel away from her face. "At least give me a chance to think. Or better yet, put up the gun and behave like a civilized human being."

"Fine." Vivian removed the firearm further from

Gracie's head. "If you or anyone else does something stupid." She waved the weapon in the air. "Consider yourself a goner."

Quinn wadded her empty wrappers and stuffed them in the bag she'd carried the food in. She wiped her mouth with a napkin and looked at Vivian. "So you offed Mike?"

"Offed?" Vivian laughed. "You have such a crude way of putting things, Quinn. I'm not in the mafia. But yes, I killed Mike. His demise was a business decision, not so much personal. "

"I thought you loved him."

"My feelings are not open for discussion. Besides, I discovered long ago, love is for fools." Vivian scanned the group, her eyes wild. "Then again, this isn't about sentiments or emotions."

"Or lack of," Quinn mumbled.

Vivian shot an angry glare at Quinn but didn't respond. She raised the pistol. "I need each of you to put your cells on the table. Don't try anything funny either, like alerting someone. I've killed before. I'm not afraid to do it again."

Quinn leaned down and dug inside her purse sitting next to her chair, then slid her phone across the flat surface toward Vivian. "Don't see why it matters since we never have a signal out here."

Gracie and Krystal also turned over their cells.

Vivian picked up the devices and dropped them on the floor. She aimed her gun downward and pointed to a phone, then she pulled the trigger. Loud blasts echoed through the small room as plastic, remnants of carpet, and unrecognizable components splintered from the explosion. A sulfur odor filled the air as she continued her target practice on the remaining phones.

Quinn leaped from her chair and leaned over the table. "Hey, I just signed a new contract." Vivian spun and aimed the pistol at her. Quinn quickly sat down. "I don't think my insurance will cover this.'

"Up." Vivian motioned with her gun. "Everybody stand."

Gracie exchanged a worried look with Krystal as they rose from their seats.

She always thought Vivian was strange, though she never would've guessed she was downright nuts. She was certifiable. Her plans were to kill them unless they found a way to overpower her, and with her in possession of the lone weapon, that idea was doubtful.

Vivian continued to use her pistol to direct. "This way."

She nudged them toward Mike's office. The three followed her instructions. Vivian walked at the end of the line, her weapon ready. She ushered them into a windowless, stinky, storage closet in the back of the room. They crowded inside and huddled close together.

Vivian stopped at the doorway's edge and flipped a switch to on. A small, yellow light beamed from the top, lighting the drab space with a faded dimness. Empty shelves were lined on either side of the long, narrow straightway. The ceiling hung low, the entire area was tight and closed in.

Vivian lowered her gun and levelled the barrel at the lower wall. A pop followed by a hot breeze whizzed past the backside of Gracie's knees. A blast exploded behind her.

Gracie eyed the new hole pitted in the sheetrock. Fragments of dark paneling spread across the faded linoleum as the smoke from gunpowder overwhelmed the tiny area.

"Why did you do that?" Quinn asked.

"I'm making a point." Vivian's weapon arm dropped to her side. "You ladies enjoy your time here. I'll be back for you later. You may quietly talk among yourselves. No screaming or yelling. The door will be locked from the outside, and I'm posting a guard with strict orders to kill anyone who misbehaves." Her eyes narrowed at Quinn before she closed the door followed by a soft click.

"She's lost it," Krystal said after several moments of quiet.

"The woman's evil on steroids. Though it doesn't matter where her malice comes from." Quinn's gaze shifted from Gracie to Krystal. "Nothing changes the fact we're about to end up dead."

"What is she doing so secretive that she thinks she needs to kill?" Krystal asked. "I'm assuming she has something to do with the missing plants."

"I had an idea," Gracie said. "Last night, Ethan and I passed a truck pulled over by border patrol. It was full of people, you know, trying to get into the country illegally. I wondered if maybe somebody was using this place for smuggling, and the missing plants are a cover."

Krystal pulled at her chin. "That actually makes sense."

"I thought so too, but Ethan didn't agree."

Quinn threw her an aggravated glace. "Why would you say anything to him, Gracie? I'm telling you again, that guy is bad news."

"This isn't the time, Quinn," Krystal said. "If we

come out of this alive, we'll need to give the police something. Let's concentrate on what she might be trafficking. I'm thinking drugs."

"No drugs." Quinn rolled her eyes and shook her head. "Guns."

Both women turned a surprised gaze at her.

"Guns are banned in Mexico, so I'm betting she's running them over the border. They're worth a lot of money over there."

"Never would've thought of weapons," Krystal said. "Where did you get the idea, Quinn?"

"On the Internet. People pay big bucks for 'em in Mexico because they're unable to own them in their country. I'm sure there's a substantial profit involved for her to want to murder us so she won't be discovered."

Fear charged through Gracie. She was in the midst of the last hours of her life. So much lie ahead of her, although she couldn't remember a single ambition at the moment.

"She's very clever," Krystal said. "To pull this off without getting caught."

"Yeah," Gracie agreed. "I bet she stayed close to us to keep tabs on what we were doing."

"Okay, so she's smart. We're a lot smarter." Quinn scratched her head. "So how are we going to get out of this mess? What's our plan?"

"Plan?" Gracie and Krystal repeated simultaneously as they exchanged doubtful glances.

"You two can do what you want, but I'm not gonna roll over and let her kill me without a fight."

Krystal and Gracie looked at one another again.

Quinn had a point. To allow Vivian take their lives

minus a struggle would be giving up. They needed to prepare for a battle. If they won, they may live. A loss means the end results would be the same, but at least they'd made an effort. Seemed like a more dignified way to die.

Gracie nodded. "We do need to come up with something."

Quinn's eyes brightened. "We should jump her when she comes back to get us."

Krystal slide down the wall and sat on the floor. She turned and put a finger inside the bullet hole next to her. "It's not a good idea to take her on in a physical attempt. She's armed and we aren't."

"Whatever we do, we need to maintain our composure. Emotions are running pretty high. I suggest we keep a close watch on her. We know her well enough. She has a huge ego, and she believes she's smarter and superior to us because she'd gotten away with this for so long. Definitely a flaw."

"Ego, weaknesses, and composure. Then what?" Quinn asked. "Kick her ass?"

Krystal shook her head. "There will be no ass kicking, Quinn. I mean seriously, what about that sounds like a good plan to you?"

"I'm all for doing whatever it takes to keep our heads from not ending up the same as our phones. If beating the crap out of her will do it, then I'm for it. We stand a good chance at beating her. There are three of us and only one of her."

"And her gun," Krystal reminded. "One or more of us could end up dead if we attempt to overtake her."

"We'll have to get down and dirty and fight her to live. Three against one, I still like the odds." Quinn chuckled. "What do you think, Gracie?"

"I'd be in favor of us too if it weren't for her having a gun."

Quinn folded her arms over her middle and turned away. "You two are useless."

"I'm guessing she won't leave us in here," Krystal said. "Maybe one of us can escape when she lets us out."

Quinn spun around to face them. "*Maybe one of us can escape?* That's not a plan."

"Quinn, we don't have a lot to work with. Plus, I'm sure there are more people in this operation, and we don't have a clue as to who to trust and who the enemy is." Krystal gave Gracie an understanding glimpse. "I wonder where Ethan fits into this."

Gracie didn't speak. She'd been pushing all scenario's that popped into her head away, not wanting to think about Ethan's involvement. "I don't want to know."

Quinn's brows dropped as her gaze centered on Gracie. "You really fell for the guy, didn't you?"

Gracie tucked her bottom lip beneath her teeth. She so preferred not to answer Quinn's question.

"Don't blame you. It's hard to ditch feelings once they've formed." Quinn gave her a genuine smile for the first time ever. "He did seem like a straight up guy when he first came around."

"I hope he is a good man. As a matter of fact, I believe he is, though he knows something about Vivian's operation he's not sharing with anyone." Krystal sighed with a smile. "At least now we can be relatively sure Mike wasn't taking his plants and making bogus insurance claims. His name will be cleared."

Heavy footsteps pounded from behind the door, the knob turned, then slowly opened.

"Time, ladies," Quinn whispered. "Let's put this bitch down."

Chapter 27

Vivian stood on the other side of the door, the gun still in her hand. Using the barrel as a pointer, she wagged the weapon toward the door. "Let's go."

Gracie's legs resembled soggy noodles as she uneasily made her from the middle of the closet to the exit. Nobody said a word as they filed out one by one, walking through the office and out the backdoor. Vivian guided them onto the porch outside where two of Mike's employees waited. Both had pistols visible and trained in their direction.

Though Krystal and Quinn's faces showed shock at their coworker's involvement, Gracie's expression remained impassive at the sight of the men. At this point nothing shocked her, although the thought of Mike's workers' betrayal turned her stomach. She hoped when this ended, the money would be worth it.

The group left the building and continued into the compounds, marching across the nursery. Vivian led the way, a guard walked in the middle next to Gracie, and another at the rear, close to Krystal.

Gracie looked into the fading sky as the warm breeze caressed her skin. Little by little the sun had transformed into a reddish sphere, until the fiery ball drifted behind a group of pines. The wispy, summer wind rustled the leaves keeping in tune with the cricket's lively chirps. The scene was pure perfection.

But excellence was far gone along with the world she'd once known. The proverbial noose around her neck had constricted a notch as her universe came unwound.

If she and her friends were to come out of this alive, they needed to do something now.

Krystal was behind her. She leaned up to Gracie and whispered, "Our escape strategy isn't going very well."

"We didn't really have one in place, did we?"

"No," Krystal said with a sigh. "I guess we'll move on to plan B."

"We have a plan B?"

"We always can go with Quinn's ass kicking idea."

"I was afraid you'd suggest that. Let's try something else before we get so drastic." Gracie stepped closer to her guard and tapped him on the shoulder. "What kind of business is she running anyway?"

Vivian stopped and snapped around. The crowd also came to a halt. "No talking."

"Sorry, Vivian. I'm curious as to what you were doing out here. It wouldn't hurt for us to know since I'm assuming you intend to kill us." Gracie almost smiled. "I mean who are we going to tell if we're dead?"

Vivian paused for a minute to consider Gracie's suggestion. "I suppose there's no harm in telling you." The corners of her mouth lifted. "Guns. We transport weapons across the Mexican border for sale."

"How did you come up with such an idea?"

"I've always enjoyed firearms. I own many, all varieties. I read an article about smuggling operations in Mexico. I viewed this as a prime market to earn extra cash. I did research, made some connections, and invested." Her smile broadened. "Actually I used the nursery's money—"

"You were stealing from Mike?" Quinn interrupted.

"He shouldn't've given me access to his bank accounts."

Quinn's face reddened with anger. "You embezzled to start your venture, and then you used the nursery to run an illegal business?"

"In all fairness, Mike was cheap and didn't pay his employees enough to live on. If he had, I wouldn't have to take on this second job." Vivian gave Quinn an aggravated glare. "Anyway, after a lot of trial and error, I was on my way. Only two years in business, and I've turned this into a *very* profitable conglomerate."

"And you helped yourself to Mike's plants for a cover too?" Krystal asked.

Vivian merely shrugged.

"Wouldn't border patrol search your contraband for possible drug trafficking when you cross into Mexico?"

"I haven't had any issues. Drugs are more apt to come into the U.S. from the south as opposed to going out. And yeah, they might inspect the plants, but they won't find anything. I designed and had special racks made for transport. There is hidden compartments where the guns can be stored, and you'd have to know where to look." She shook her head. "We were running great until Mike interfered."

Krystal raised her eyebrows. "Mike spoiled things?"

"The man cost me a fortune, Krystal. I had to cease

shipments after he discovered my business." Vivian's pupils dilated, her eyes empty. "Then he went and willed you the nursery. Definitely put a kink in my plans."

"I don't understand how Krystal's inheritance would've hurt you if she weren't aware of what was going on," Gracie said. "How would it be any different if it's been willed to Mickey?"

"I brought Mickey on as my partner when I first started." Vivian's grin turned evil. "He's my insurance policy."

Even in the evening dusk, Krystal's skin paled. "Is Mickey aware you killed his father?"

"He was there when it happened."

The women stared wordlessly. Vivian was crazy for sure, but she was also deviously brilliant. Bringing Mickey in was a smart move. Although Mickey didn't seemed to be bright, as he was involved in so many "get rich quick" schemes and had lost tons of money, Mike would never turn on his son.

Too bad Mickey wasn't as loyal. Gracie had thought of him as harmless, but this latest revelation showed him to be quite cold hearted.

"We'd have been free and clear if Mike would've left the company to Mickey like he promised." Vivian sneered. "Bastard."

Quinn stepped out of line and bolted to Vivian. She shoved the gun arm out of the way and grabbed Vivian's shirt collar. She hoisted her legs around Vivian's waist, still holding onto her blouse. She got into her face, nose to nose. "You shouldn't speak ill of the dead."

"Get her off me," Vivian shrieked at her thugs,

trying to push her away. "Shoot her."

The two goons rushed to their superior in an attempt to detach Quinn. They managed to separate her legs from Vivian's middle, but the little woman hung on, wiggling like a worm, slipping away from the guys again and again. Quinn swung a foot trying to kick at her capturer and the men as she tightened her grip on Vivian's shirt.

A light tap touched Gracie. She glanced over her shoulder. Krystal nodded and put a finger to her lips. Not sure what her friend was trying to tell her, Gracie frowned and returned to the excitement.

The men finally succeeded in wrenching Quinn away. The second they dragged her from Vivian, she twisted free, throwing punches at anyone within reach. Gracie continued to stare, her mouth opened. While she mentally applauded Quinn's spirit, she also hoped her actions didn't get her, or the rest of them, killed earlier than planned.

One of the men grabbed an arm and swung her to the ground. Quinn landed on her butt with an *oomph*. She started to get up but stopped. Vivian aimed a gun at her forehead, the trigger cocked. She glanced at her helpers and shouted, "Why didn't you kill her?"

"What if we missed? She was all over the place. We'd have hit you," one answered.

"Too public here anyway," said the other. "We might have attracted too much unwanted attention."

"You're lucky this isn't a good spot to shoot you dead." Vivian dropped her arm holding the pistol. "Get up."

Quinn scrambled to her feet and wiped the dirt from the seat of her jeans.

"Let's move," Vivian commanded.

Gracie turned for Krystal's reaction. She froze. Krystal was missing. Her signal. What was she telling Gracie? Did she use the diversion to make an escape? She was going for help. A wave of relief swept through her. Silently, she prayed her friend made it to safety and was bringing in the troops.

"Wait." Vivian swirled around to face them. "Where is Krystal?"

Gracie and Quinn glanced at one another, Quinn looked surprised.

Gracie raised a shoulder. "Don't know."

"This is trouble we don't need," Vivian grumbled, then said to one of her men. "Go find her."

"And what do you want me to do then?"

"You know."

The guy made a face. "You realize she might be leading the cops right to us. If we get caught, we'll spend the rest of our lives in jail."

She raised her gun again. Her trigger finger twitched. "Then she needs to be taken care of before that happens."

"I'm not as heartless as you. I can't easily shoot someone who I've worked with for years."

"You need to grow a pair and do what needs to be done. Our financial well-being, freedom, *and* your life depend on it."

"I'm in for a lot less prison time if I chose not murder if we get caught."

"Don't count on it," Vivian countered. "You're in this past your hairline. Go take care of her, or it'll be your ass on the line, and not from the law."

He threw Vivian a menacing glare, whirled around,

and vanished into the darkness.

"Remember, I'm on a time table here, so make it fast," Vivian yelled after him.

"Where's Krystal?" Quinn whispered to Gracie.

"I don't know. I hope she's bringing help and soon. She's our only chance."

They walked deeper into the nursery. The sky darkened as night fell around them, the entire range had turned black. The only exception was a corner of the area where they were being led. A bright glow highlighted the blackness. Loud noises ricocheted, suggested activity going on.

Gracie put the inevitable from her mind and focused on the positive. She hoped her friend escaped and was able to call the authorities, and help was on the way. She glanced at the weapons directed at her and Quinn. She prayed they wouldn't be too late.

The commotion became more apparent as they approached. Huge spotlights shined on a semi-truck with the hatch lifted. The vehicle sat near a once hidden, opened gate located to the rear of a greenhouse, behind brush and trees. A low glow shimmered from within the truck as long shadows paraded back and forth.

"In there."

Vivian indicated for them to get into the trailer. Gracie squinted to see in, trying to make out the workers' faces as they pushed loaded racks further inside. But the glare against the darkness prevented her from making out anything clear. She carefully put a foot onto the lift gate and hoisted up. Quinn did the same. Vivian and her guard dog were already in place.

"We're gonna die in a stinking truck,'" Quinn said

in a low voice. "We need to take them on if we want to live."

"We're outnumbered and everyone is armed." Gracie gazed at the multitude of artillery each member carried. "She must pay her people in weapons."

"Yeah, they're packing some major heat, but I don't know what else to do. You got any ideas?"

"Let's give Krystal a few minutes to bring help."

"We don't have a few minutes."

Vivian stuck her face between them. "Forget about any and all thoughts of escape." She shook her head and grinned. "Not going to happen."

A movement in the shadows near the opening of the truck caught her attention.

"Reed." Quinn squealed, and her face lit up as the man strolled into the light. "Gracie." She gave Gracie an excited push. "It's Reed."

Reed walked toward them. But something appeared off. She bent into Quinn and whispered, "This is very wrong, Quinn. He's not here to help us."

"What are you talking about? Of course he is."

Quinn beamed as Reed continued upon their group. He brushed past her and Quinn, ignoring everyone until he reached Vivian, where he halted. There was a definite difference about him. He seemed older, more mature. A coldness shrouded his aura.

Another shift in the shadows caught Gracie's eye. She looked beyond Reed and froze. The color drained in her face.

The countless fears, the agonizing anguish, every one of those warning bells she'd disregarded these past few days brimmed over in her mind.

Her head swam. She braced her backbone and

forced the jelly out of her knees as Ethan emerged from the dimness.

Chapter 28

Ethan swiftly moved toward them. The trailer's interior lights threw a harsh shadow over his rugged face giving him almost a menacing appearance. He came to a halt next to Reed. Side by side, they stared straight ahead, their expressions unreadable.

Vivian smirked. "I believe you know my associates."

Unable to breathe, Gracie stepped to Ethan and gazed into his eyes. He didn't blink. It was almost as if he looked right through her.

Vivian spoke quietly from behind her. "To his credit, Gracie. He did try to keep you out of this. That's why he left you at that God forsaken Deluxe Inn, to keep you out of harm's way." Vivian *tsked*. "But you wouldn't listen."

"That makes everything so much better."

She blinked away a tear. She would not give him the satisfaction of letting him see her cry. Somewhere in all the craziness, she'd totally fallen for the guy. She'd hoped and prayed the gossip was unfounded, and after Mike's murder was solved, everything would be explained. Like he promised. She continued to gaze at him. A brief flicker of—something, zipped across his face before his expression returned to stoniness.

"Gracie, I don't wanna say I told you so, but I told you so. He fooled everybody. Not me though. I knew he was no good." Quinn glared at Reed. "I never expected for you to be involved."

"Enough chit chat." Vivian turned to the men. "We have much work to do."

She spun to where Gracie and Quinn stood. "Now I expect you to take care of your former girlfriend and her little *amigo*." She leaned close to Ethan and whispered, but loud enough for everyone to hear, "No loose ends, baby."

"You're gonna kill us now?" Quinn sighed. "That sucks."

"You wouldn't keep your noses out of my business." Vivian placed her hands onto her hips and swirled her head back and forth. "We need to get busy. I have a plane to catch."

Gracie gazed at Vivian, her brows raised.

"I'm leaving in a few hours for a tropical island without extradition until this Mike situation blows over. I can't wait to lie on a sandy beach, gazing into the clear, blue water with some sweet thing bringing me spiked drinks with little umbrellas."

"Sounds lovely. At least someone will come out of this with a happy ending." Gracie paused. "What about Mickey? Is he going with you?"

Vivian shook her head. "I brought Mickey on as leverage in dealing with Mike. The guy's useless. He talks a good game, but he'd sell me out in a heartbeat.

I can't believe he's Mike's son. No balls whatsoever. I cannot keep a nutless man on my team." She twisted to the men. "If our good friend Ethan did his job, they'll soon find Mickey's body, along with a suicide note confessing to being brains to this operation and murdering his father."

Gracie's heart crashed into her chest and fell into the pit of her stomach. Ethan had killed Mickey in cold blood and set him up for his father's murder. God, she could pick 'em.

Vivian gazed pointedly at Ethan. "Are we ready?"

"Plants are loaded. Should I send the people on their way?"

Gracie eyed Vivian's gun. She wondered if this would be a good time to push Quinn and attempt an escape. How far would they get before Vivian could set her site to aim and shoot. But she also had to consider Ethan and Reed were probably armed.

"We do have one small problem."

Vivian's hackles rose. "Which is, Mr. McCarthy?"

"One of the taillights in the semi was broken and needs to be fixed before the shipment leaves."

"Not an issue." Vivian pressed her palm against her forehead. "Still, it pisses me off these things always happen when I'm in a hurry. Replace the bulb. We don't want to draw any added attention on the road."

"That's the catch. The light is already swapped, but it's still out. Malcolm believes a ground wire has gone bad or maybe there's a connection problem. Someone's left for a power meter and some wire now. The lamp can be repaired, though not quickly."

"Do whatever. As fast as possible. We need to rush and wrap this up. I'm getting a bad feeling." Vivian's gaze rested on Gracie and Quinn. "In the meantime, take them to the back woods behind the nursery and do what is needed to be done." She spun to leave but stopped. "Do either of you know if that nitwit took care of Krystal?"

"I didn't see Krystal," Ethan said.

Reed nodded at Gracie and Quinn. "I didn't realize Krystal was with them."

"Then one of you will have to handle that little hitch, too. Let's get moving, gentlemen."

Ethan snatched Gracie's upper arm. He jerked her forward and attempted to guide her to the truck's opening.

Reed nudged Quinn's shoulder. "Come on, Quinn."

"It's now or never, Gracie." Quinn ducked to dodge Reed, and then stepped around him. Hands out, she shoved him hard enough that he lost his balance and toppled onto the dirty, truck's floor.

Everything stopped. Except for Quinn. She took off in a full run toward a stunned Vivian. Quinn leaped in the air and clutched onto Vivian's shoulders, attaching to her. Vivian turned in circles, her arms flailed as she screamed. "Shoot her. Somebody put a bullet in the little bitch, damn it."

Quinn was small but had large hands. She placed a palm over Vivian's face, her legs wrapped around the larger woman's middle again, and holding on as if she was taming a bronco upside down.

Ethan tugged at Gracie's arm. She planted her feet using her weight to anchor herself. If Quinn was willing to put everything all on the line, so was she.

Ethan yanked her to him, his face in hers. "Stop fighting me."

"You're not killing me."

With an exasperated expression, he released her and stepped away. An astonished Gracie stood motionless. Ethan swiftly closed in on her, scooped her into his arms, and flung her over his shoulder. He placed an arm over her butt and rushed her out of the truck.

Gracie knew it was useless to fight him. Her fate appeared to be sealed.

She fought to keep focused. She'd find a way out, and she would live through this. He couldn't kill her on his shoulder. He'd have to put her down to set up and finish her off. The moment her feet touched the ground, she'd be hauling ass.

A flicker caught her attention. She managed an upward peek. Flashing red and blue lights entered the nursery and sped in their direction. Relief shrouded over her. Krystal was alive and had called the authorities. Within seconds the scene shifted into mass chaos. Sirens blasted; people screamed and scattered in all directions. A gunshot rang out into the mess.

Ethan ignored the happenings and carried Gracie into a blackened, wooded area beyond the gate. A shadowy figure followed them. Gracie wanted to shriek from elation. The police were here. Within the matter of seconds, she'd be free.

She pounded on Ethan's back. "It's over. Someone's behind us. The judge will go easier if you release me."

But he ignored her and kept traveling. He stopped at a small clearing and dropped her to her feet. The person behind came into view and closed in on them. Gracie's heart sank. Reed. She was sandwiched between the two men. The ordeal may be over, although she feared they'd kill her before they made an escape. She knew too much. But Gracie wanted answers first. She wanted the truth.

"Where is Quinn?" Ethan asked Reed. "You were supposed to get Quinn."

Reed ran a hand over his bruised jaw. "I tried, but she was a quick. I managed to wrestle her off Vivian. She popped me in the chin. Then she went back to Vivian and started pounding her. After that, the authorities showed up and I needed to evacuate."

"Good call."

"Speaking of call, we got the word to disappear."

"'Bout time."

Gracie waved a hand. "Um, excuse me?"

They looked to her.

"So, what am I supposed to be doing?"

Ethan grinned. "This is an excellent opportunity for you to escape." He closed in, stepping to her, and lightly brushed his lips over hers. "Take care and be happy, sweet Gracie." Ethan spun her in the direction of the strobe lights and gave her a gentle push. "Go."

"Bye, Gracie," Reed called.

Gracie took a few stumbling steps, and then whirled around to look behind her. Both men were gone. Confused, she continued forward and arrived to much shouting, flashing lights, and people everywhere. A line of about twenty people, all Mike's employees, stood with their hands on top of their heads, while uniforms marched in front and behind the group.

A stretcher was being wheeled out of the truck. Quinn lay on her stomach atop the gurney. Gracie gasped and rushed to Quinn's side as she was guided down the ramp.

She clutched her hand between her own. "Quinn. What happened?"

"I was shot. Vivian put a bullet in me. My life flashed before my eyes."

"She's going to be fine," said the technician who

walked beside them.

"No, I'm not. I keep seeing the light, and my grandma keeps telling me to come with her."

Gracie glanced at the EMT, alarmed.

He shook his head. "A flesh wound."

"Where was she shot?"

"In my butt." Quinn turned toward the EMT. "Don't you have pain killers? I'm dying here. The least you could do is give me something to be comfortable while I pass on into my next life."

The technician nodded to his partner, and they stopped. The man dipped into a kit and produced a needle and inserted the medicine into Quinn's IV bag. "This ought to make you better."

"I don't feel anything. That wasn't enough. I need more drugs."

"Quinn," came a voice from behind. "Calm down."

"Krystal." Gracie dashed to her. "I'm so glad you're all right."

"I'm fine and happy you are too, although everything has certainly turned chaotic since we were last together." Krystal smiled as she looped an arm through Gracie's. She glanced at Quinn, who snored loudly. "What happened to her?"

"Somebody shot her."

Krystal chuckled. "Told you."

"Got her in the butt." Gracie continued to relate the version of the craziness that occurred, concluding with Ethan's and Reed's odd meeting, ending with the men vanishing like ghosts.

"So Ethan and Reed are both involved?"

Gracie shrugged. "I'm clueless." She paused. "You took quite a chance sneaking off the way you did, but

I'm happy you made it to call in reinforcements. Quinn and I were close to being goners."

"I'd love to take the credit, except I didn't do anything but get away. The police were already here before I reached a phone." Krystal lifted a shoulder. "I guess we'll never get the whole story."

"Ms. Desoto, Ms. Laine?" A uniformed man came up behind them. "My name is Officer Ted Cheek. Your assistance is needed. Will you come with me, please?"

She and Krystal glanced at each other then followed him to a waiting SUV.

He opened the back door and indicated for them to get in. "My superior wants to speak with you." He gestured to a female sitting inside. They stopped in their tracks, their mouths dropped.

The well-dressed blonde woman sat in the backseat. "Gracie, Krystal. I'm Special Agent Becca Bonatch, and I work for the Bureau of Tobacco, Firearms, and Explosives."

Chapter 29

Gracie sat on her pier, her bare feet dangled in the water. She drew a deep breath, mixed with contentment and frustration. Early evening. Yet the finality of the day seemed incomplete. Like something was missing.

A light touch on the top of her shoulder startled her out of her own little world. "Am I interrupting?"

She glanced at her guest before her gaze returned to the river. "No, of course not."

Krystal slipped out of her flip-flops and lowered next to Gracie.

She peered at Krystal's belly with a grin. "How's the mamma to be feeling?"

"Queasy." Krystal slid her hand over her stomach. "I still can't believe I'm forty and pregnant again. After three kids, I thought I was done birthin' babies."

"It's wonderful." Gracie's grin stretched across her face. "And Charlie is so happy."

Krystal chuckled. "I swear the man turns bright red every time someone brings up how I got this way. They rib him constantly at the nursery."

"I'm glad the two of you decided to run the place together."

"Me too, since he's more familiar with the business end. The financial and employment factors are going to be challenges because the company wasn't doing well economically, and I've got to replace all the employees who are sitting in jail because they worked for Vivian on the side."

"I have faith in you two."

There was a short pause.

"Speaking of work, I heard from Quinn today. She sends you her best and said to tell you her butt's healing nicely."

"Good. How does she like Florida?"

"Loves it. She met a guy at the beach, and she's crazy about him." Krystal paused to roll her eyes. "A professional alligator wrestler."

Gracie giggled. "The heart wants what the heart wants."

Another peaceful quiet settled between the friends as they watched the lazy river flow past them.

"How's your heart?" Krystal finally asked.

"Better." Gracie swallowed hard. "I only wish I'd gotten closure. An honest goodbye."

Ethan's mysterious departure four weeks ago left her riddled with questions. Becca explained as much as the law allowed the night of the bust, but she wondered where she'd fit in to all this.

Krystal gazed at the water's swirls for a long moment, deep in thought. "Would you take an honest hello?"

"Huh?"

A tiny grin played at her lips. "What would you do if Ethan showed up, right now?"

Gracie couldn't imagine where Krystal dreamed this up. The pregnancy must've affected her. "Won't happen. He's gone, and he's not coming back. Even Becca said he can't return."

"He cared for you. Maybe that's enough to make

him reappear."

"Doubtful."

"Could be he's afraid you'll reject him."

"If he were truly interested, he'd still do something to see me."

Krystal glanced toward the backyard and smiled. Gracie gradually turned to follow Krystal's gaze. Her insides froze. Krystal slowly stood, offering a hand to Gracie. Gracie clutched onto her friend. Her legs morphed into rubber as she struggled to her feet.

Krystal released Gracie and gave her a gentle push. "He's waiting for you." Krystal stepped around her and strolled the short distance over the dock. She waved before she headed around the house and disappeared.

Gracie's world remained suspended in the moment as she watched Ethan standing at the top of the pier. His gray eyes smoldered, his gaze attached to hers. Hands in his pockets, he slowly walked to where she waited. Her heart sped up with each step. He stopped in front of her.

"Hello."

Gracie opened her mouth, but the words became trapped in her throat. She couldn't believe he was here.

"You're not talking to me? Do you want me to leave?"

"No."

His lips curved. "No, you're not speaking to me or no, you don't want me to go?"

"I want you to stay. I haven't decided if I'm talking to you yet."

He scrubbed a hand over his face. "Fair enough."

"I have questions."

"Of course you do. But if you won't talk to me,

you can't ask them, can you?"

"It's been a month."

Ethan ducked his head. "I needed to tie up loose ends."

"Okay." Gracie combed her fingers through her hair and cleared her throat. "So you and Reed are U.S. firearm agents for the American Tobacco and Firearms. Becca told us that much. What she didn't explain, was your actual relationship with her."

"We used to be partners, Gracie. She recently became my boss. We still have a connection, but there isn't nor was there ever anything romantic between us.

What you witnessed the day of the funeral was just me comforting her. This was her first big case, and Mike's death was a definite blemish on her record." A corner of his mouth lifted. "You didn't notice that double sized rock on her left hand? I couldn't afford something like that on my salary."

She took a moment to digest the information. "You work on task forces undercover, right?"

"We're specifically assigned to anti-smuggling operations. In this case, our task was to capture gunrunners. Since most illegal arms traders go unnoticed, they're hard to track down. Vivian was especially difficult to pin because she was so good at covering her tracks."

"How did you end up at the nursery?"

"Mike suspected the plants were stolen for a specific reason and internal. He called in a private detective friend, and he made the discovery. Mike summoned the department. From the amount of product disappearing meant lots of weapons had to be going across the border. Agents were covertly put inside the plant farm." He looked at her. "Gracie, this was big. Vivian had people shipping her weaponry from all over the country and filtered them through Mike's place."

This news stunned Gracie. She'd known Vivian for years, and while she thought of her as odd, her amount of deviousness continued to shock.

"We advised Mike not to tell anyone about this, unfortunately we were too late, he'd already confided in Mickey. He had no idea his son was involved."

"Did you know Vivian was in charge when you first came in?"

"Not right away. After we arrived, we discovered Vivian's link immediately, although we thought her a middleman and someone else ran the show, which is what she wanted everyone to believe. She created the illusion an individual above her called the shots. It was brilliant. She understood, correctly, the authorities wouldn't be interested in a middleman. They'd want the people on top and take their time for the big capture."

"When did you discover she was the top dog?"

"The night you and your little team was at the nursery. We come to believe she might be running the show, but had no proof. Then Reed and I surmised she may be arrogant enough to keep her records right in the open. Sure enough, Reed was able to break into her work computer and found she kept her logs and manifests in plain sight."

"You were involved in the actual smuggling?"

"Yep. Reed and I are always a part of the whole shebang, documenting everything. Undercover means we participate." Ethan smiled. "I can't give you any details on infiltration or our duties. We don't reveal our secrets."

"Did you tell Mike after you discovered Vivian's activities?"

"We went to our superiors, first. Although unusual, we explained the situation to Mike as a courtesy. But he wanted to confront Vivian and insisted we turn a blind eye to Mickey's involvement. I tried to convince him to keep quiet or he might mess up our whole investigation, instead he did things his way. In the end, it cost him his life, and Mickey's still going to prison."

"Did Vivian try to kill you and set you up for Mike's death?"

"No. Ortiz did that. He'd joined Vivian's organization before me, and she counted on me instead of him. He even made an attempt on his own life to throw us off. He was jealous. We had a showdown at the nursery. After I took care of him, a couple of his besties turned up at my place—well you met them."

Ethan wet his lips, his eyes darted about before setting his gaze on Gracie. He looked her square in the eye. "Just so you know, finding you with Vivian was one of the scariest moments in my life."

"Frightening for me, too." Gracie raised both shoulders in a careless shrug. "Sad she got away."

"I'm good at what I do. I don't make errors or do stupid stuff to put myself in any more danger than possible, but I made a lot of mistakes on this assignment. My ass got reamed from the bigwigs."

She eyed him. "Was I one of your mistakes?"

He held his arms out from his sides. "I've never tried so hard to not be with someone as I did with you. I kept pushing you away, though I think I wanted you to pull me closer." Ethan took a step nearer and scooped up her hands and clutched them tight between his. "We haven't known each other long and what little time we had, I either tried to run from you or get you into bed." He hesitated as he struggled for his next words. "Can you forgive me? I can't keep you out of my mind, my dreams, or my heart." He leaned in and gently kissed her cheek. "There are some things you just know. I'm supposed to be with you. You make me a better man. I want you, Gracie. Do you feel the same about me?"

Stunned by his admission, Gracie stood motionless for several seconds, unsure how to respond. Could she trust this man? She certainly wanted to. "What about your issue? Your PTSD?"

"In therapy. Understand, it's something I'll always deal with, but I'm going to do my best to keep it under control from now on, especially since I'm aware aspects of my job can trigger it, which is another issue. I will be away because of what I do." He smiled. "I've come to like the idea of having someone to come home to."

"It'll take a while for me to trust you again. And I understand your behavior had to do with your job, but this showing up and disappearing in the middle of the night without reason won't be happening."

"I know. I'll work hard to make you feel safe and secure with me. I just want to make you happy." He squeezed her hands as he stared at her for a long time. "So are we okay? Can we do a restart?"

"Hmmm, not sure. A guy breaks up with a woman, saves her life, disappears for a month without a word, reappears and convinces her to sleep with him again, disappears again and again." Gracie's mouth twisted as she let several seconds pass. "Sounds like if I say yes, you'll be getting a truck load of sex points."

"Nope." Palms on her shoulders, he tugged her closer. "No more points and all past points are null and void. This is just you and me, Gracie."

"You and me." Gracie smiled. "I like that."

A word about the author...

Debra was born in Waco, Texas, and is a lifetime Texan, living in different areas throughout her adult life. She enjoyed creating stories growing up, though the idea of becoming an author did not occur to her until 2004. Since then, she has worked on learning to write while pursuing her bachelor's degree, which she earned in 2011 in business.

She now resides in her hometown of Waco and is an active member of the Central Texas Chapter of Romance Writers of America, where she is secretary of the group.

In her spare time, she loves being with her son Stephen and his wife Astrid, and daughter Hannah and her husband Ryan. Besides writing, she also enjoys traveling, shopping, a relaxing pedi, and a good plate of Mexican food.

debrajupe@gmail.com
debrajupe.wordpress.com
www.debrajupe.com

~*~

Other Debra Jupe titles
available from The Wild Rose Press, Inc.
ECHOES IN THE WIND
TOMORROW DOESN'T MATTER TONIGHT

Thank you for purchasing
this publication of The Wild Rose Press, Inc.

If you enjoyed the story, we would appreciate your
letting others know by leaving a review.

For other wonderful stories,
please visit our on-line bookstore at
www.thewildrosepress.com.

For questions or more information
contact us at
info@thewildrosepress.com.

The Wild Rose Press, Inc.
www.thewildrosepress.com

Stay current with The Wild Rose Press, Inc.

Like us on Facebook

https://www.facebook.com/TheWildRosePress

And Follow us on Twitter
https://twitter.com/WildRosePress